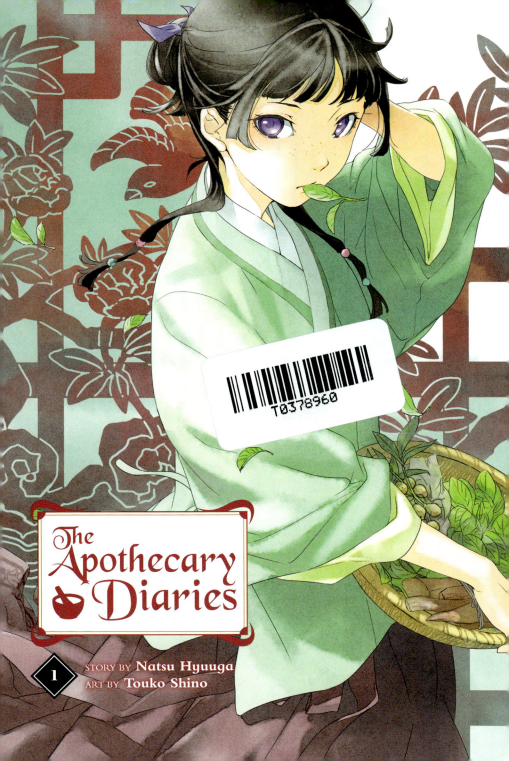

Lihua

"May I whisper in milady's ear?"

And then, quietly so that no one else would hear her, she gave Consort Lihua some advice. Lihua's face went as red as an apple when she heard it. What Maomao might have told her was a subject of lively debate among Lihua's ladies-in-waiting for some time afterward.

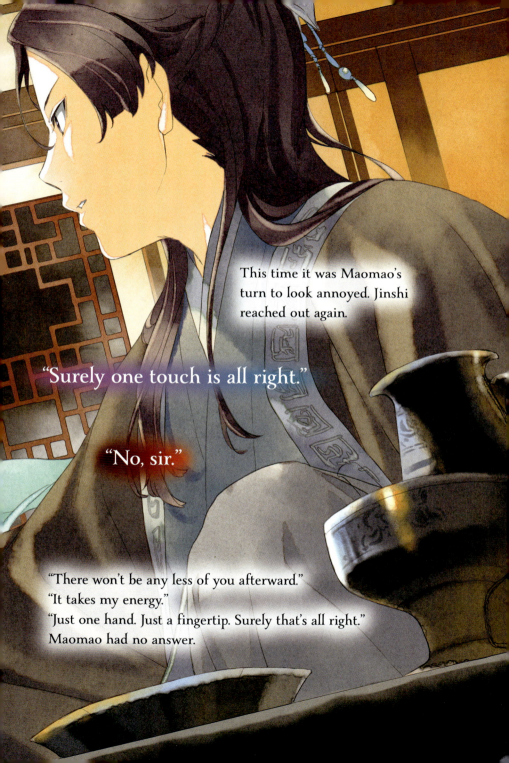

This time it was Maomao's turn to look annoyed. Jinshi reached out again.

"Surely one touch is all right."

"No, sir."

"There won't be any less of you afterward."
"It takes my energy."
"Just one hand. Just a fingertip. Surely that's all right."
Maomao had no answer.

A NOTE FROM THE AUTHOR

It was a simple story of a young girl, a food taster in a medieval palace who could solve the most perplexing mysteries. Against that bracing backdrop, my heroine—a woman who could be as outwardly prickly as she was inwardly sweet—turned out to be well received. It's been two years now since the trade volumes went on sale, and by popular demand, the story is now being reissued in mass-market paperback format.

These new versions have been much revised from the trade releases, hopefully in ways that will make them even more exciting and suspenseful. In fact, I dare say I think a new name is about to be added to the annals of the great light-novel detectives. I hope you'll find our heroine Maomao's deductions and discoveries thrilling and surprising!

The Apothecary Diaries

～1～

Story by Natsu Hyuuga
Art by Touko Shino

English Adaptation by
Kevin Steinbach

SQUARE ENIX
BOOKS

The Apothecary Diaries

Volume 1

Story: Natsu Hyuuga
Art: Touko Shino

Translator:	Kevin Steinbach
Cover Designer:	Ti Collier
Interior Designer:	Laura K. Corless
Editor, Print Edition:	Jennifer Sherman
Editor, Digital Edition:	Sasha McGlynn

KUSURIYA NO HITORIGOTO
© Natsu Hyuuga 2014
Originally published in Japan by Imagica Infos Co., Ltd.
Translation rights arranged with Shufunotomo Co., Ltd.
English translation © 2021 by J-Novel Club LLC

The names, characters, and incidents portrayed in this publication are fictitious. No identification with actual persons (living or deceased), places, buildings, and products is intended or should be inferred.

No portion of this book may be reproduced in any form or by any electronic or mechanical means without permission in writing from the copyright holders.

Library of Congress Cataloging-in-Publication Data

Names: Hyūga, Natsu, author. | Shino, Tōko, artist. | Steinbach, Kevin, translator.
Title: The apothecary diaries / written by Natsu Hyuuga ; art by Touko Shino ; English adaptation by Kevin Steinbach.
Other titles: Kusuriya no hitorigoto. English
Description: First edition. | El Segundo, CA : Square Enix, 2024–
Identifiers: LCCN 2023042712 | ISBN 9781646092727 (v. 01 ; trade paperback) | ISBN 9781646092734 (v. 02 ; trade paperback) | ISBN 9781646092741 (v. 03 ; trade paperback)
Subjects: CYAC: Healers--Fiction. | Courts and courtiers--Fiction. | China--History--Fiction. | LCGFT: Historical fiction. | Detective and mystery fiction. | Light novels.
Classification: LCC PZ7.1.H97 Ap 2024 | DDC [Fic]--dc23
LC record available at https://lccn.loc.gov/2023042712

Manufactured in the USA
First Edition: May 2024
5th Printing

Published by Square Enix Manga & Books, a division of SQUARE ENIX, INC.
999 N. Pacific Coast Highway, 3rd Floor
El Segundo, CA 90245, USA

square-enix-books.com

TABLE OF CONTENTS

CHAPTER 1: Maomao 1

CHAPTER 2: The Two Consorts 6

CHAPTER 3: Jinshi 13

CHAPTER 4: The Nymph's Smile 18

CHAPTER 5: Attendant 23

CHAPTER 6: Poison Tester 27

CHAPTER 7: Branch 34

CHAPTER 8: Love Potion 41

CHAPTER 9: Cacao 49

CHAPTER 10: The Unsettling Matter of the Spirit (Part One) 55

CHAPTER 11: The Unsettling Matter of the Spirit (Part Two) 67

CHAPTER 12: The Threat 74

CHAPTER 13: Nursing 82

CHAPTER 14: The Fire 88

CHAPTER 15:	Covert Operations	96
CHAPTER 16:	The Garden Party (Part One)	107
CHAPTER 17:	The Garden Party (Part Two)	114
CHAPTER 18:	The Garden Party (Part Three)	122
CHAPTER 19:	After the Festivities	135
CHAPTER 20:	Fingers	144
CHAPTER 21:	Lihaku	155
CHAPTER 22:	Homecoming	163
CHAPTER 23:	Wheat Stalks	170
CHAPTER 24:	A Misunderstanding	185
CHAPTER 25:	Wine	193
CHAPTER 26:	Two 'Cides to Every Story	203
CHAPTER 27:	Honey (Part One)	212
CHAPTER 28:	Honey (Part Two)	228
CHAPTER 29:	Honey (Part Three)	234
CHAPTER 30:	Ah-Duo	244
CHAPTER 31:	Dismissal	253
EPILOGUE:	The Eunuch and the Courtesan	259

CHAPTER 1

Maomao

What I wouldn't give for some good street-stall meat skewers. Maomao looked up at the overcast sky and sighed. She lived in a world that was at once a place of unparalleled, sparkling beauty and a noxious, foul, suffocating cage. *Three months already. Hope my old man's eating properly.*

It seemed just the other day she had gone into the woods to gather herbs, and there she had met three kidnappers; let us call them Villagers One, Two, and Three. They were after women for the royal palace, and one could say they offered the world's most forceful and unpleasant marriage proposal.

Now, it wasn't that she wouldn't be paid, and with a couple years' work, there was that glimmer of hope that she might even be able to come back to her hometown. There were worse ways to earn a living—*if* one went to the royal city of one's own accord. But Maomao, who had been making her way just fine as an apothecary, thank you very much, saw it solely as so much trouble.

What did the kidnappers do with the nubile young women they captured? Sometimes they sold the girls to the eunuchs, putting the proceeds toward a night of drinking for themselves. Sometimes the young ladies were offered in lieu of someone's own daughter. To Maomao, it was a moot question, for now she found herself caught up in their schemes, regardless of the reason. Else, she would never in her life have wished to have anything to do with the *hougong*, the "rear palace": the residence of the Imperial women.

The place was so thick with the odors of makeup and perfume as to turn the stomach, and even more full of the thin, forced smiles of the court ladies in their beautiful dresses. In her time as an apothecary, Maomao had come to believe there was no toxin so terrifying as a woman's smile. That one rule held true whether in the halls of the most ornate palace or the squalid chambers of the cheapest pleasure house.

Maomao hefted the laundry basket at her feet and headed into a nearby building. Unlike the dazzling front façade, the dreary central courtyard housed flagstone-paved washing areas, where the court's servants—people who were neither quite man nor quite woman—did laundry by the armload.

Men, in principle, were not allowed in the rear palace. The only men who could enter were either members and blood relations of the most noble family in the country, or former men who had lost a very important part of themselves. Naturally, all the men Maomao was looking at right now were the latter. It was twisted, she thought, but admittedly a logical thing to do.

She set down her basket and spotted another one sitting in the next building over. Not dirty clothes, but clean laundry that had dried in the sun. She glanced at the wooden tag dangling from the handle; it bore an illustration of a leaf along with a number.

Not all the palace women were literate. It wasn't that surprising: some of them had been brought here by force, after all. And though the rudiments of etiquette were beaten into them before they arrived, letters were not. It would probably be lucky, Maomao reflected, if half the girls who got snatched from the countryside turned out to know how to read. It was, one might say, a hazard of the rear palace growing too populous. Quality was being sacrificed for quantity. It in no way equaled the "flower garden" of the former emperor. Still, the consorts and ladies-in-waiting together numbered two thousand people, and with the eunuchs that number came to three thousand. A vast place indeed.

Maomao was a serving girl, a post so lowly she didn't even have an official rank. What more could she expect, as a girl who had no one to back her at court—who had arrived by way of kidnappers to fill out the palace staff? If she had perhaps possessed a body as shapely as a peony, or skin as pale as the full moon, she might at least have aspired to the status of one of the lower concubines, but Maomao possessed only ruddy, freckled skin and limbs with all the elegance of withered branches.

I need to just get this job done.

Maomao picked up the basket with its tag depicting a plum flower and the number seventeen, and she trundled off as quickly as she could manage. She wanted to get back to her room before the frowning sky began to weep.

One of the low-ranked consorts was the owner of the laundry in the basket. Her room was rather more lavish than those accorded to the other low consorts—in fact, it was downright ostentatious. The occupant, Maomao surmised, must be the daughter of some affluent noble family.

When a woman was assigned a palace rank, she was also permitted her own ladies-in-waiting. A minor consort, however, could have two ladies at most, which was why Maomao, a serving girl with no mistress of her own on which to attend, was carting around the woman's laundry like this.

A low consort was permitted personal rooms in the rear palace precincts, but they were inevitably on the fringes of the grounds, where the Imperial eye was unlikely ever to fall upon her. If she should, nonetheless, be graced with a night with His Majesty, she would be granted new rooms, while a second such night meant she had truly found a place in the world.

As for those who ultimately never excited the Emperor's interest, after a certain age a consort (assuming her family didn't wield particular influence) could expect to see herself demoted, or even granted as a wife to some member of the bureaucracy. Whether that was a blessing or a curse depended on whom she was granted to, but the fate the women feared most was being bestowed upon one of the eunuchs.

Maomao knocked discreetly on the door. A lady-in-waiting opened it and snapped, "Just leave it there." Within, a consort, redolent of the sweetest perfume, was sipping some alcohol from a cup. She must have been much admired for her beauty in those halcyon days before she had arrived at the palace, but when she got here, she discovered she had known as much about the outside world as a frog who had spent its life in a well. Crowded out by the array of dazzling flowers in this garden, she had lost her will to continue fighting for a place here, and of late had ceased to come out of her room at all.

You know no one is going to come visit you in your own room, right?

Maomao traded the basket in her arms for the one sitting outside the door and went back to the laundry area. There was so much work to do still. She may not have come to the palace of her own volition, but they were at least paying her, and she intended to earn her keep. Maomao the apothecary was diligent, if nothing else. If she kept her head down and did her job, she could hope to leave this place someday, and never, she assumed, to gain royal notice.

Sadly, Maomao's thinking was—let us say—naïve. She didn't know what was going to happen. No one does; that's the nature of life. Maomao was a relatively objective thinker for a girl of seventeen, but she had a few qualities that continually dogged her. For one, curiosity; for another, a hunger for knowledge. And then there was her budding sense of justice.

A few days hence, Maomao would uncover a mysterious and terrible truth concerning the deaths of several infants in the rear palace. Some said it was a curse laid upon any concubine who dared to produce an heir, but Maomao refused to regard the matter as anything supernatural.

CHAPTER 2

The Two Consorts

"Huh! So it's true?"

"It is! She said she saw the doctor go into their rooms with her own eyes!"

Maomao sipped her soup and listened. Hundreds of serving girls were having their breakfast in the vast dining room. The meal consisted of soup and a porridge of mixed grains. She was listening to two women diagonally across from her as they traded gossip. The women took pains to look chagrined about the story, but it was an unseemly curiosity that lit their eyes.

"He visited *both* Lady Gyokuyou and Lady Lihua."

"Gracious, both of them? But they're only six months and three months, aren't they?"

"That's right! Maybe it really is a curse."

The names were those of the emperor's two favorite consorts. Six months and three months were the ages of the ladies' children.

Rumors were rife in the palace. Some of them sprang from contempt

for His Majesty's companions and the heirs they bore him, but others had more the savor of simple ghost stories, the sorts of tales told during the summer doldrums to beat the heat by chilling the blood.

"It must be. Otherwise, why would three separate children have died?"

All the offspring in question had been born to consorts; that is to say, they could in principle have been heirs to the throne. One of the poor victims had been born to His Majesty before his accession, while he still lived in the Eastern Palace, and two more since he had assumed the throne, but all three had passed away in infancy. Mortality was common among infants, of course, but that three of the emperor's own progeny should die so young was strange. Only two children, those of the consorts Gyokuyou and Lihua, still survived.

Poisonings, perhaps? Maomao mused, sipping her porridge, but she concluded it couldn't be. After all, two of the three dead children had been girls. And in a land where only men could inherit the throne, what reason was there to murder princesses?

The women across from Maomao were so busy talking about curses and hexes that they had stopped eating entirely. *But there's no such thing as curses!* Maomao thought. It was stupid, that was the only word for it. How could you destroy an entire clan with one curse? Such questions bordered on the heretical, but Maomao's expertise, she felt, constituted proof of this pronouncement.

Could it have been some kind of sickness? Something blood-borne, maybe? How exactly did they die?

And that was when the detached, quiet maid began talking to her chatty dining companions. It would not be long before Maomao regretted succumbing to her curiosity.

The Two Consorts

"I don't know the whole story, but I heard they all wasted away!" Apparently inspired by Maomao's show of interest, Xiaolan, the talkative maid, thereafter regularly brought her the latest rumors. "The doctor's been to see Lady Lihua more often than Lady Gyokuyou, so I guess Lady Lihua must be worse." She wiped at a window frame with a rag as she spoke.

"Lady Lihua herself?"

"Yes, it's mother and child both."

Maomao supposed the doctor paid closer attention to Lady Lihua not necessarily because she was sicker, but because her child was a little prince. Consort Gyokuyou had borne a princess. The Imperial affection fell more upon Gyokuyou, but when one child was a boy and the other a girl, which one should receive preferential treatment was clear.

"Like I said, I don't know everything, but I've heard she has headaches and stomachaches, and even some nausea." Satisfied that she had divulged all her newest gleanings, Xiaolan busied herself with another task. By way of thanks, Maomao gave her some tea flavored with licorice. She'd made it with some herbs that grew in a corner of the central garden. It smelled strongly medicinal but was in fact quite sweet. Xiaolan was thrilled—serving girls had all too few opportunities to enjoy sweet things.

Headache, stomachache, and nausea. Maomao had some ideas as to what illnesses these might portend, but she couldn't be sure. And her father had never tired of admonishing her not to do her thinking based on assumptions.

Maybe I'll just pay her a little visit.

Maomao was determined to finish her work as quickly as possible. The rear palace was in fact a vast place, housing more than two thousand women and five hundred eunuchs on the premises. Lowly workers like Maomao slept ten to a room, but the lower-ranked consorts had their own chambers, mid-ranking ones had whole buildings to themselves, and the highest-ranking consorts virtually had their own palaces, sprawling complexes including dining halls and gardens, large enough to dwarf a small town. Thus, Maomao rarely left the eastern quarter where she lived; there was no need. She had neither the time nor the means to leave unless she was sent on some errand.

Well, if I don't have an errand, I'll just have to make one.

Maomao spoke to a woman holding a basket. This basket contained fine silk that would have to be washed over in the laundry area in the western quarter. No one seemed to know whether there was something different about the water there, or perhaps about the people who did the washing, but apparently the silk would be ruined if handled here in the eastern quarter. Maomao understood that silk degraded more or less depending on whether it was dried out in the sun or kept in the shade, but she felt no particular need to tell anybody that.

"I'm just dying to get a look at that gorgeous eunuch they say lives in the central area," Maomao said, invoking one of the other rumors Xiaolan had mentioned in passing, and the woman gladly gave her the basket. Chances for anything resembling romance were few and far between in this place, so that even the eunuchs, men who were not really men, soon became something to swoon over. Stories were even told, from time to time, of women who became the wives of eunuchs after they left palace service. Presumably this was healthier than the women lusting after each other instead, but still it puzzled Maomao.

Wonder if I'll end up like everyone else one day, she thought to herself. She crossed her arms and grunted. Romantic matters held scant interest for her.

She delivered the basket of laundry as quickly as she could, and then a red-lacquered building of the central area came into view. Carvings were everywhere, every pillar like a work of art unto itself. Each detail had been attended to so that the whole was far more refined than anything on the fringes of the eastern quarter. At present, the largest quarters in the rear palace were occupied by Consort Lihua, the mother of the prince. The emperor was without an empress proper, which made Lihua, the only one of his women with a son, the most powerful person here.

The scene Maomao discovered looked almost as if it could have come from the city itself. One woman fulminated, one hung her head in gloom, while others fussed and fretted, and a man tried to make peace among them all.

It's hardly different from a brothel, Maomao thought, a cold observation made possible by her status as a third party, if not a gawker.

The upset woman was the most powerful person in the rear palace, the one hanging her head the next most powerful, and the fussy women were attendants. The man (no doubt a man no longer at this point) interceding was the doctor. Maomao gathered so much from the whispering she heard and the general state of things around her. That first woman would have to be Consort Lihua, mother of the Imperial prince, and the second woman would be Consort Gyokuyou, blessed—though not quite so blessed as Lihua—with a daughter. As for the eunuch doctor, Maomao knew nothing about him, but she had heard that in this whole great palace there was only one person who could truly be called a practitioner of medicine.

"This is your doing. Just because you had a girl, you got it into your head to curse my prince to death!" A beautiful face distorted by anger is a frightful thing. Eyes as furious as a demon's, set in a face as pale as a ghost's, were turned upon the beautiful Gyokuyou, who held a hand to her cheek. There was a red mark under her fingers; she had, Maomao surmised, been slapped with an open hand.

"That isn't true, and you know it. My Xiaoling is suffering just as much as your son." The second woman had red hair and eyes the color of jade, and she answered the charges calmly, referring to the young Princess Lingli by an affectionate nickname. Consort Gyokuyou's looks suggested no small amount of western blood in her veins. Now she raised her head and glared at the doctor. "And that is why I request that you not neglect to attend to my daughter as well."

It seemed the doctor himself was the reason intercession had been needed between the two women. He had been spending all his time looking in here at the young prince, and Gyokuyou was appealing on her daughter's behalf. One sympathized with her, but this was the rear palace, and male children were more prized than female ones. The doctor, for his part, looked caught between trying to make an excuse and total speechlessness.

What a knave, that sawbones, Maomao thought. Failing to notice with the two consorts right in front of him. How could he not have figured it out already, anyway? The dead infants, the headaches, the stomach pains, the nausea. To say nothing of Consort Lihua's ghostly pallor and frail appearance.

Muttering to herself, Maomao put the raucous scene behind her. *I need something to write on,* she thought. She was so busy thinking it, in fact, that she didn't even notice the person passing by.

CHAPTER 3

Jinshi

"They're at it again," Jinshi muttered glumly to himself. It was unseemly, the way the blossoms of the palace carried on sometimes. It fell to Jinshi—one among his many responsibilities—to quiet things down.

As he waded into the crowd, Jinshi saw one person walking along as if the uproar didn't concern her. She was a petite girl with freckles peppering her nose and cheeks. There was nothing else distinctive about her, except that she paid no heed at all to Jinshi as she walked along muttering to herself.

And that could well have been the end of it.

It was not quite a month later that word spread the young prince had died. Consort Lihua was consumed with weeping and was thinner now than ever; she no longer looked anything like the woman who had once been considered the blooming rose of the court. Perhaps she suffered from the same illness as her son, or perhaps it was an affliction of the spirit that blighted her. Regardless, in such condition, she could hardly hope for another child.

Princess Lingli, the half sister of the deceased prince, soon recovered from her indisposition, and she and her mother became a great comfort to the bereaved emperor. Indeed, it seemed likely Consort Gyokuyou might soon bear another child, given how often His Majesty visited.

The prince and princess had both suffered from the same mysterious illness, yet one had recovered while the other had succumbed. Could it be the age gap between them? It had been just three months, but such a span could make a significant difference in an infant's resilience. And what of Lihua? If the princess had made a recovery, then there was every reason the consort should be able to as well. Unless she was suffering chiefly from the psychological shock of losing her son.

Jinshi turned these thoughts over in his head as he reviewed some paperwork and pressed his chop to it. If there was any difference between the two children, perhaps it lay with Consort Gyokuyou.

"I'm going out for a while," Jinshi said as he stamped the final page with his chop, and promptly left the room.

The princess, cheeks as full and rosy as steamed buns, smiled at him with all the innocence a child could muster. Her tiny hand clasped into a fist around Jinshi's finger.

"No, child, let him go," her mother, a red-haired beauty, scolded gently. She wrapped the infant in swaddling clothes and put her down to sleep in her crib. The princess, apparently too warm, kicked the coverings off and lay watching the visitor, gurgling happily.

"I presume you wish to ask me something," said the consort, always a perceptive woman.

Jinshi got right to the point. "Why did the princess recover her health?"

Consort Gyokuyou allowed herself the smallest of smiles before pulling a piece of cloth from a pouch. The cloth had been torn off of something and was adorned with ungainly characters. Not only was the handwriting uneven, but the message appeared to have been written using grass stains, so in places it was faded and difficult to read.

Your face powder is poison. Don't let it touch the baby.

Perhaps the faltering quality of the handwriting was deliberate. Jinshi cocked his head. "Your face powder?"

"Yes," Gyokuyou said, entrusting the child in the crib to a wet nurse and opening a drawer. She took out something wrapped in cloth: a ceramic vessel. She opened the lid to a puff of white powder.

"This?"

"The very same."

Perhaps, Jinshi conjectured, there was something in the powder. He remembered that Gyokuyou, already possessing the pale skin that was so prized at court, didn't need to use the powder to try to make herself more beautiful. Consort Lihua, in contrast, looked so sallow that she used more of it every day to conceal her condition.

"My little princess is quite a hungry girl," Gyokuyou said. "I don't make enough milk for her, so I hired a nurse to help." Sometimes mothers whose children had died shortly after birth found work as wet nurses. "This face powder belonged to that woman. She favored it because she felt it was whiter than other powders."

"And where is this nurse now?"

"She took ill, so I dismissed her. With ample funds for her livelihood, of course." Spoken like a woman who was both intellectual and perhaps too kind for her own good.

So, say there was some kind of poison in the face powder. If the mother were to use it, it would impact the child; if whatever was in the powder got into the mother's milk, it might even end up in the child's body. Neither Jinshi nor Gyokuyou knew what such a poison might be. But if the mysterious message was to be believed, it was how the young prince had met his end. By simple face powder, makeup used by any number of people in the rear palace.

"Ignorance is a sin," Gyokuyou said. "I should have taken more care with what was going into my child's mouth."

"I'm guilty of the same crime," Jinshi said. It was ultimately he who had allowed the emperor's son to be lost. And there may have been others who had died in the womb.

"I told Consort Lihua about the face powder, but anything I say only makes her dig in her heels," said Gyokuyou. Lihua had dark bags under her eyes even now and used ample helpings of the white makeup to conceal the poor color of her face, never believing it was poisonous.

Jinshi gazed at the simple cotton cloth. He thought it looked strangely familiar. The hesitant quality of the characters appeared to be a ruse, but the hand had an unmistakably feminine quality. "Who gave this to you, and when?"

"It came the day I demanded the doctor examine my daughter. I'm

Jinshi

afraid I only succeeded in causing you trouble, but this was by the window afterward. It was tied to a rhododendron branch."

Jinshi remembered the commotion that day. Had someone in the crowd noticed something, realized something, left a word of warning? But who? "No doctor in the palace would resort to such circuitous methods," he said.

"I agree. And ours never did seem to know how to treat the prince."

All that commotion. On reflection, Jinshi did remember a serving girl who had seemed distanced from the other rubbernecks. She had been talking to herself. What was it she had been saying?

"I need something to write on."

Jinshi felt the pieces fall into place. He started to chuckle. "Consort Gyokuyou, if I were to find the author of this message, what would you do with her?"

"I would thank her profusely. I owe her my daughter's life," the consort said, her eyes sparkling.

Ah, so she was keen to discover her benefactor. "Very well. Perhaps you would allow me to keep these for a short while."

"I eagerly await whatever you may discover." Gyokuyou looked happily at Jinshi. He returned her smile, then collected the jar of face powder and the cloth with the message on it. He searched his memory for any cloth that felt quite like this.

"Far be it from me to disappoint His Majesty's favorite lady." Jinshi's smile had all the innocence of a child on a treasure hunt.

CHAPTER 4

The Nymph's Smile

Maomao first learned of the prince's passing when black mourning sashes were distributed at the evening meal. The women would wear them for seven days to demonstrate their sorrow. But what caused more frowns than anything was the announcement that their serving of meat, already miserly, would be eliminated entirely for the duration. The women servants ate two meals a day, chiefly millet and soup, with the occasional vegetable. It was enough for the petite Maomao, but many of the women found the meals less than filling.

There were many kinds of women among this lowest class of servants. Some came from farming families, others were city girls, and although uncommon, a few were the daughters of officials. Children of the bureaucracy could expect a modicum more respect, but even so, the work a woman was given depended on her own accomplishments. A girl who couldn't read or write could certainly not expect to become a consort with her own chambers. Being a consort was a *job*. You even got a salary.

The Nymph's Smile

I guess maybe it didn't matter, in the end.

Maomao was aware of what had killed the young prince. It was Consort Lihua's and her serving women's liberal use of white powder to cover her face. That powder was so expensive, the average citizen couldn't expect to use it a day in her life. Some of the more established ladies in the brothel had it, though. Some of them made more money in a single night than a farmer would earn in his entire lifetime, and they could afford their own makeup. Others received it as an expensive present.

The women would cover themselves in it from their faces down to their necks, and it would eat away at their bodies. Some of them died from it. Maomao's father had warned them to stop using it, but they ignored him. Maomao, attending at her father's side, had witnessed several courtesans waste away and die with her own eyes. They had weighed their lives against their beauty, and in the end had lost them both.

That was why Maomao had broken off a couple of convenient branches, scrawled a brief message to each of the consorts, and left it for them. Not that she had expected them to heed a warning from a servant girl who couldn't get her hands on so much as paper or a brush.

After the mourning period was over and the black sashes disappeared, she began to hear rumors about Consort Gyokuyou. People said that after the loss of the prince, the emperor, sick at heart, had begun to take comfort with Gyokuyou and his surviving daughter. But to Consort Lihua, who had lost her child just as he had, he did not go.

How convenient for him. Maomao drained her bowl of soup—today furnished with the smallest sliver of a piece of fish—then cleaned up her utensils and headed to work.

"A summons, sir?" Maomao was carrying a laundry basket when a eunuch stopped her and told her to report to the office of the Matron of the Serving Women.

The Office of Serving Women was one of the three major divisions of service in the rear palace, and encompassed responsibility for the lowest ranking of the women servants. The other two divisions were the Office of the Interior, which dealt with the consorts, and the Domestic Service Department, to which the eunuchs were attached.

What could she want with me? Maomao wondered. The eunuch was talking to other serving girls nearby, as well. Whatever was going on, it involved more than just Maomao. They must need more hands for some chore or other, she reasoned. She set the basket outside its proper room, then went following after the eunuch.

The Matron of the Serving Women's building was situated just to one side of the main gate, one of the four gates that separated the rear palace from the world outside. When the emperor visited his ladies, this was the entrance through which he passed.

Despite being there on an official summons, Maomao didn't feel comfortable in the place. Although it was somewhat lackluster compared to the headquarters of the Office of the Interior, located next door, it was still noticeably more ornate than the residences of the mid-level consorts. The railing was worked with elaborate carvings, and brightly colored dragons climbed the vermilion pillars.

Urged inside, Maomao was somewhat less impressed than she had expected to be: the only furnishing in the room was a single large

The Nymph's Smile

desk. Ten or so other serving girls besides her were present, and they seemed animated by anxiety, anticipation, and a strange sort of excitement.

"All right, thank you. The rest of you may go home," the eunuch said.

Huh? Maomao felt unnatural, being singled out this way. She went alone into the next room as the remaining women left with suspicious glances in her direction.

Even for the chamber of an appointed official, it was a large space. Maomao looked around, intrigued, whereupon she noticed that all the serving women in the room were looking in one particular direction. A woman sat unobtrusively in the corner, attended by a eunuch. Another, somewhat older woman was not far away. Maomao remembered the middle-aged woman to be the Matron of the Serving Women, but she didn't recognize the haughty-looking lady.

Hmm? Now she registered that the person's shoulders were rather broad for a woman's, and their dress was so plain. Their hair was mostly held back by a sort of scarf, the rest of it cascading down behind them. *He's a man?*

He was surveying the female servants with a smile as soft and gentle as that of a heavenly nymph. Even the Matron was blushing like a girl. Suddenly Maomao understood the flush in everyone's cheeks. This had to be the immensely beautiful eunuch of whom she had heard so much. He had hair as fine as silk, an almost liquid presence, almond-shaped eyes, and eyebrows that evoked willow branches. A heavenly nymph on a picture scroll could not have competed with him for loveliness.

What a waste, Maomao thought, not remotely blushing herself. The men in the rear palace were all eunuchs, deprived of their ability to reproduce. They now lacked the equipment they needed to bear children. Precisely how gorgeous the offspring of this man would have been would remain a matter for the imagination.

Just as Maomao was thinking (with no small amount of impertinence) that such almost inhuman beauty might ensnare even the attentions of His Majesty, the eunuch stood up with a flowing motion. He went over to a desk, took up a brush, and began to write with elegant movements of his hand and arm. Then, with a smile as sweet as ambrosia, he displayed his work to the women.

Maomao froze.

You there, with the freckles, it said. *You stay here.*

That, at least, was the gist of it. The beautiful man must have noticed Maomao's reaction, because he turned his fullest smile on her. He rolled up the paper again and clapped his hands twice. "We're done here for today. You may all go back to your rooms."

The women, with plentiful disappointed glances back over their shoulders, exited the room. They would never know what had been written on the nymph's paper.

Maomao watched them leave, and after a moment it occurred to her that they were all petite women with prominent freckles. But they hadn't heeded the sign, which must mean that they couldn't read.

The message hadn't been for Maomao alone. She made to leave the room with the others, only to feel a hand placed firmly on her shoulder. With much fear and trembling, she turned around to find herself confronted with the almost blinding smile of the nymph-man.

"Now, now, mustn't do that," he said. "I want you to stay behind."

That smile—so bold, so bright—wouldn't take no for an answer.

CHAPTER 5

Attendant

"Most interesting. I was given to understand that you couldn't read," the beautiful eunuch said slowly, deliberately. Maomao followed uncomfortably behind him as he walked along.

"No, sir. I am of lowly birth. There must be some mistake."

Who the hell would teach me? she thought, but she would hardly have said the words if she'd been under torture. Maomao was set on acting as ignorant as she could. Maybe her language was a little off, but what could she do about it? Someone of such mean origins could be expected to do no better.

The lower-ranked serving girls were handled differently depending on whether or not they could read. Those who were literate and those who were not each had their uses, but if one could read yet pretended ignorance—ah, now that was the way to walk the fine line in the middle.

The beautiful eunuch introduced himself as Jinshi. His gorgeous smile suggested he wouldn't hurt a flea, but Maomao felt something shifty behind it. How else could he needle her so remorselessly? Jinshi had told Maomao to be silent and follow him. And that brought them to this moment. Maomao was aware that, as a servant of no import, shaking her head at Jinshi might be the last thing she ever did with it, so she had obediently done as he said. She was busy calculating what might happen next, and how she would deal with it.

It wasn't as if she couldn't guess what might have inspired Jinshi to summon her. What remained mysterious was how he had figured out that she had delivered the message to the consort.

A piece of cloth dangled with affected nonchalance in Jinshi's hand. It was festooned with unkempt characters. Maomao had told no one she could write and had likewise kept silent about her background as an apothecary and her knowledge of poisons. He could never have tracked her by her handwriting. She thought she had been careful to ensure there had been no one around when she delivered the message, but perhaps she had missed something, been seen by someone. The witness must have reported a petite servant girl with freckles.

No doubt Jinshi had begun by canvassing all the girls who could write, collecting samples of their calligraphy. One could attempt to appear a less competent wielder of the brush than one was, but telltale signs and identifying characteristics would remain. When that search had proved in vain, he would have turned to the girls who could not write.

Suspicious fart. Too much time on his hands . . .

As Maomao was having these uncharitable thoughts, they arrived at their destination. It was, as she might have expected, Consort Gyokuyou's pavilion. Jinshi knocked on the door and a placid voice responded, "Come in."

So they did. Inside, they discovered a gorgeous woman with red

Attendant

hair, lovingly cradling an infant with curly locks. The child's cheeks were rosy, her skin the same pale tone as her mother's. She was the picture of health as she lay dozing sweetly in the consort's arms.

"I have brought the one you wished to see, milady." Jinshi no longer spoke in the jocular manner of earlier but comported himself with perfect gravity.

"Thank you for your trouble." Gyokuyou smiled, a smile that was warmer than Jinshi's, and bowed her head to Maomao.

Maomao looked at her in surprise. "I possess no station to warrant such acknowledgment, milady." She chose her words carefully, trying not to offend. Although, not having been born to a life where such care was necessary, she wasn't sure she was doing it right.

"Oh, but you do. And I will do much more than this to show my gratitude to you—my daughter's savior."

"I'm certain there's been some misunderstanding. Perhaps you have the wrong person," Maomao said. She felt herself break into a cold sweat: she was being polite, but she was still contradicting an Imperial consort. She wished for her head to remain attached to her shoulders, but she did not wish to be a part of anything involving people such as this—to be pressed into any kind of service for any kind of noble or royal.

Jinshi, alert to the concern on Gyokuyou's face, displayed the cloth to Maomao with a flourish. "Are you aware that this is the material used in the maids' work clothes?"

"Now that you mention it, sir, I see the resemblance." She would play stupid to the bitter end. Even though she knew it was useless.

"It's more than a resemblance. This came from the uniform of a girl connected to the *shang* of sartorial affairs."

The palace serving staff were grouped into six *shang*, or main offices of employment. The *shang fu*, or Wardrobe Service, dealt with the dispensation of clothing, and it was this group to which Maomao, who was largely charged with doing laundry, belonged. The unbleached skirt she wore matched the color of the fabric in Jinshi's hands. If anyone were to inspect her skirt, they would find an unusual seam, hidden carefully on the inside.

In other words, the proof was there before them. Maomao doubted Jinshi would do anything so uncouth as to check for himself right in front of Consort Gyokuyou, but she couldn't be sure. She decided she had best own up before she was publicly humiliated.

"What exactly is it that you both want from me?" she asked.

The two of them looked at each other, apparently taking this for confirmation. Both had the sweetest of smiles on their faces. The only sound in the room was the whispering breath of the sleeping child and, almost as soft, Maomao sighing.

The very next day, Maomao was obliged to pack up her meager belongings. Xiaolan and all the other women who shared a room with her were properly jealous and pestered her endlessly about how this turn of events had come about. Maomao could only give her most strained smile and try to pretend it was no great matter.

Maomao was to be a lady-in-waiting to the emperor's favored consort.

That is to say, she had made it.

CHAPTER 6

Poison Tester

Jinshi found this a most congenial turn of events. The unusual girl he had discovered by sheer chance would now help him solve one of his many problems.

Lady Gyokuyou, the emperor's favored consort, was presently served by four ladies-in-waiting. That might be enough for some concubine of mean account, but for a high-ranking consort like Gyokuyou, it seemed too few. The ladies-in-waiting, however, insisted that the four of them were perfectly sufficient to take care of everything that needed doing, and Gyokuyou herself didn't seem inclined to press for more servants.

Jinshi understood well why this was the case. Consort Gyokuyou was a cheerful and generally tranquil person, but she was also intelligent and careful. In the garden of women that was the rear palace, a woman who received Imperial favor and was not suspicious of others was in mortal danger. There had, in fact, been several prior attempts on Gyokuyou's life. Notably, when she had become pregnant with the child who would go on to be Princess Lingli.

And so, although she had had ten ladies-in-waiting at first, she now had less than half that number. Typically, a lady only brought her own servants with her when she first arrived at the rear palace, but Gyokuyou had called on special privilege to bring in that nursemaid. She would never accept an anonymous servant girl from some far-flung corner of the rear palace as one of her ladies-in-waiting. But she had her station as a high consort to think of. Surely she could take on at least one more woman.

And this was where the freckled girl came in. She had saved Gyokuyou's daughter; certainly the consort wouldn't be averse to her. What was more, the girl knew something about poisons. That could only be useful. There was always the possibility that this freckled girl would put her knowledge to evil ends, but if she tried anything, they would simply have to corner her somewhere she couldn't do anything harmful. It was all so simple.

If all else failed, Jinshi thought with a grin, he could always use his charms. Yes, he found it just as repugnant as everyone else that he was so ready to take advantage of his ethereal beauty. But he had no intention of changing his ways. Indeed, his looks were what gave Jinshi his value in life.

When one became a servant assigned to a specific mistress, and a lady-in-waiting to the emperor's favorite consort at that, one found that one's treatment improved. Maomao, who had heretofore been squarely at the bottom of the palace hierarchy, suddenly found herself in the middle ranks. She was told her salary would see a significant increase, although twenty percent of what she earned went to her "family," which was to say, the merchants who had sold her into this life. A distasteful arrangement, in her opinion. A system created so greedy officials could line their pockets.

She was also given her own room—cramped, but a far cry from the overcrowded accommodations she had shared in the past. From a meager reed mat and a single sheet for bedding, she now found herself with an actual bed. Granted, it took up half her room, but Maomao was frankly happy to be able to get up in the morning without treading all over her coworkers.

She had one more cause for celebration as well, although she wouldn't know it until later.

The Jade Pavilion, in which Gyokuyou lived, was home to four other ladies-in-waiting besides Maomao. A nursemaid had lately been dismissed, allegedly because the princess was beginning to be weaned, but Maomao thought she had an inkling of the real reason. It was an awfully small number of women, in view of the fact that Consort Lihua had more than ten ladies-in-waiting attending her. Gyokuyou's ladies were more than a little taken aback to discover that one of the least important people in the palace had suddenly been elevated to their colleague, but they never harassed Maomao in the way she had half expected. If anything, they seemed sympathetic toward her.

But why? she thought.

She would find out soon enough.

———◇———

A palace meal, packed with ingredients traditionally believed to be of medicinal benefit, sat before her. One by one, Hongniang, the head of Gyokuyou's ladies-in-waiting, took samples and put them on little saucers, placing them in front of Maomao. Gyokuyou observed the scene apologetically but gave no indication that she was going to stop what was happening. The other three ladies-in-waiting likewise watched with pitying gazes.

The location was Gyokuyou's room. It was appointed in the highest style, and it was where the consort ate all her meals. Before the food reached her, it would pass through the hands of many others, and being the emperor's favorite, it behooved her to consider the possibility that one or more of those hands might try to poison the product.

Thus, a food taster was necessary. Everyone was on edge because of what had happened to the young prince. Rumors were rampant that the princess might have been sickened by the same poison the infant boy died from. The ladies-in-waiting hadn't been informed of what the toxic substance had ultimately been, and so they were understandably paranoid that it might be in anything or everything.

It would not have been strange if they'd viewed the lowly servant girl sent to them at that moment, specifically to be a food taster, as nothing but a disposable pawn. Maomao was charged not only with tasting Consort Gyokuyou's meals, but also the baby food served to the princess. On those occasions when His Majesty was present, she was also responsible for sampling the luxurious edibles offered to him.

After it was discovered that Gyokuyou was pregnant, Maomao was given to understand, there had been two separate instances of attempted poisoning. In one, the taster had gotten off without real injury, but another had found themselves subject to a nerve toxin that had left their arms and legs paralyzed. The remaining ladies-in-waiting, with much fear and trembling, had to check the food themselves, so they frankly must have been grateful for Maomao's arrival.

Maomao furrowed her brow as she looked at the plate in front of her. It was ceramic.

If they're so scared of poison, they should be using silver. She picked up the little bit of pickled vegetable in her chopsticks and regarded it critically. She took a sniff. Then she placed it on her tongue, checking to see whether it caused a tingling sensation before she swallowed it.

I don't think I'm actually qualified to be tasting for poisons, she reflected. Fast-acting agents were one thing, but with regard to slower toxins she expected to be somewhat useless. In the name of science, Maomao had accustomed her body to a variety of poisons by gradual exposure, and she suspected there were few left that would have a serious effect on her. This was not, let it be said, a part of her work as an apothecary, but purely a way of satisfying her intellectual curiosity. In the west, she heard, they had a name for researchers who did things that made no sense to people: mad scientists. Even her father, who had taught her the apothecary's trade, grew exasperated with her little experiments.

When she was satisfied that there were no untoward physical effects and that she detected no poisons she knew of, the meal could finally make its way to Consort Gyokuyou.

Next would come the flavorless baby food.

"I think it might be best to change the plates to ones made of silver," she said to Hongniang, as flatly as possible. She had been called to

Hongniang's room to provide a report on her first day of work. The chief lady's chambers were generous in size, but unadorned with any frivolous objects, bespeaking Hongniang's practical bent.

Hongniang, an attractive, black-haired woman not quite thirty years of age, let out a sigh. "Jinshi really had it all figured out." She confessed with some chagrin that they had deliberately not used silver tableware at the eunuch's instruction.

Maomao had a distinct suspicion that it was also Jinshi who had ordered her appointed food taster. She struggled not to let her already cold expression turn into one of outright disgust as she listened to Hongniang talk. "I don't know why you decided to hide your knowledge, but it's amazing that you know so much about poisons and medicine both. If you'd told them from the start that you knew how to write, you could have gotten a lot more money."

"My knowledge comes from my vocation—I was an apothecary. Until I was abducted and sold into this place. My kidnappers receive a portion of my salary even now. The thought turns my stomach." Maomao's hackles were up now, and her words came in a sharp rush, but the chief lady-in-waiting didn't rebuke her.

"You mean you were willing to put up with receiving less than you were worth to make sure they had one less cup of wine when they were carousing." Hongniang, it seemed, was more than perceptive enough to grasp Maomao's motives. Maomao found herself simply relieved that Hongniang hadn't scolded her for what she said. "Not to mention that women of no special distinction serve a couple of years and then go on their merry ways. Plenty of replacements out there."

She didn't have to understand quite that *well.*

Hongniang took a carafe from the table and gave it to Maomao.

Poison Tester

"What's this?" Maomao asked, but almost as soon as the words were out of her mouth, a pain shot through her wrist. She dropped the carafe on the floor in shock. A large crack spidered through the ceramic vessel.

"Oh, my goodness, that's quite an expensive piece of pottery. Certainly not something a simple lady-in-waiting could afford. You won't be able to make remittances to your family anymore with that hanging over your head—in fact, we should probably bill *them*."

Maomao understood immediately what Hongniang was saying, and the slightest ironic smile crept over her otherwise expressionless face. "My profound apologies," she said. "Please, deduct it from the amount of my salary that's sent home each month. And if that isn't enough, by all means, take from my own share as well."

"Thank you, I'll make sure the Matron of the Serving Women knows to do that. And one more thing." Hongniang put the broken carafe back on the table before taking a wood-strip roll out of a drawer and writing on it in quick, short strokes. "This details your additional salary as a food taster. Hazard pay, you might call it."

The amount was almost as much as Maomao was currently receiving. And insofar as nothing would be taken from it to pay her captors, Maomao came out ahead.

This woman does know how to use the carrot, she thought as she bowed deeply and left the room.

CHAPTER 7

Branch

The four ladies-in-waiting who had always attended Consort Gyokuyou were exceptionally hard workers. Granted, the Jade Pavilion was not the largest place, but they kept it humming along neatly, just the four of them. Serving girls from the *shangqin*—the Housekeeping Service, those charged with keeping rooms clean—did come sometimes, but by and large the four ladies-in-waiting handled all the cleaning and tidying themselves. That was not, for the record, something ladies-in-waiting typically did.

All this meant that the new girl, Maomao, had little to possess her other than tasting the food. Besides Hongniang, none of the other ladies-in-waiting ever asked Maomao to do anything. Maybe they felt bad that she was stuck with the most unpleasant job, or maybe they simply didn't want her intruding on their turf. Whatever the reason, even when Maomao offered to help, they would gently rebuff her with an "Oh, don't worry about it," and urge her to go back to her room.

How am I supposed to settle in here?

Cooped up in her room, she was summoned twice daily to meals, once to afternoon tea, and every few days to try one of the sumptuous banquets offered when the emperor came calling. That was all. Hongniang was kind enough to try to find little tasks for Maomao to do, but they were never anything difficult and didn't occupy her for long.

In addition to her tasting duties, she found her own meals became more elaborate. Sweet treats were offered at tea, and when there were extras, they would be sent to Maomao. And because she was no longer working like an ant as she once had been, all those extra nutrients went to flesh.

I feel like some kind of livestock.

Her new appointment as food taster had brought with it another thing Maomao didn't like. She had always been rather slim, but this meant that if a poison caused her to waste away, it would be hard to detect. What was more, the dosage of any given toxin that might be deadly was in proportion to one's body size. A little extra weight could improve her chances of survival.

In Maomao's mind, there was no way she could miss a poison so powerful as to make her waste away, and meanwhile, she was confident she could survive an ordinarily fatal dose of many toxins. But no one around her seemed to share her optimism. They only saw a small, delicate girl being treated like a disposable pawn, and they pitied her for it. And so, they plied her with congee even after she was full, and always gave her an extra serving of vegetables.

They remind me of the girls from the brothels. Maomao could be cold, reticent, and unsentimental, but for some reason, the women had always doted on her. They always had an extra treat or a bit of something for her to eat.

Although Maomao didn't realize it, there was a reason people were so inclined to look kindly on her. Running along her left arm was a collection of scars—cuts, stabs, burns, and what seemed to be repeated piercings with a needle. To others, Maomao looked like a petite, overthin girl with wounds on her arm. Her arms were frequently bandaged, her face sometimes pale, and once in a while she was given to fainting. People simply assumed, with a tear in their eye, that her coldness and reticence were the natural result of the treatment she had suffered to this point in her life. They were sure she had been abused, but they were wrong.

Maomao had done it all to herself.

She was most interested in discovering the effects of various medicines, analgesics, and other concoctions firsthand. She would take small doses of poison to inure herself to them and had been known to let herself be bitten by venomous snakes. And, as for the fainting, well, she didn't always get the dosage quite right. This was also why the wounds were concentrated on her left arm: it was preferable to her dominant limb, her right.

None of this sprang from any masochistic proclivity for pain but was fueled entirely by the interests of a girl whose intellectual curiosity inclined rather too much in the direction of medicines and poisons. It had been her father's burden to cope with her for her entire life. Yes, it was he who had taught Maomao her letters and first instructed her in the ways of medicine, in the hopes that she would see a way forward in life other than prostitution, even though he had been obliged to raise her in and around the red-light district. By the time he realized he had far too apt a student on his hands, it was too late, and the calumnies about him had already begun to spread. There were a few who understood, just a few, but most turned cold, hard gazes on Maomao's father. They never for a moment imagined that a girl of her age might commit self-harm in the name of experimentation.

And so, the story seemed to be complete: after suffering long abuse at the hands of her father, this poor child had been sold off to the rear palace, where she was now to be sacrificed to discover poison in the consort's food. A sorrowful tale indeed.

And one of which the protagonist was entirely unaware.

I'm going to be a pig at this rate! About the time Maomao began to fret about this particular possibility, her woes were compounded by a most unwelcome visitor.

"It's rather late for you," Consort Gyokuyou said as a newcomer entered the room.

The caller in question was the nymphlike eunuch, this time with one of his compatriots in tow. The gorgeous youth evidently made routine rounds of the upper consorts' chambers. The compatriot had brought sweets. Maomao tasted them for poison, then withdrew discreetly behind Consort Gyokuyou, who reclined on a chaise longue. Maomao was standing in for Hongniang, who had gone to change the princess's diaper. These men may have been eunuchs, but they were still not allowed an audience with the consort without the presence of a lady-in-waiting.

"Yes, there's been word that the barbarian tribe has been successfully subdued."

"Has it? And what's to come of it?" Gyokuyou's eyes glowed with curiosity; this subject was more than enough to excite the interest of a bird trapped in the cage that was the rear palace. Though she was the emperor's favorite, Gyokuyou was also still young, not more than a few years older than Maomao herself, as Maomao understood it.

"I'm not certain it's appropriate to discuss in front of a lady such as yourself . . ."

"I wouldn't be here if I couldn't endure both the beautiful and the terrible in this world," Gyokuyou said boldly.

Jinshi glanced at Maomao, an appraising look that swiftly vanished. He insisted there was nothing interesting about the subject but proceeded to speak of the world outside the birdcage.

Some days before, a band of warriors had been sent out, on information that a tribe was once again plotting ill. This country was largely a peaceful one, but issues such as this did sometimes mar its tranquility.

The warriors successfully drove back the barbarian scouts who had ventured into the territory, with hardly a casualty to speak of. The trouble started on the way home. The food in the encampment was compromised, and almost a dozen men came down with food poisoning. Many more were deeply demoralized. They had obtained the provisions at a nearby village just prior to coming into contact with the barbarians. The villages in this area were technically part of Maomao's nation, but historically they were not without their ties to the barbarian tribes.

One of the armed soldiers arrested the village chieftain. Several villagers who attempted to resist were killed on the spot for conspiring with the barbarians. The rest of the villagers would learn their fate after it was determined what would happen to their chief.

When Jinshi had delivered this précis of events, he took a sip of tea.

That's outrageous. Maomao wanted to grab her head in her hands. She wished she had never heard the story. There were so many things in the world one would be happier not knowing. The eunuch saw the furrow in her brow and turned his fine countenance on her.

Don't look at me.

Ah, if only wishes made things so.

Jinshi's lips formed a gentle arch as he took in Maomao's expression. He almost seemed to be testing her with his smile. "Something on your mind?"

It was as good as an order to say something, so she had to find something to say.

Will it even matter? she asked herself. But one thing was for certain: if she said nothing, then at least one village would disappear off the map of the frontier.

"I offer you only my personal opinion," Maomao said, and picked a branch out of a nearby vase in which some flowers had been arranged. This branch, which had no blossoms itself, was from a rhododendron.

The same kind of branch upon which Maomao had left her message. She plucked off a leaf and put it in her mouth.

"Is it flavorful?" Consort Gyokuyou asked, but Maomao shook her head.

"No, ma'am. Touching it can induce nausea and difficulty breathing."

"And yet you've just had it in your mouth," Jinshi said with a probing look.

"You needn't fret," Maomao said to the eunuch, setting the branch on the table. "But you see, even here on the grounds of the rear palace, there are poisonous plants. The rhododendron's poison is in the leaves, but others contain their toxins in the branches or roots. Some release poison if you so much as burn them up." These hints, Maomao suspected, would be enough to lead the eunuchs and the clever Gyokuyou where she wanted them to go. Despite doubting it was necessary to continue, she did so: "When encamped, soldiers make their chopsticks and campfires from local materials, do they not?"

"Ah," Jinshi said.

"But that—" Gyokuyou added.

It would mean the villagers had been punished unjustly.

Maomao watched as Jinshi rubbed his chin thoughtfully.

I don't know how important this Jinshi is . . .

But she hoped that he might be able to help in some way, however minor. Hongniang came back with Princess Lingli, and Maomao left the room.

CHAPTER 8

Love Potion

There was the young man with his inhuman beauty and his perpetual, divine smile. Even the way he sat on the cloth-draped sofa in the sitting room was elegant.

What's he want today? Maomao thought. Her cold detachment was not shared by the three ladies-in-waiting who blushed and bustled off to make tea for the guest. Maomao could hear them arguing in the next room over who would have the honor of preparing it. Finally, an exasperated Hongniang made the drink herself, sending the other three ladies back to their rooms. They went with their shoulders slumped, the very picture of dejection.

Maomao, the food taster, picked up the silver teacup and gave it a delicate sniff before taking a mouthful of tea. Jinshi had been watching her this entire time, and it made her fidgety. She squinted so she wouldn't have to meet his eyes. Most young women would have been quite satisfied to have the attention of such a fine man, even if he was a eunuch. But not Maomao. She didn't much share the interests of the common run of people, so even if she acknowledged intellectually that Jinshi was intensely beautiful, she remained aloof.

"Someone gave me some treats. Would you be so kind as to taste them, too?"

Jinshi indicated a basket filled with *baozi*. Maomao took one of the buns and pulled it open, discovering a filling of minced meat and vegetables. She took a sniff; it had a faintly medicinal odor she recognized. It was the same as a stamina booster from the other day.

"An aphrodisiac," she said.

"You can tell without tasting it?"

"It's not harmful to speak of. Go ahead and take them home with you. Enjoy them."

"I don't think I could, knowing who they came from."

"Indeed. I think you might have a visitor this evening." Maomao made sure to sound downright nonchalant. Jinshi, who had clearly not expected this reaction, looked at a loss. He was just lucky she didn't give him her staring-at-a-worm look. Giving her a bun to taste when he knew there was an aphrodisiac in it!

There remained the question of *who* had given him the *baozi*. Consort Gyokuyou laughed to overhear their conversation, her voice like the tinkling of a bell. Princess Lingli slept peacefully at her feet.

Maomao bowed and made to leave the room.

"Just a moment, if you please."

"Do you need something further, sir?"

Jinshi and Gyokuyou shared a look, then nodded at each other. It seemed they had already discussed whatever was going on—and it involved Maomao.

Love Potion

"Perhaps you could make a love potion."

For just an instant, Maomao's eyes lit up with a mixture of surprise and curiosity. *What's that supposed to mean?*

She couldn't imagine what they wanted with such a thing, but the subject was one she would be more than happy to entertain. Forcing herself not to smile, she replied, "I need three things: tools, materials, and time."

Could she make a love potion? Oh, yes. Yes, she could.

Jinshi wondered what was the matter. His eyebrows furrowed like drooping willow branches, and he crossed his arms. Jinshi was a person of such beauty that some said if he had only been born a woman, he could have had the country under his thumb; indeed, it was held that had he wished to, he could have convinced the very emperor to affirm that gender meant nothing. But such "praise" brought him no pleasure.

Today, as he went about the rear palace, he had once again found himself the object of something like catcalls by one of the middle-ranked consorts and two of the lower-ranked ones, and even by two separate male officials in the palace, one military and one bureaucratic. The military official had gone so far as giving him dim sum laced with a stamina tonic, so Jinshi decided to forgo his rounds tonight and retire to his rooms in the palace instead. He wasn't slacking off; it was for his own protection.

He quickly noted some names on the scroll lying open on his desk—the names of the consorts who had called out to him today. Even if she had scant visits from the emperor, it was awfully audacious of a woman to try to invite another man into her bedchamber. Jinshi's list was not an official report, but he suspected they would be even less likely to receive an Imperial visit after this.

He wondered how many of the little birds trapped in this cage understood that his own beauty was a testing stone for the women of the rear palace. Women were chosen to be consorts based first and foremost on family background, but beauty and intelligence played their part, too. Compared to the first two qualities, intelligence was trickier to measure. They also needed an upbringing befitting a mother to the nation, and of course they must be of chaste outlook.

The emperor, in a nasty little tweak, had made Jinshi the standard for selecting his consorts. It was in fact Jinshi who had recommended both Gyokuyou and Lihua. Gyokuyou was thoughtful and perceptive. Lihua was more emotional but possessed unimpeachable manners. And both had unquestioned loyalty to His Majesty, without a shadow of untoward feelings.

Consort Lihua, though, now seemed to have no place in His Majesty's adoration.

The emperor might have been Jinshi's master, but he was also, in Jinshi's estimation, terrible. He set up concubines purely based on their usefulness to him and the country, got them pregnant, and then when the children showed no aptitudes, he would cut them loose.

In the future, Jinshi surmised, the Imperial affection would continue to incline ever more toward Gyokuyou. The death of the young prince had marked the emperor's final visit to Lihua, who now seemed as insubstantial as a ghost. Lihua was not the only consort for whom it seemed His Majesty no longer had any need. Those women would be quietly returned to their homes at an opportune moment, or else gifted as wives to various officials.

Jinshi pulled a particular paper out of his pile. It referred to a middle consort of the Upper Fourth rank, Fuyou by name. She had just been promised in marriage to the leader of the assault on the barbarian tribe in recognition of his military valor. Truth be told, they were less appreciative of the man's energetic destruction of the enemy than of his restraining certain short-tempered elements among his own troops. That a certain small village had been blamed and punished for something it hadn't done was not a fact that had been made public. Such were politics.

"Now then, I wonder if it will all go well."

If everything went just as he had calculated in his head, there would be no problems. He might have to lean on the chilly apothecary to help him out with a few things, though. She had turned out to be even more useful than he'd expected.

She wasn't the only one who showed no special desire for him, but she was the first to regard him as though she were looking at a worm. She seemed to think she hid the feeling well, but the disdain was clear on her face.

Jinshi smiled in spite of himself. That smile, like nectar from heaven, some said, contained just a hint of something mean in it. He wasn't a masochist as such, but he found the girl's reaction intriguing. He felt like a child with a brand-new toy.

"Yes, where *will* this all lead?"

Jinshi placed the papers under a weight and decided to go to sleep. He made sure to lock his door in case he should have any uninvited visitors during the night.

People spoke of "cure-alls," but in fact there was no medicine that would cure all. Her father had always insisted as much, but Maomao had admittedly gone through a phase in which she had rejected his claim. She had wanted to create a medicine that could work on anyone, for any condition. That was what had led her to inflict those ugly wounds on herself and had indeed resulted in the creation of some new medicines, but a true panacea remained nothing more than a dream.

As much as she hated to admit it, the story Jinshi brought her was enough to pique Maomao's interest. Since arriving in the rear palace, she'd been unable to make much more than sweet *amacha* tea. To her surprise, a variety of medicinal herbs did grow on the grounds of the rear palace, but she lacked the implements necessary to make proper use of them, and trying to do anything with them would have attracted undesirable attention in her crowded quarters anyway, so she forced herself to leave the plants alone.

This was what she liked best about having her own room. Now she just needed excuses to go gather ingredients—laundry was a convenient one. She suspected Hongniang would soon see to it that Maomao was entrusted with all the washing.

Now she arrived at the room she had been told was the doctor's, ostensibly to deliver clean laundry. She entered the room to discover the lamentable quack himself along with the eunuch who so frequently accompanied Jinshi. The doctor had a mustache that made him look like a loach fish, which he stroked as he gave Maomao an appraising glance. He seemed to be wondering what this petite young woman was doing on his turf.

Love Potion

I'll thank you not to stare so hard at a young lady, Maomao thought. The eunuch, by comparison, was as polite as if Maomao were his own master, ushering her gracefully into the room. When Maomao saw the space, surrounded by medicine cabinets on three sides, she was overcome by the biggest smile she'd smiled since coming to the rear palace. Her cheeks flushed, her eyes brimmed, and her lips went from a thin, implacable line to a gentle arch.

The eunuch looked at her in surprise, but what did she care? She gazed at the labels on the drawers, doing a sort of little dance when she spotted an especially unusual pharmaceutical. The joy was simply too much to keep inside.

"Is she under some sort of spell?" Maomao had been indulging this rapture for a good half an hour, unaware that Jinshi had appeared in the room. He watched her with a mixture of curiosity and sheer bewilderment.

M aomao went row by row, collecting any ingredients she might be able to use. Each one went into a separate baggie, the name written carefully on the package. In an era when most writing was still done on rolls of wood strips, such extensive use of paper was a luxury. The loach-mustached doctor came peeking into the room, wondering who or what was in there, but the eunuch closed the door on him. The eunuch's name, Maomao learned, was Gaoshun. He had a steady countenance and a well-built body, and if he hadn't been here in the rear palace, she would certainly have taken him for some sort of military official. He appeared to be Jinshi's aide, and was often seen in his company.

Gaoshun politely fetched any medicines that were in drawers too high for Maomao to reach. His superior, meanwhile, did nothing. Maomao maintained a neutral expression but privately wished that if he wasn't going to make himself useful, he would go away.

Maomao spotted a familiar name on one of the topmost drawers and craned her neck for a better look. Gaoshun passed the stuff to her, and she looked at it in wonder. Several small seeds rested in the palm of her hand. They were exactly what she needed, but there weren't enough of them.

"I need more of these."

"Then we shall simply get them," the indolent eunuch said with an indulgent smile. As if it were so easy.

"They're from all the way in the west, then farther west, then south."

"Trade's the thing. We'll check the goods that come in, and I suspect we'll find some." Jinshi took one of the seeds between his fingers. It resembled the seed of an apricot but had a unique aroma. "What is it called?"

"Cacao," Maomao replied.

CHAPTER 9

Cacao

"At least I grasp its effectiveness now," Jinshi said with an annoyed glance at Maomao.

"As do I," Maomao said.

Jinshi looked almost overcome by the catastrophic scene in front of him. "Ugh," he said, and there was no hint of his usual detached smile. There was only fatigue on his face. "How did this happen?"

To answer that question, we'll have to go back in time a few hours.

The cacao they were sent was no longer in seed form, but had been powdered. All the other ingredients Maomao had requested had already arrived at the kitchen of the Jade Pavilion. Three of the ladies-in-waiting were busy trying to look on, but a word from Hongniang sent them scurrying back to their work.

Milk, butter, sugar, honey, distilled spirits and dried fruits, and some oils derived from aromatic herbs to give everything a pleasant odor. All nutritious—and expensive—ingredients, and all useful in a stamina concoction.

Maomao had tasted cacao only once. It had been in a hardened, sweetened form called chocolate, and she had received it from one of the prostitutes. It had been a piece hardly the size of the tip of her finger, but on eating it, she felt she had drunk an entire cup of some especially sharp liquor. It made her oddly giddy.

The chocolate was, the woman had explained, a gift from an especially nasty customer who had hoped to buy the affections of a girl who had been sold into prostitution by offering her a rare treat. When the girl noticed Maomao's altered state, however, she was deeply angry, and the madam of the brothel forbade the customer from coming back. It came to light later that a trading concern had started to sell the stuff as an aphrodisiac. Maomao had managed to obtain a handful of seeds since then, but she had never used them as medicine. No one in the red-light district came to the apothecary seeking something so extravagant for a simple medicament.

Even now, Maomao remembered the chocolate for the way it had been hardened with oil and fat. Her wide experience with an eclectic collection of medicines and poisons in all their various flavors and aromas naturally also gave her an excellent memory for ingredients.

It was still the hot season, and she suspected butter wouldn't set well, so she decided to cover some fruit instead. A bit of ice would be perfect, but that was of course impossible and didn't make the ingredients list. Instead, she asked for a large, unglazed water jug to be prepared. It was filled half full with water. As the water evaporated, the inside of the jug would become cooler than the outside air, cool enough to help harden the fats.

Maomao dipped a spoon into the mixture and tasted a bit of it. It was bitter and sweet at the same time, and her knowledgeable tongue likewise detected elements that would improve the mood. She was far more resistant to things like alcohol and toxins now than she had been when she'd had that first taste of chocolate, and it didn't affect her nearly as much. But she could still tell it was powerful stuff.

Maybe I should make the portions a bit smaller.

She chopped the fruit in half with a simple cleaver, then dipped them in the brownish liquid. She put them on a plate, then placed them in the jug. She put a lid on the jug, then covered it with a straw mat to hide it. The only thing left was to wait for the chocolate to harden. Jinshi would come by to collect it that evening; that should be plenty of time.

Guess I've got a little extra . . .

She hadn't used all the brownish liquid. The ingredients were extremely expensive, and it was quite nutritious. Aphrodisiac or not, it had a minimal effect on Maomao, so she decided to eat it herself later. She chopped some bread into cubes and soaked them in the stuff; this way she wouldn't have to worry about any cooling process, either.

She put a lid on the jar of cacao liquid and set it on the shelf. The rest of the ingredients she put in her own room, then headed for the washing area to clean the utensils. She should have put the dipped bread in her room, too, but she was already thinking about other things. Maybe her taste-testing *had* left her a little inebriated.

Well, it was too late now.

It happened after that, while Maomao was out running errands for Hongniang, stopping off along the way to pick some medicinal herbs for herself. The bread, and the fact that it should have gone on the shelf, were chased clear out of Maomao's mind. She returned with a laundry basket full of herbs, thoroughly pleased with herself, only to be greeted by Hongniang and Consort Gyokuyou, looking deathly pale and rather disturbed, respectively. Gaoshun was there too, which implied Jinshi was somewhere about.

Hongniang could only put a hand to her forehead and point to the kitchen, so Maomao pressed her laundry basket into Gaoshun's arms and headed over.

She discovered Jinshi, looking annoyed. The delicate way to put it would be to say that a great medley of peach and light-red colors spread before her. Which is to say, more plainly, that three ladies-in-waiting were all leaning against each other, sound asleep. Their clothes were in disarray, their disheveled skirts revealing lascivious glimpses of thigh.

"What *happened* here?" Hongniang demanded of Maomao.

"I'm afraid I'm not best placed to answer that question," she replied. She went over to the three young women and crouched down, flipping down their skirts and examining them. "It's all right, this attempt failed to—"

Hongniang, blushing furiously, smacked Maomao on the back of the head.

Sitting on the table was the brown-colored bread. Three pieces were missing.

The girls had mistaken it for an afternoon snack.

The fatigue caught up with her after they had put each of the girls to bed in her own room. In the sitting room, Gyokuyou and Jinshi were looking at the chocolate bread with some wonder.

"Is this your aphrodisiac?" Gyokuyou inquired.

"No, ma'am, this is." Maomao gave her the chocolate-covered fruit. Approximately thirty pieces, each the size of a thumbnail.

"What *is* this, then?" Jinshi asked.

"It was supposed to be my bedtime snack." Everyone seemed to recoil a little at that. Had she said something wrong? Gaoshun and Hongniang both looked like they could hardly believe their eyes. "I'm very accustomed to spirits and stimulants, so I don't feel them much."

Maomao had once, in the name of science, pickled a venomous snake in alcohol and drunk it, so she could safely be called an experienced drinker. She considered alcohol to be a kind of medicine. The more susceptible one was to new forms of stimulation, the better medicine worked on one. Take this bread, for instance: here in the Jade Pavilion, it passed for an aphrodisiac, but she had to think that in the land where the ingredients had come from, it would be substantially less effective.

Jinshi picked up one of the pieces of bread and looked at it doubtfully. "I wonder if I might safely try a piece, then," he said.

"*No, sir, don't!*" Hongniang and Gaoshun cried almost in unison. Maomao thought this was the first time she had heard Gaoshun speak.

Jinshi put the bread back, remarking that he had only been joking. It would, of course, have been improper for him to consume a known aphrodisiac in the presence of the emperor's own favorite consort, but perhaps even more to the point, hardly anyone could have resisted him had he come to her with that nymphlike smile and a flush in his cheeks. His face, if nothing else, Maomao reflected, did him credit.

"Perhaps I should have some made for His Majesty," Gyokuyou said with amusement. "It might keep him from his usual ways."

"It would most likely work about three times better than a typical stamina medication," Maomao informed her.

At this, Gyokuyou's face took on a cast that was hard to read. "Three times . . ." She mumbled something about whether she could endure so long, but those present affected not to have heard her. It seemed it wasn't easy being a concubine.

Maomao put the aphrodisiacs in a covered jar and handed it to Jinshi. "They're quite potent, so I recommend taking just one at a time. Taking too many could overstimulate the blood flow and produce a nosebleed. Also, consumption should be limited to when the patient is alone with their partner."

With these instructions duly conveyed, Jinshi stood up. Gaoshun and Hongniang left the room to prepare for his departure. Consort Gyokuyou likewise nodded to him, then left with the sleeping princess in a carrier.

As Maomao went to clean up the plate of bread, she smelled a sweet aroma from behind her.

"Thank you. I put you through quite a bit of trouble." The voice was sweet, too, like honey. Maomao felt her hair being lifted up, and something cold was pressed against her neck. She turned in time to see Jinshi waving at her as he left the room.

"I get it." When she looked at the plate, she discovered one of the pieces of bread was missing. She had an idea where it was. "I just hope no one gets hurt," Maomao muttered, but she didn't seem to think it had much to do with her.

The night was still young.

CHAPTER 10

The Unsettling Matter of the Spirit
(PART ONE)

Yinghua, lady-in-waiting to the emperor's favorite consort, Gyokuyou, was faithfully at her work, as she was every day. All right, so she had fallen asleep on the job the other day, but her gracious mistress had forborne to punish her. The only way to repay her, then, was to work herself to the bone. She would make sure she polished every windowsill, every railing, until it gleamed. This was not normally something a lady-in-waiting would be expected to do, but Yinghua was not above doing a serving girl's work. Consort Gyokuyou had said how much she liked hard workers.

Consort Gyokuyou and Yinghua both came from a town in the west. The climate there was dry, and the area had no special resources to speak of and was periodically subject to drought. Yinghua and the other ladies-in-waiting were all officials' daughters, but she didn't recall her life in her hometown as especially luxurious. It had been the sort of impoverished place where even a child of the bureaucracy had to work if she didn't want to starve.

And then Gyokuyou was taken into the palace, and the world began to take note of her home. When the consort received the special attentions of the emperor, the central bureaucracy could no longer hide where she had come from. But Gyokuyou was an intelligent woman. She wasn't content simply to be a pampered ornament. And Yinghua was bent on following her lady wherever she might go, including into the rear palace. Not all Gyokuyou's ladies showed the same dedication, but those who remained simply resolved to work even harder to make up the difference.

When Yinghua went into the kitchen to organize the utensils, she discovered the new girl there, making something. Maomao was her name, Yinghua recalled, but she had proven so taciturn that nobody was sure what kind of person she really was. Consort Gyokuyou was an uncommonly strong judge of character, however, so it was unlikely Maomao was a bad egg.

Indeed, Yinghua felt sorry for her. The scars on her arm obviously bespoke a history of abuse, after which she had been sold into service and now brought on to taste food for poison. It was enough to bring a tear to a lady-in-waiting's eye. They kept increasing her portions at dinner, hoping to plump up the spindly girl, and they refused to let her do the cleaning so that she wouldn't have to reveal her injuries to the wider world. Yinghua and her two fellow ladies-in-waiting were of one mind in all this, and as a result Maomao frequently found herself with little to do.

Yinghua was happy enough with that. She and the other girls were

The Unsettling Matter of the Spirit (Part One)

more than capable of handling the work by themselves. Hongniang, the chief lady-in-waiting, didn't precisely agree, and at least gave Maomao the washing to take care of. It was just carrying the laundry around in a basket, so her scars wouldn't be obvious. She also engaged Maomao for miscellaneous chores when necessary.

Carting around laundry baskets also wasn't the work of a lady-in-waiting but was properly done by serving girls from the large communal rooms. But ever since a poison needle had been discovered in Consort Gyokuyou's clothing once, Yinghua and the others had taken to handling the wash themselves. It was incidents like this that inspired them to debase themselves as if they were simple serving women. Here in the rear palace, they were surrounded by enemies.

"What are you making?"

Maomao was boiling something that looked like grass in a stewpot. "It's a cold remedy." She always answered with the absolute minimum of words. It was understandable—poignant, in fact—to realize how hard she must find it to get close to people as a result of her abuse.

Maomao was profoundly knowledgeable about medicine and occasionally made some like this. She always cleaned up after herself neatly, and the anti-chapping ointment she'd given Yinghua recently was precious stuff, so Yinghua didn't object. Sometimes Maomao even produced the concoctions at Hongniang's request.

Yinghua took down some silver dishes and began diligently polishing them with a dry cloth. Maomao rarely said much, but she knew how to be a polite listener in a conversation, so it never hurt to talk to her. And that's what Yinghua did, telling her about some rumors she'd heard recently. Stories of a pale woman who danced through the air.

Maomao headed for the medical office with her completed cold remedy and a basket of laundry. It was the doctor's right to give his imprimatur to any medicine, even if it was only for form's sake.

Did this spirit suddenly pop up in the last month? Maomao shook her head at the garden-variety ghost story. She hadn't heard anything of the sort prior to arriving at the Jade Pavilion, and because she trusted Xiaolan to tell her anything worth hearing, she had to think the rumor was a recent one.

The rear palace was surrounded by what amounted to castle walls. The gates in each wall were the only ways in or out; a deep moat on the far side of the barrier prevented both intrusion and escape. Some said there were former concubines, would-be escapees from the rear palace, sunk at the bottom of that moat even now.

So, the ghost is supposed to show up near the gate, huh?

There were no buildings in the immediate area, just a spreading pine forest.

Started around the end of summer.

It was the time for harvesting a certain something.

No sooner had she had this naughty little thought than Maomao heard a voice, one she was not pleased by, but which always seemed to be after her specifically.

"Hard at work again, I see."

Maomao met the man's smile, lovely as a peony blossom, with studious indifference. "Hardly working, sir, I assure you."

The medical office was beside the central gate to the south, near

The Unsettling Matter of the Spirit (Part One)

the headquarters of the three major offices that oversaw the running of the rear palace. Jinshi could be seen there often. As a eunuch, his proper place was in the Domestic Service Department, but this man seemed to have no specific place of employment; indeed, he almost seemed to oversee the entire palace.

It's almost like he's over the Matron of the Serving Women.

It was always possible he was the current emperor's guardian, but considering Jinshi looked to be about twenty years old, it was hard to imagine. Maybe he was the son of the emperor or something, but then why become a eunuch? He seemed close with Consort Gyokuyou; maybe he was her guardian instead, or perhaps . . .

The emperor's lover . . . ?

Relations between the emperor and Gyokuyou always seemed perfectly normal when His Majesty came for his visits, but things weren't always what they seemed. Maomao got tired of trying to play out the possibilities, though, and so settled on this last one. That was easiest.

"Your face says you're having the world's most impertinent thought," Jinshi said, squinting at her.

"Are you sure you're not imagining it?" She bowed to him and ducked into the medical office, where the loach-mustached quack of a doctor was industriously pulverizing something in a mortar. Maomao grasped that in his case, this wasn't a step in making some medical concoction, but simply a way of passing the time. Otherwise, why would he need her to give him any medicine she made? The doctor didn't seem to know but the most rudimentary medicinal recipes or techniques.

The medical staff was perpetually shorthanded, as one might surmise of the rear palace. Women were not allowed to become doctors, and while many men might wish to be, few wished also to become eunuchs. The old quack here had at first treated Maomao like a distracting little girl, but his attitude softened when he saw the medicines she made. Now he would put out tea and snacks and gladly share with her any ingredients she needed, but while she was grateful for this, she did question what it said about him as a physician. Confidentiality seemed of little concern to him.

I wonder if this is remotely all right. Maomao would entertain the thought, but she wouldn't say anything. The current arrangement was far too convenient for her.

"Would you be so kind as to check this medicine I've made?"

"Ah, hullo, young lady. Of course, hold on just a moment." He brought out snacks and some kind of tea. No more sweet buns; there were rice crackers today. That was fine by Maomao, who preferred a hotter flavor. It seemed the doctor had been so gracious as to remember her preferences. She'd had the continual feeling that he was trying to ingratiate himself with her, but it didn't bother her. He might have been a quack, but he was a decent person.

"Surely there's enough for me, too?" a honeyed voice said from behind her. She didn't have to turn around; she could practically feel his effulgence in the air. You must know by now who it was: Jinshi, in the flesh.

The doctor, with a mixture of surprise and excitement, promptly changed the crackers and *zacha*—old tea with flavorings—for more-desirable white tea and mooncakes.

The Unsettling Matter of the Spirit (Part One)

My rice crackers...

The beaming smile seated itself beside Maomao. By dint of social difference, they should never have found themselves sitting side by side, and yet, here they were. It might have looked like a gesture of utmost magnanimity, but Maomao felt something very different in it, something pointed and forceful.

"I'm sorry for the trouble, Doctor, but could you go in the back and fetch these for me?" Jinshi handed the quack a slip of paper. Even without getting a clear look at it, Maomao could see an abundant list of medicines. It would keep the doctor occupied for a while. The quack squinted at the list, then retreated ruefully into the back room.

So that was the plan all along.

"What exactly do you want?" Maomao asked bluntly, sipping her tea.

"Have you heard about the commotion concerning the ghost?"

"No more than rumors."

"Then have you heard of somnambulism?"

The sparkle that lit Maomao's eyes at that word wasn't lost on Jinshi. A naughty bit of satisfaction entered his lovely smile. He brushed Maomao's cheek with his broad palm. "And would you know how to cure it?" His voice was as sweet as a fruit liqueur.

"I haven't the foggiest idea." Maomao refused to be self-deprecating, but she didn't want to overstate her abilities, either. She'd encountered virtually every kind of illness, though, and seen many of them in patients. Thus, she could say with confidence what she said next: "It can't be helped with medicine."

It was a disease of the spirit. When a prostitute had been afflicted with this illness, Maomao's father had done nothing to treat it, because there was no treatment to give.

"But with something other than medicine . . . ?" Jinshi wanted to know any potential cure at all.

"My specialty is pharmaceuticals." She thought that was about as emphatic as she could be, but then she realized she could still see the lovely face, now wreathed in distress, floating in her peripheral vision.

Don't look him in the eye . . .

Maomao avoided his gaze, as if he were a wild animal. Or at least, she tried to, but it just wasn't possible. He slid around so he was facing her. Talk about persistent. Talk about annoying. Maomao had no choice but to admit defeat.

"Fine. I'll help you," she said, but she was careful to look very unhappy about it.

Gaoshun arrived to fetch her around midnight. They were going out to witness the illness in question. Gaoshun's taciturn nature and often expressionless face could have made him seem unapproachable, but Maomao actually rather liked it. Sweet treats went best with pickled foods. Gaoshun made the perfect complement to Jinshi's saccharine attitude.

He doesn't come across like a eunuch.

Many eunuchs became effeminate because their biological yang had been forcibly removed. They grew minimal body hair, had gentle personalities, and were disposed to obesity as their sexual appetites were replaced by culinary ones.

The Unsettling Matter of the Spirit (Part One)

The quack doctor was the most obvious example. He looked like any other middle-aged man, but his speech made him sound like the mistress of some well-to-do merchant household. Gaoshun, for his part, didn't have much body hair, but what was there was thick and black. If he hadn't lived in the rear palace, it would have been easy to take him for a military official.

I wonder what brought him to choose this path. Wonder she might, but even Maomao understood that actually asking would be beyond the pale. She simply nodded in silence and went with him.

Gaoshun led the way, holding a lantern in one hand. The moon was only half full, but it was a cloudless night, and all its light reached them.

Maomao had never been out in the rear palace so late at night: it was like a different world. Once in a while she thought she heard rustling, and maybe some moaning, from the bushes here or there, but she determined to ignore it. The emperor was the only proper man allowed in the rear palace, so it wasn't the ladies' fault if romantic encounters here started to take on less typical forms.

"Miss Maomao," Gaoshun began, but Maomao felt some compunction at the polite mode of address.

"Please, you needn't call me that," she said. "Your station is so far above mine, Master Gaoshun."

Gaoshun ran his hand along his chin as he considered this. Finally, he said, "Xiao Mao, then," a diminutive form of her name that was very much the polar opposite of "Miss Maomao."

That's maybe a little too familiar, Maomao thought, realizing that perhaps Gaoshun had a lighter heart than it first appeared, but nonetheless she nodded.

"Perhaps," Gaoshun ventured now, "I might ask you to stop regarding Master Jinshi in the same manner in which you might look at a worm."

Damn. They noticed.

Her reactions had been growing too automatic recently; her poker face could no longer hide them. She didn't expect to be beheaded for it on the spot or anything, but she would have to control herself. From the perspective of these notables, it was Maomao who was the worm.

"Why, today he reported to me that you gazed at him as though he were a slug."

Well, he certainly seemed especially slimy.

The fact that he informed Gaoshun of Maomao's every disparaging glance, she thought, spoke to both his tenacity and his sliminess. It didn't say much for him as a man . . . or former man, perhaps.

"He smiled so broadly as he told me, his eyes brimming and his whole body trembling. Truly, I have never seen joy so singularly expressed."

Maomao greeted Gaoshun's description (surely he knew it could only possibly cause misunderstanding?) with total seriousness. As a matter of fact, she was privately demoting Jinshi from worm to filth as she replied: "I'll be more mindful in the future."

"Thank you. Those with no immunity do tend to swoon at a glance. It's quite an effort to keep on top of it." The sigh with which Gaoshun accompanied this remark carried an unmistakable note of frustration. Maomao surmised that this was not the first time he'd had to clean up after Jinshi. Having a superior who was too pure was its own kind of difficulty.

The course of this tiring conversation brought them to the gate on

The Unsettling Matter of the Spirit (Part One)

the east side. The walls were about four times as tall as Maomao. The great deep moat on the other side necessitated a bridge be lowered when provisions or supplies were brought in, or at the occasional changes of serving girls. In short, to flee the rear palace was to face the ultimate punishment.

The entry was a double gate with a guardhouse on both sides, and the gate was always guarded—two eunuchs on the inside, two soldiers on the outside. The drawbridge was too heavy to raise or lower by manpower alone, so two head of oxen were on hand to do the job. Maomao was seized by the desire to go into the nearby pine forest to look for ingredients, but with Gaoshun there, she had to restrain herself. Instead, she sat down in the open-air pavilion of the garden.

And then, there in the light of the half-moon, she appeared.

"There she is," Gaoshun said, pointing. Maomao looked and saw something unbelievable: the figure of a pale woman almost floating through the air. Her long dress trailed behind her, her feet moving gracefully atop the wall as if in a dance. She shivered, and her clothing rippled as if it were alive. Her long, black hair shimmered in the dark, lending her a sort of faint halo. She was so beautiful she seemed almost unreal. It was like something out of a fantasy, as though they had wandered into the legendary peach village.

"Like a hibiscus under the stars," Maomao said suddenly.

Gaoshun looked surprised, but then murmured, "You're a quick study."

The woman's name was Fuyou, "hibiscus," and she was a middle-ranked consort. And the next month, she was to be given in marriage to a certain official, as a reward for his fine work.

CHAPTER 11

The Unsettling Matter of the Spirit
(PART TWO)

Somnambulism was a most mysterious condition. It caused one to move around as though awake, even when one was asleep. The cause could be some sort of disturbance in the heart, something no amount or type of medicine could cure. For there was no medicine to soothe a troubled spirit.

Maomao knew of a courtesan who had suffered from the condition. She had been of sunny disposition, a good singer, and one man had even been talking about buying her out of prostitution. But the negotiations fell through, for every night she would wander the brothel like a woman possessed. Ugly rumors began to dog her. When the madam tried to restrain her and stop her from walking around one night, the woman scratched her so badly she bled.

The next day, the other women confronted her about her behavior, but the courtesan said cheerfully, "My goodness, ladies, what *are* you talking about?"

The woman remembered nothing, but her bare feet were covered with mud and scratches.

"And what happened to her?" Jinshi asked. He, Maomao, and Gaoshun were in the sitting room together, along with Consort Gyokuyou. Hongniang was looking after the little princess.

"Nothing," Maomao said curtly. "When the discussions of her emancipation ended, so did her wandering around."

"Was it that the discussions upset her, then?" Gyokuyou asked with a puzzled look.

Maomao nodded. "It seems likely. The suitor was the head of a large business, but he was a man with not only a wife and children already, but even grandchildren. The woman's contract was going to be up with another year's work, anyway." Perhaps she found the idea of working another year better than being married off to a man she had no interest in. In the end, the woman had worked out the remainder of her contract with no further offers to buy her out.

"Exceptional emotional agitation commonly results in wandering like this, so we tried to give her perfumes and medicines that might help calm her down. They relaxed her a little but didn't do much more." Maomao had always been the one to mix the concoctions, not her father.

"Hmm," Jinshi said with more than a touch of boredom. "And that's really all there is to that story?"

"That's all." Maomao struggled not to sneer at Jinshi's languid look. Gaoshun sat beside him, silently encouraging her in this effort. "If

The Unsettling Matter of the Spirit (Part Two)

that's all you need, I must get back to work," Maomao said. Then she bowed and left the room.

Let's turn back the clock a bit. The day after she had witnessed the spirit, Maomao had gone to see her favorite chatterbox, Xiaolan. Xiaolan was forever trying to pry information about Gyokuyou out of Maomao, so this time Maomao fed her some innocuous tidbits in exchange for what she knew about the ghost.

The trouble had begun about two weeks before. The spirit had first been spotted in the northern quarter. Shortly after that, it began to be seen in the eastern quarter and started to appear every night. The guards, frightened by the entire situation, did nothing about it. But as the situation didn't seem to be causing any harm, no one punished them for their inaction.

It seemed that the deep moat, the high walls, and the overall impenetrability of the rear palace had left the guards susceptible to such fears. Worthless for security.

Next, Maomao had headed to see the quack. His loose lips told her something new—about Princess Fuyou, how she had been unwell lately. She was the third princess of a vassal state so small it could have been flicked away with a finger; though she was given the title "Princess," she was really little more than a highly ranked concubine. She had a building in the northern quarter. She liked to dance, but she was nervous and high-strung, and she had once made a mistake while dancing for His Majesty. The other consorts in attendance had laughed at her, and since then she had refused to come out of her room. A sensitive soul, one might say.

Princess Fuyou had no conspicuous qualities other than her dancing, and it was said that in the two years since she had come to the rear palace, His Majesty had not spent the night with her once. Now she was to be given in marriage to a military official, an old friend of hers, and one hoped, might be happy.

Father always said not to say anything based on assumptions, Maomao thought.

And so, she resolved not to.

The princess, pale and demure, was blushing as she passed through the central gate. She was not uncommonly beautiful, but her palpable happiness excited cries of admiration from the onlookers. A collective expectant gaze turned on the gate.

If one was going to be given in marriage, this was the ideal. This was how it should look.

"Surely you can at least tell me," Consort Gyokuyou said with a lustrous smile. Though she was already the mother of a little girl, she was in fact not quite twenty years old, and the smile had a hoydenish quality about it.

What should I do? Maomao thought. Consort Gyokuyou had fixed her with her best stare and wasn't letting up, and at length Maomao gave in. "If you understand that what I'm going to say is ultimately just speculation," she said with a sigh. "And if you promise not to get angry."

"Of course I won't get angry. I was the one who asked."

The Unsettling Matter of the Spirit (Part Two)

Hmm. It was looking like she had no choice but to talk. Maomao braced herself. "And you won't tell anyone else."

"My lips are sealed." Gyokuyou sounded almost flippant, but Maomao decided to trust her. Then she told the consort the story of the sleepwalking courtesan. Not the one she had told Jinshi and the rest of them the day before. A different story.

Just like the other courtesan, the condition had first manifested when a suitor proposed to buy her out of her contract. The talks fell through—this much was the same as the other story. But this woman didn't stop sleepwalking, and the perfumes and medicines that had given the first courtesan some relief didn't help this one at all.

Then someone else offered to buy the woman out of her contract. The madam said she couldn't foist a sick person off that way, but the suitor insisted they were still interested. And so, the agreement was sealed, at half the price in silver of the first man's offer.

"We learned later that it had been a con all along."

"A con?"

The first man who had come with an offer was a friend of the second. Knowing that the woman would feign illness, he then broke off the negotiations. Then his friend swooped in and got her for half the price.

"This courtesan still had a substantial amount of time left on her contract, and the silver the man paid for her wasn't enough to cover it."

"And you're suggesting these women and Princess Fuyou have something in common?"

The military official, the old friend, might have been from the same vassal state, but he was nonetheless not really of high enough social standing to seek to marry a princess. He had hoped to perform enough valorous deeds that he might one day be able to ask for her hand. Politics intervened, and Fuyou found herself in the rear palace. Still longing for her official, the princess deliberately botched her otherwise accomplished dancing to ensure she would not draw the emperor's attention. Then she shut herself up in her room until she seemed no more than a shadow in the palace.

Just as she had intended, she was still pure at the end of two years, the emperor never having visited once. The military official had performed his valorous deeds, and now, when he was to receive Princess Fuyou in marriage, she began to manifest these mysterious wanderings. She was trying to ensure that His Majesty would have no cause to have second thoughts about sending her away, no reason to suddenly make her his bedfellow.

There are, after all, some unscrupulous men of power who cannot stand to see a woman go to someone else, even a woman they never valued. If His Majesty were to take Princess Fuyou into his bedchamber, she could not be married off until later. And Fuyou herself, fastidious about her chastity, would be unable to face her childhood friend after she had spent the night with the emperor.

Then, too, perhaps her dancing by the eastern gate was in part a prayer for her friend's safety on his expeditions.

"Again, I have to stress that this is just speculation," Maomao said calmly.

"Well . . . I can't say you're wrong as far as His Majesty is concerned."

The lusty emperor could conceivably find his interest kindled in someone that one of his subordinates obviously valued so much. He visited Gyokuyou once every few days, and some of the nights on

The Unsettling Matter of the Spirit (Part Two)

which he did not visit could be accounted for by the need to attend to official business. But not all of them. One of His Majesty's duties was to produce as many children as possible.

"I suppose it would make me the most awful person to say I felt jealous of Princess Fuyou."

Maomao shook her head. "I don't think so." She was more or less convinced that she had things figured out correctly, but she felt no special impulse to tell Jinshi. All the women involved would be happier that way. His ignorance was their bliss. She wanted her smile to stay as soft and innocent as it was.

It seemed everything had been resolved . . .

But in fact, one mystery still remained.

"How *did* she get all the way up there?" Maomao asked, gazing up at a wall four times as tall as she was. Perhaps she would have to look into it sometime.

As she danced that night, Princess Fuyou had looked truly beautiful, like the heroine of one of the illustrated story scrolls the women so enjoyed. It was almost hard to believe she was the same woman as the stoic, reticent princess.

Maomao went back to the Jade Pavilion, but her thoughts were less elevated than this: if only she could bottle love. What a medicine it would be, that could make a woman so beautiful!

CHAPTER 12

The Threat

There was a crash. The porridge of boiled potatoes and grains went flying, along with the tea and the crushed fruits. Maomao, her clothes soaked in porridge, looked up at the person in front of her.

"You would dare serve this tripe to Lady Lihua? Make it again, and do it right this time!" A heavily made-up young woman was glaring at Maomao. One of Consort Lihua's ladies-in-waiting.

Ugh, what a pain. Maomao sighed and started gathering the dishes and cleaning up the spilled food.

She was in the Crystal Pavilion, Lady Lihua's residence. Unfriendly gazes surrounded her. Mocking looks, scornful eyes, and downright hostile expressions. For a servant of Consort Gyokuyou like Maomao, this was truly enemy territory, a bed of nails.

———◇———

The Threat

His Majesty had come to Gyokuyou's chambers the night before. Maomao had tasted the food for poison, as she always did, and had been about to leave the room when the emperor himself had spoken to her: "I have a request for the apothecary of whom I've heard so much."

Wonder what exactly he's heard.

The emperor was a robust man and handsome, only in his mid-thirties. And he was the absolute ruler of this nation—no wonder he dazzled the women of the rear palace. Maomao was one of the few exceptions. Basically the only thing she thought of the emperor was: "That's a really long beard. I wonder what it feels like to touch."

Now she asked, "What might that be, Your Majesty?" with a deferential bow of the head. She knew that she was insignificant before the emperor, that a breath from His Majesty could blow away her life, and she wanted to get out of the room before she accidentally breached etiquette somehow.

"Consort Lihua is feeling unwell. Perhaps you could look after her for a while."

Well, there it was. And as Maomao wanted her head and her shoulders to maintain close relations for a long time to come, the only possible answer was, "Of course, sire."

By *look after her,* Maomao understood His Majesty to mean *make her better.* The emperor no longer favored Consort Lihua with his visits, but perhaps some vestige of his affection remained—or perhaps he simply knew he couldn't neglect the daughter of a powerful man. It made no difference. If Maomao didn't help her, she couldn't expect to hold on to her head for very long. In a manner of speaking, she and Lihua would share the same fate.

The fact that the emperor had asked this of a young girl like Maomao meant either that he knew perfectly well that the doctor of the rear palace could not be relied upon, or that he didn't care if either, or both, of them died. In either case, it was a reckless request to make. The more time Maomao spent with these people who ruled in the Imperial Palace—who lived "above the clouds," as the traditional expression went—the more she found herself thinking how much trouble their every command and desire caused.

Still, did he really have to ask me right in front of his other consort?

She almost marveled at a man who could make a request like that of her, then eat a luxurious meal and be intimate with Consort Gyokuyou immediately afterward. Maybe that was just an emperor for you.

When Maomao began to "look after" Consort Lihua, the first thing she turned her eye to was improving the woman's diet. The poisonous face powder had been banished from use in the rear palace on Jinshi's command, and thorough punishment appointed for the merchants who had brought it in the first place. It would not be possible to get more of the stuff from here on out.

In which case, the priority had to be expunging the remaining toxins from Lihua's body. Her current meals were based on bland congee, but it was frequently topped with things like deep-fried fish, broiled pork, red-and-white bean buns, and other rich foods like shark fin or crab. Nutritious, true enough, but too heavy for the stomach of a convalescent.

Forcing herself not to salivate, Maomao told the cook to change the menu. The weight of an Imperial assignment gave even an unimportant lady-in-waiting like Maomao a certain amount of authority, and Lihua's meals were made to consist of porridge (rich in fiber), tea (an excellent diuretic), and fruit (easily digested).

Unfortunately, all of these were now scattered on the ground. Maomao, raised in the red-light district as she was, was appalled by the waste of food.

The women of the Crystal Pavilion were less impressed by whatever Imperial commission Maomao might have had than they were displeased by the fact that she served their rival, Consort Gyokuyou. Maomao would have gladly given them all a piece of her mind, but instead, she bit her tongue and cleaned up the mess.

Lihua's ladies-in-waiting brought the consort sumptuous meals, but over time they came back more and more untouched. Presumably, the ladies got to enjoy the leftovers.

Maomao would have liked to perform a proper physical examination of the patient, but Lihua's canopied bed was surrounded by a phalanx of ladies-in-waiting, collectively performing a rather ungracious and ineffective nursing duty. When they provoked a cough by slapping whitening powder on Lihua's face while she was asleep, they would exclaim, "The air is bad in here. It's this noxious worm!" and chase Maomao out of the room. She couldn't get at Lihua to do an exam.

No question in my mind. At this rate, she'll keep wasting away until she dies.

Maybe she had taken in too much of the poison, and it was too late to get it out of her system. Or perhaps she simply wasn't strong enough. If a person didn't eat, they would die. Lihua appeared to be losing the will to live.

Maomao was leaning against a wall, counting the number of days her head was likely to remain attached to her body, when she heard a shrill of coquettish voices.

She had a very bad feeling about this. She raised her head very slowly and found herself confronted with a gorgeous face, smiling like the sun. It was the beautiful eunuch.

"You look troubled," he said.

"Do I?" Maomao replied tonelessly, her eyes half closed.

"I wouldn't have said it if you didn't." He stared straight at her, so she tried looking away instead. He leaned in, his eyelashes noticeably long, to counter her, and when their eyes met again, Maomao very much broke her promise to Gaoshun by adopting the expression of someone looking at a piece of garbage.

"What is with that girl?" The words were soft but venomous. Maomao was referring to the woman who had spilled the food. She was insufferable, and she veritably exuded menace.

A woman's wrath was a terrible thing, but Jinshi nonetheless said softly into her ear with his honeyed voice, "Shall we go inside?" Maomao found herself pushed into the room before she could object.

The chamber's self-appointed guardians looked even more dangerous than before. But when they saw the nymph beside Maomao, they immediately put on nonchalant smiles, even though they were all obviously forced. Truly, women could be terrifying creatures.

"Surely you agree it's unbecoming for lovely, talented young ladies to make a hash of the emperor's good offices."

The women paused, they bit their lips, and then one by one they backed away from the bed.

"There now, go," Jinshi said, giving Maomao a little shove on the

The Threat

back that almost toppled her over. She bowed and approached the bed, then took Lihua's hand. It was pale; the veins stood out prominently.

Maomao had some experience of medicine—the practice of healing—if not as much as she had of *medicine*—the concoctions that did the healing. Lihua's eyes were closed, and she didn't fight Maomao. It was hard to tell if she was even awake or asleep. She already seemed to have one foot in the grave.

Maomao placed a finger on Lihua's face, hoping to get a better look at her eye. She was greeted by a slick, slippery texture. Lihua's skin was as pale as it had ever been.

It hasn't changed? Maomao frowned, then went over to the ladies-in-waiting. She stood in front of one of them, the one who had been making the consort up earlier. In a deliberately soft, restrained voice, Maomao asked, "You. Are you the one who does the lady's makeup?"

"I certainly am. It's a lady-in-waiting's duty, you know." The woman seemed mildly intimidated by Maomao's searing look. It obviously took everything she had to remain defiant. "We want Consort Lihua to be as beautiful as she can, always." The girl sniffed; she sounded so sure of herself.

"Is that right?"

A *crack* echoed through the room. The girl stumbled aside, in the direction of the force, hardly knowing what had happened. She felt an unfamiliar heat in her cheek and ear. Maomao's right hand smarted; it burned almost as much as the girl's left cheek. Maomao *had* smacked her about as hard as she was able.

"What's wrong with you?!" one of the other ladies-in-waiting demanded. Several of them were openly astounded.

"Me? I'm just giving an *idiot* her due." Maomao grabbed the girl by the hair, pulling her to her feet.

"Ow! That hurts. Stop!" the lady-in-waiting wailed, but Maomao paid her no heed. She dragged the girl over to the makeup stand and picked up a carved jar with her free hand. She opened the lid and smeared the contents on the face of the lady-in-waiting. White powder went everywhere, causing coughing fits. Tears brimmed in the young woman's eyes.

"There! Now you can be as beautiful as your lady. Lucky you!" Maomao gave a tug of the girl's hair, forcing her to meet her eyes, and leered like a beast with its prey in its claws. "You can have poison in your pores, in your mouth, in your nose, in every part of your body. You can wither away just like your beloved Lady Lihua, until your eyes are sunken and your skin is bloodless."

"No . . . I don't believe you . . ." the newly powdered lady-in-waiting simpered.

"You don't understand why this stuff was forbidden, do you?! It's poison!" Maomao was well and truly angry now. Not because of the sneers and glares, not because of the spilled porridge, but because of this fool of a lady-in-waiting who thought of nothing, but simply assumed she was right about everything.

"But it's the prettiest! The most beautiful . . . I thought Lady Lihua would be happy . . ."

Maomao dipped her hand in the powder scattered on the floor, then grabbed the girl's cheek, pulling, distorting her lips. "Who would be happy to be continually covered in poison that sucks their life away?" It was like listening to a child trying to explain why they'd done something wrong. Maomao gave a click of her tongue and let the woman go.

The Threat

A few long strands of dark hair remained wrapped around her fingers. "All right, go rinse your mouth out. And wash your face."

She watched the girl all but flee the room, weeping, and then she turned to the other ladies-in-waiting, who were now thoroughly frightened. "Go on. You want that stuff to get on the patient? Clean it up!" She pointed to the powdery floor, deciding to ignore the fact that she was the one who had spilled it. The other ladies-in-waiting winced, but then went to get the cleaning supplies. Maomao crossed her arms and snorted. Some of the powder was on her clothes, but she didn't care.

One person had remained calm and collected throughout all this. "Women are indeed terrifying," Jinshi said now, tucking his hands into his wide sleeves.

Maomao had completely forgotten he was there. *"Argh!"* she said as the rush of blood to her head subsided. She squatted down right where she was.

Now she'd done it.

CHAPTER 13

Nursing

Consort Lihua's condition was worse than Maomao had thought. She changed the millet porridge for thin gruel, but Lihua could hardly sip it from the spoon. Maomao had to work Lihua's mouth open, pour the gruel in, and gently help her to swallow. Not the most decorous routine, but then, this wasn't the moment to be worrying about decorum.

This was the biggest problem: Lihua wasn't eating. An old proverb held that a healthy diet was as restorative as good medicine, and Maomao knew her patient wouldn't get better if she didn't have some food. And so, she persisted obstinately in trying to feed Lihua.

She had the air in the room changed, and the cloying scent of incense lessened, replaced by that characteristic odor of a sick person. They must have been burning the incense in hopes of covering the smell of Lihua's body. How long had it been since she'd had a bath? Maomao felt ever more enraged at the witless ladies-in-waiting.

Nursing

At least the young woman Maomao had upbraided seemed to have learned something from it. The whitening powder she'd been using on Lihua had been from her own secret stash. Sad to say, the eunuch who had failed to find and confiscate the powder was condemned to be beaten. Birth could affect even the punishments one received.

Maomao derided the eunuch in charge of all this as a worthless idiot to his face, but it didn't seem to mean much. He turned out to be one of those highborn people with "special" proclivities.

Maomao had a cloth and a bucket of hot water prepared, then summoned the other ladies-in-waiting to help her wash Consort Lihua. The ladies looked uncomfortable, but at a glare from Maomao, they meekly went along.

Lihua's skin was so dry the water hardly beaded on it, and her lips were painfully cracked. They applied honey rather than red makeup to her lips, and her hair was tied back in a simple knot. Now they just had to get her to take some tea whenever they could. Once in a while, she was given watered-down soup instead. It would help her get some salt. This would cause her to use the toilet more, expelling the toxins from her body.

Maomao had thought the consort might reject this unusual new caretaker, even think of her as an enemy, but Lihua was as pliant as a doll. Looking at her vacant eyes made one doubt whether she even knew one person from another. But then they were able to increase her portion of gruel from half a bowl to an entire bowl, and then to add some rice and grains. When Lihua was able to chew and swallow without help, meat stock was added, making a savory soup, along with mashed fruits.

One day, when she had managed to use the toilet on her own, Lihua suddenly spoke: "Why. . . . . . . ie?"

Maomao stood closer to catch the whispered words.

"Why didn't you just let me die?" The voice was vanishingly small.

Maomao frowned. "If that's what you want, then just stop eating. The fact that you keep taking your gruel tells me you don't want to die." And then she offered Lihua some warm tea.

The woman gave a gentle cough. "I see . . ." She smiled, however faintly.

Lihua's ladies-in-waiting tended to have one of two reactions to Maomao: either they were terrified of her, or they were terrified of her but still fought back.

Guess I went a little too far.

Once Maomao's emotions hit a boiling point, she was wont to boil over herself. She knew it was a bad habit. She'd even abandoned the delicate language of the court for more uncouth expressions. Maomao might not show much emotion, but she had a warm heart, and it honestly hurt her to see people regard her from afar as if looking at a devil or a monster. She rationalized this latest outburst: it had been in the service of taking care of Lady Lihua. It had been necessary.

Jinshi himself put in frequent appearances. Whether on the orders of the emperor or at the behest of Consort Gyokuyou, Maomao didn't know. Bent on making use of anything that was provided to her, though, she asked him to have a bath added to the Crystal Pavilion. The extant bathing facilities were expanded to include a steam bath.

Maomao tried, indirectly of course, to communicate to Jinshi that he could not help and was not wanted here, but he still stopped by to smile at her at every opportunity with the tenacity of a ghost that was

Nursing

haunting her. He clearly, Maomao concluded, was a eunuch with far too much time on his hands. She wished he would take a cue from Gaoshun, who at least had the decency to bring treats whenever he showed up. A person as thoughtful as that might make someone a good husband—even if he was a eunuch.

Lihua, meanwhile, was encouraged to consume fiber, drink water, and to sweat—anything that would help move the poison out of her system. Two months passed focused on this and only this, and finally Consort Lihua was even able to walk on her own.

She had already been in a severe condition on account of her emotional malaise. Maomao judged that as long as she didn't take in any more of the toxins, she would be all right. It would take some time yet for her to regain her healthy figure and the flush in her cheeks, but she no longer seemed to be standing on the banks of the river that divided this world from the next.

The night before Maomao was to return to the Jade Pavilion, she went to pay her formal respects to Consort Lihua. She half expected to be dismissed as someone too lowly to merit the consort's notice, but this was not the case. Lihua, she learned, had her pride, but she wasn't prideful. With all that had happened surrounding the prince, Maomao had come to think of Lihua as quite a disagreeable woman, but in fact she had the comportment and personality of a true Imperial consort.

"I'll take my leave tomorrow morning, milady," Maomao told her. She added some instructions regarding what the lady was to eat, and a few other cautionary pieces of advice, and then went to leave the room.

But Lihua said from behind her: "Young lady, do you suppose I will ever be able to bear another child?" Her voice was flat and affectless.

"I don't know. The only way to find out is to try."

"But how, when His Majesty no longer has any interest in me?"

Her meaning was clear enough. She had only conceived the prince because the emperor happened to visit her after his time with his favorite, Consort Gyokuyou. The fact that there was three months' difference in age between the little princess and the little prince revealed the truth of the matter.

"It was His Majesty who ordered me to come here in the first place. Now that I'm leaving, I must think you will see him again." It wasn't a political or emotional problem. The issue was the same for both of them. The rear palace being what it was, love and romance had no place here.

"Do you think I can yet win out over Consort Gyokuyou? I, who ignored her advice and killed my own child doing so?"

"I don't think it's a question of winning. And as for our mistakes, we can learn from them." Maomao took down a vase that was decorating the wall, a slim thing designed to hold a single flower. At the moment, it was occupied by a star-shaped bellflower. "There are hundreds, even thousands of kinds of flowers in the world, but who would dare say whether the peony or the iris is the more beautiful?"

"I don't have her jade eyes or fiery hair."

"If you have something else instead, then there is no problem." Maomao's gaze traveled down from Consort Lihua's face. They always said *those* were the first things to go when you lost weight, but Lihua still had her ample endowment. "I think size like that is quite a treasure."

Maomao had seen a great deal in the brothels, so she should know.

Nursing

She would keep to herself the fact that she'd been struck by a certain amount of amazement every time they bathed the consort.

Given that Lihua was the rival of her own mistress, Maomao couldn't help her out *too* much, but she decided to give the woman a last gift before she left. "May I whisper in milady's ear?" And then, quietly, so that no one else would hear her, she gave Consort Lihua some advice. A secret technique one of the older ladies of the night had told her it "couldn't hurt to know." Sadly, Maomao lacked equipment of the necessary size. But this particular technique seemed the perfect thing for Consort Lihua.

Lihua's face went as red as an apple when she heard it. What Maomao might have told her was a subject of lively debate among Lihua's ladies-in-waiting for some time afterward, but it was all the same to Maomao.

There was a period after this when His Majesty's visits to the Jade Pavilion became noticeably less frequent. With a mixture of irony and real relief, Consort Gyokuyou only said: *"Phew!* Finally, I can get a little sleep!"

Maomao gawked in surprise. But that's a story for another time.

CHAPTER 14

The Fire

There. I knew it. Balancing a laundry basket in one arm, Maomao smiled. Those were red pines growing in a grove near the eastern gate.

The gardens of the rear palace were deftly manicured. Once each year, the dead leaves and withered branches were cleared out of the pine forest, as well. And Maomao knew that a well-tended pine forest encouraged a certain kind of mushroom to grow.

Right now, she held a small-capped matsutake mushroom in her hand. Some people didn't like the way they smelled, but Maomao loved them. Quartered matsutake mushrooms, grilled on a grate with a dash of salt and a squeeze of citrus over them, were her idea of heaven.

It was a modest copse, but as she'd found a convenient cluster of the mushrooms, she put five of them in her basket.

Should I eat them at the old fogey's place or in the kitchen?

The Fire

She couldn't do it at the Jade Pavilion; there would be too many questions about where she'd gotten the ingredients. They might not smile upon a serving woman admitting she had gathered the mushrooms herself from the grove. So, Maomao went instead to see the doctor, the man who was so good with people and so bad at his job. If he liked matsutake mushrooms, too, then all was well; and if not, she figured he would still be kind enough to look the other way. Maomao had by now completely ingratiated herself with the loach-mustached man.

She couldn't forget to go by Xiaolan's place on the way. Xiaolan was an important source of information for Maomao, who otherwise had few friends.

When Maomao had come back from Lihua's residence, looking thinner than ever from the effort of helping the consort, the other ladies-in-waiting had undertaken to plump her up. On the one hand, Maomao was happy about this—it showed she hadn't fallen out of the ladies' good graces despite having been with a rival consort almost two months—but on the other, it was nearly as frustrating as it was gratifying. She had a little basket that began to bulge with the extra treats she received every time tea was served.

Xiaolan, however, would never turn down something sweet. Her eyes would light up at the sight of whatever Maomao had brought her, and she would be more than happy to take a short break, munching on sweets and chatting Maomao's ear off in equal measure.

Now they sat behind the laundry area on a couple of barrels, talking about this and that. Stories of strange happenings made up the bulk of it, as usual, but among other things, Xiaolan told Maomao:

"I heard one of the palace women used a potion to get some hardhearted soldier type to fall in love with her, and it worked!"

Maomao broke into a cold sweat at that. *Probably nothing to do with me, right? Probably.*

Looking back on it, she realized she never had thought to ask who that love potion was for. But did it really matter? "The palace" meant the actual palace, not the rear palace, which meant it had happened safely outside. The palace proper had actual, functioning men, so appointment there was a popular prospect for which competition was fierce. Unlike the women who served in the rear palace, these were elites who had passed serious tests to gain their positions.

Let it be said that, insofar as actual, functioning men were absent, the rear palace could seem a rather lonelier assignment. Not that it mattered to Maomao.

When Maomao arrived at the medical office, she found the loach-mustached old man in the company of a pale-faced eunuch whom she didn't recognize. He was continually rubbing his hand.

"Ah, just the young woman I wanted to see," the doctor said with his most welcoming smile.

"Yes, what is it?"

"This man has developed a rash on his hand. Do you think you could whip up a salve for him?"

Not very becoming words for the man who was ostensibly the palace's doctor, Maomao thought. One would expect him to do it himself. But this was nothing new, and Maomao was content to go into the room full of medicine cabinets and get her ingredients.

The Fire

First, though, she set the basket down and produced the matsutake. "Do you have any charcoal?" she asked.

"Oh ho, what fine specimens you've found!" the quack said jovially. "We'll be wanting some soy paste and salt as well."

She seemed to have found a winner. That would make things easy. The doctor all but danced out of the room on his way to the dining hall to find suitable seasonings. Perhaps if he put this much passion into his work . . .

Sadly for the patient, he was left quite by himself.

Maybe I'll give him a consolation mushroom, if he likes them, Maomao thought, watching the disconsolate eunuch as she mixed the ingredients. By the time the quack returned with spices, a small charcoal grill, and a grate, she had a good, thick ointment going. She took the eunuch's right hand, gently spreading the stuff on the angry red rash. The salve wasn't the most pleasant-smelling thing in the world, but he would just have to bear with it.

When she had finished, his previously pale face seemed to have regained some of its luster. "My, but she's a very kind young woman." There were some among the serving women who looked down on the eunuchs. They saw them as uncanny things, neither women nor really men, and the serving women didn't hide it in their faces.

"Isn't she, though? She's forever helping me with little things like this," the doctor said with a hint of pride.

There had been times in history when the eunuchs had been treated as villains who lusted after power, but in fact, only a few of them had ever been like that. The majority were calm and pleasant, like these two.

Maybe not all *of them, though* . . . An unwelcome face flashed through

Maomao's mind, and she deliberately chased it away. They lit the charcoal, set the grate in place, then tore the mushrooms into pieces by hand and left them to cook. Maomao had helped herself to a small *sudachi* citrus from the orchard, and now they cut it into slices. When they started to smell that unique fragrance of cooking matsutake mushrooms, the fungus delicately blackened, they put it on dishes and seasoned it with salt and citrus juice.

Maomao waited to take her first bite until she was sure the other two had started eating: the moment the older men took bites of the stuff, they became Maomao's accomplices. She munched away while the quack doctor chatted contentedly. "This young lady has been all kinds of help to me. She can do just about anything, you know. She mixes up every type of medicine under the sun, not just ointments."

"Huh! Most impressive."

The old man sounded like he was bragging about his own daughter. Maomao wasn't sure she thought that was ideal. She suddenly found herself thinking about her father, whom she hadn't seen in more than six months now. She wondered if he was eating properly. She hoped the expense of keeping his medicines stocked wasn't snowing him under.

It was just when Maomao was feeling this emotional pitch that the quack had to go and say something especially tone-deaf. "Why, I do believe she can make *any* kind of medicine at all."

Guh?

But before Maomao could tell the old man to keep his hyperbole to himself, the eunuch sitting across from them said, *"Any* kind?"

"Yes, anything you need." The doctor gave a triumphant little snort, which in Maomao's mind only confirmed his quackery. The other eu-

The Fire

nuch looked at Maomao with new interest. He had something on his mind, she was sure.

"In that case, might you be able to make something to cure a curse?"

He was rubbing his inflamed hand pathetically. His face was once again pale.

It had happened the night before last.

The last thing he always did was to pick up garbage. He would gather all the litter and trash around the rear palace in a cart, then wheel it over to the western quarter, where there was a great pit where it would be burned. Typically, fires were not allowed after sunset, but as the air was damp and there was no wind, it was deemed safe, and he was granted permission.

His subordinates pitched the trash into the pit. He lent a hand himself, eager as he was to be done with the chore. Bit by bit they flung the stuff from the cart into the hole.

Then something in the pile on the cart caught his eye. It was a woman's outfit. Not silk, but certainly of high quality. A waste to get rid of. When he held it up to inspect it, a collection of wood writing slips tumbled out. There was a noticeable burn mark on the sleeve of the outfit that had been cradling them.

What could this mean?

But he knew his job wouldn't be done any sooner for puzzling over it. He grabbed the wooden slips one by one and tossed them into the pit.

"And then you say the fire blazed up in unnatural colors?"

"That's right!" The old man's shoulders shook as if he found the very memory horrible.

"And you say the colors were red, purple, and blue?" Maomao asked.

"Yes, that's what they were!"

Maomao nodded. So this was the source of the rumors Xiaolan had reported to her that morning.

Who knew something from the western quarter would make it all the way here? Apparently, it was true what they said, that rumors among women traveled faster than a swift-footed *skandha*.

"It's got to be the curse of the concubine who died in a fire here many, many years ago. It was wrong of me to set a fire at night, I know that now! That's why my hand got this way!" The rash on the eunuch's hand had appeared after the incident with the fire. He was pale and trembling as he said, "Please, miss. Make me a medicine that can cure a curse." The man looked at her beseechingly. She thought he might fling himself face-first onto the reed mat.

"There is no such medicine. How could there be?" Maomao said coldly. She got up and started rifling through the drawers of the medicine cabinets, quite ignoring the old man and the doctor, who both looked thoroughly out of sorts. Finally, she set something down on the table. Several varieties of powder, and bits of wood.

"Is this the color you saw in that fire of yours?" Maomao asked. She placed the bits of wood among the charcoal embers, and when they were burning, she took a teaspoon and scattered some of the white powder into the flames. The fire took on a red hue.

"Or perhaps this?" She added a different powder, and a blue-green

The Fire

color resulted. "I can even do this." She took a pinch of the salt they'd put on the mushrooms and tossed it into the flames, which turned yellow.

The two eunuchs watched her, astonished. "Miss, what *is* this?" the flabbergasted doctor asked.

"It's the same principle as colored fireworks. The colors change depending on what you burn."

One of the visitors to their brothel had been a fireworks maker. He was supposedly sworn never to share the secrets of his craft, but in the bedroom, trade secrets became simple pillow talk. And if a restless child happened to be listening from the next room, well, no one was the wiser.

"What about my hand, then? Are you saying it's not cursed?" the old eunuch asked, still rubbing the afflicted appendage.

Maomao held out some of the white powder. "If this stuff gets on bare skin, a rash can result. Or perhaps there was lacquer on the wooden strips. Who knows? Do you happen to be prone to rashes to begin with?"

"Now that you mention it . . ." The eunuch went as limp as if the bones had left his body. Relief was written on his face. There must have been some substance like these on the wooden strips he had handled the previous day. That was what had caused the colored fire. That was all—not some curse or devilment.

Where are all these mysterious substances coming from, though?

Maomao's ruminations were interrupted by the sound of clapping. She turned to discover a slim figure resting in the doorway.

"Superb."

When had this most unwelcome guest arrived? It was Jinshi, standing there with the same nymphlike smile as always.

CHAPTER 15

Covert Operations

When Maomao and Jinshi arrived at their destination, she found that he had brought them to the office of the Matron of the Serving Women. The middle-aged woman was inside, but at a word from Jinshi, she quickly left the room. Let us be honest about how Maomao was feeling: the last thing in the world she wanted was to be alone with this creature.

It wasn't that Maomao hated beautiful things. But when something was *too* beautiful, one started to feel that the remotest blemish was like a crime, unforgivable. It was like how a single scratch on an otherwise perfect, polished pearl could cut the thing's price in half. And though the exterior might be lovely, there was the question of what was within. And so Maomao ended up looking at Jinshi like some kind of bug crawling along the ground.

She sincerely couldn't help it.

I'd rather just admire him from afar. This was how Maomao, simple commoner that she was, truly felt. It was, then, with some relief that she greeted Gaoshun, who replaced the woman in the room. For all his taciturn disposition, this servant eunuch had become something of a refuge for her of late.

"How many colors like this exist?" Jinshi inquired, lining up the powders he had brought from the doctor's chambers.

They were just medicines as far as Maomao was concerned, so there might be more that she didn't know about. But she said, "Red, yellow, blue, purple, and green. And if you subdivide them, there are arguably more. I couldn't give you an exact number."

"And how would a wooden writing strip be made to acquire one of these colors?" The powder couldn't simply be rubbed on it; it would just rub off again. It was all very strange.

"Salt can be dissolved in water to color an object. I suspect a similar method would work here." Maomao pulled the white powder toward her. "As for the rest, some might dissolve in something other than water. Again, this is outside my field of expertise, so I can't be sure."

There were any number of white powders out there: some that would dissolve in water and some that wouldn't; others that might dissolve in oil, say. If some of the stuff was to be impregnated into a writing strip, a substance that would dissolve in water seemed a reasonable assumption.

"All right, enough." The young man crossed his arms and lost himself in thought. He was so lovely, he could have been a painting. It almost seemed wrong for heaven to have given a man such unearthly beauty. And to then cause that man to live and work as a eunuch in the rear palace was deeply ironic.

Maomao knew that Jinshi had his hand in a great number of proverbial cookie jars in the rear palace. Perhaps something she'd said had caused the pieces of some puzzle to fall into place for him. He seemed to be trying to figure them out.

Could it be a code . . . ?

They had probably each come to the same conclusion. But Maomao knew better, much better, than to say so out loud. The quiet pheasant is not shot, went the proverb. (Which country had those words supposedly come from, again?)

Feeling that she was no longer needed, Maomao made to leave.

"Hold on," Jinshi said.

"Yes, sir, what is it?"

"Personally, I like them best steamed in an earthen pot."

She didn't have to ask what "they" were. *Found me out, eh?* Perhaps it had been a little bit much, eating the matsutake mushrooms right there in the doctor's quarters. Maomao's shoulders slumped. "I'll try to find some more tomorrow."

It seemed her agenda for the next day was set: she would be going back to the grove.

When he heard the *clack* that assured him the door was shut fast, Jinshi gave a honeyed smile. His eyes, however, were hard enough to cut diamond. "Find anyone who recently suffered burns on their arms," he ordered his aide. "Start with anyone with their own chambers, and their serving women."

Covert Operations

Gaoshun, who had been sitting silently as if waiting just for this, nodded. "As you wish, sir."

He left the room, and the Matron came back in his place. Jinshi did feel bad chasing her out every time he showed up. "I must apologize for constantly stealing your office out from under you."

"O-oh, heavens, not at all," the woman said, blushing like she was many years younger than she was. Jinshi made sure the ambrosial smile was still on his face.

This was how women were supposed to react to him. But on *her*, his looks were completely ineffective. Was this all his face could get him? Jinshi allowed himself the briefest purse of his lips before his smile returned and he left the room.

A pile of woven baskets, delivered by a eunuch, awaited Maomao when she got back to the Jade Pavilion. They sat in the living area, the ladies-in-waiting busily investigating the contents. She thought at first they might be a gift from His Majesty, or perhaps a care package from home, but they didn't quite look like either of those things. The clothing they contained was too plain to be something Consort Gyokuyou might wear, and there were several duplicate outfits. From the way the other girls were holding the dresses up to themselves to check the length, Maomao surmised that they must be new uniforms.

"Here, try this on," said one of the other ladies-in-waiting, Yinghua, pushing one of the outfits at Maomao. It consisted of a plain overgarment above a light-red skirt, while the sleeves were pale yellow and somewhat wider than usual. It wasn't silk, but it was an exceptionally fine brocade.

"What's going on with these?" Maomao asked. The colors were subdued, as befitted a serving woman, but the design seemed eminently impractical. Maomao also frowned instinctively at the excessively open chest, something that had never been featured on any of her other clothes.

"What do you mean, *what*? These are our outfits for the garden party."

"I'm sorry. The garden party?"

Thoroughly insulated by the indulgences of the more experienced ladies-in-waiting, Maomao's only excursions outside of her regular regimen of food tasting and making medicine were going out to collect ingredients, chatting with Xiaolan, taking tea with the doctor, and so forth. As a result, she didn't hear much about what was going on among those over her head. Frankly, she had started to wonder if it was really acceptable for a person to make her living at a job that seemed this easy.

Yinghua, somewhat amazed that she had to spell this out, explained to Maomao what was going on. Twice a year, a party was held in the Imperial gardens. His Majesty, being without a proper queen as he was, would be accompanied by his concubines of the Upper First rank. And *they* would be accompanied by their ladies-in-waiting.

In the rear palace hierarchy, Gyokuyou held the rank of *guifei*, or "Precious Consort," while Lihua bore the title *xianfei*, "Wise Consort." In addition to these women there were two others, the *defei*, or "Virtuous Consort," and the *shufei*, or "Pure Consort." These four comprised the Upper First rank.

Covert Operations

Typically, only the Virtuous and Pure Consorts would attend the winter garden party. But due to the birth of their children, Gyokuyou and Lihua had both been absent from the most recent gathering, so this time all four would be present.

"So, all of them will be there?"

"That's right. We have to be ready to put on a good show!" Yinghua was practically vibrating. Besides being the all-too-rare chance to get out of the rear palace, this gathering of all the most important consorts would double as the debut of Princess Lingli.

Maomao was well aware that she couldn't beg off the party on the pretext of inexperience. Consort Gyokuyou had far too few ladies-in-waiting already for her to do that. Besides, the services of a food taster would be seen as particularly important at such a public gathering.

Maomao's intuition nagged at her. *It could be a bloodbath if we aren't careful.* And her intuition had an annoying habit of being right.

"Hmm, I think you'd better stuff that chest. I'll help you add a bit around the butt, too. Sound okay?"

"I leave the matter in your capable hands."

A certain voluptuousness was the standard of beauty here, which unfortunately meant Maomao's natural shape was somewhat wanting—a point Yinghua made inescapably clear. She was busy cinching belts and checking fits. "You'll have to make yourself up, too. You could at least bother to hide your freckles every once in a while." Yinghua gave Maomao a naughty little grin, and we need hardly say that Maomao replied with a scowl.

───◇───

Maomao was somewhat disheartened when Hongniang filled her in on how things would go at the party. The head lady-in-waiting, who had been at the previous year's spring event, heaved a sigh and said, "I was so looking forward to not having to deal with it this year." When Maomao inquired whether there was anything particularly bad about it, Hongniang explained that there was simply nothing to do. The ladies-in-waiting just stood around the entire time.

There would be dance performance after dance performance, then singing accompanied by a two-stringed *erhu*, then food would be presented and eaten, and then the girls would exchange forced smiles and pleasantries with the various officials in attendance. And all of it outdoors, where they would be exposed to the blowing, dry wind.

The gardens were expansive, a testament to His Majesty's power. Even a "quick" visit to the toilet could take upwards of thirty minutes. And if His Majesty, the true guest of honor, remained resolutely seated, his consorts would have no choice but to stay sitting as well.

Sounds like I'm going to need an iron bladder, Maomao thought. If the spring party had been as much trouble as all that, how much worse would it be in winter?

To combat one source of potential discomfort, however, Maomao had sewn several pockets onto her undergarment, into which warmers could be placed. She also minced ginger and tangerine rinds, boiling them with sugar and fruit juice to produce candy. When she showed these products to Hongniang, the head lady-in-waiting veritably begged her to make some for everyone else.

While she was busy working on them, a certain eunuch with too much time on his hands showed up and demanded she make some for him as well. His assistant seemed to feel bad about it and at least helped her with the work.

What was more, it seemed Consort Gyokuyou let word of Maomao's ideas slip during one of the emperor's nocturnal visits, and the next day she was approached by His Majesty's personal seamstress and chef. She obligingly taught them her methods.

I guess we aren't the only ones who have it tough at these events, she thought. Still, the hubbub over such simple ideas suggested how rotely everyone else was approaching the party. When one let oneself become too attached to custom, one ceased to be capable of discovering even the most minor innovations.

So, Maomao passed the time until the garden party in domestic endeavors. Hongniang, meanwhile, busied herself with attempting to correct Maomao's occasional lapses into less-than-deferential speech. Much as Maomao appreciated the gesture, she found the lessons trying. Unlike the other three serving girls, their leader, Hongniang, was just a bit too attuned to how Maomao really was.

When she was finally free, the night before the garden party, Maomao set about making some medicine with herbs she had on hand. A little something, just in case.

"You look absolutely beautiful, Lady Gyokuyou." Yinghua spoke for all of them, and her words were more than mere flattery.

I guess that's the emperor's favorite consort for you.

Gyokuyou exuded an exotic beauty, dressed in a crimson skirt and a robe of a lighter red color. The wide-sleeved jacket she wore over this was the same red as her skirt and worked with embroidery in gold thread. Her hair was gathered into two large rings held back with ornate hair sticks decorated with flowers, and perched between the rings of hair, she wore a tiara. Straight silver hair sticks surrounded the elaborate decoration, themselves adorned with red tassels and jade stones.

It was a mark of Gyokuyou's force of personality that, despite the elaborate designs, her own clothes in no way outshone her. The consort with the flame-red hair was said to look better in scarlet than anyone in the country. The way her eyes, green as jade themselves, shone from within all that red only added to her mystique. Perhaps this was the product of the abundant foreign blood that flowed through Gyokuyou's veins.

The skirts that Maomao and the others would wear likewise used light red to indicate that they served Consort Gyokuyou. In addition, wearing the same color as their mistress, but in a lighter hue, would make her stand out that much more.

The ladies-in-waiting all changed into their skirts and did their hair. Consort Gyokuyou, remarking that this was after all a special occasion, produced a jeweled box from her own dressing table. Inside were necklaces, earrings, and hair sticks decorated with jade.

"You are my own ladies-in-waiting. I have to mark you out, to make sure no little birds try to go flying off with you." And then she bestowed an accessory on each of them, in their hair or on their ears or around their necks. Maomao was given a necklace to wear.

"Thank you, milad—"

Hrk!

Before she could properly finish her expression of gratitude, she

found herself choked. Yinghua had wrapped her arms around Maomao. "All right! Time for some *makeup!*"

Hongniang was standing there with eyebrow tweezers and a grin on her face. Was it just Maomao's imagination, or did she look a bit more jovial than usual? The other two ladies-in-waiting had items of their own: a pot of lip color and a brush.

Maomao had forgotten that the other women had of late been deeply interested in getting her to wear some makeup.

"Hee hee. I'm sure you'll look lovely."

It seemed they had a coconspirator! Consort Gyokuyou's laugh was like the ringing of a bell. Maomao couldn't hide her distress, but the four waiting-women were merciless.

"First, we need to wipe your face and get some scented oil on there."

A damp cloth was assiduously applied to Maomao's face.

But then Yinghua and the others exclaimed in unison: "Huh?"

Ugh... Maomao stared at the ceiling, beaten. The girls were looking from the cloth to her face and back, their mouths hanging open. *Guess the jig is up.* Maomao closed her eyes, not pleased.

We should say something here. The reason Maomao hated to be made up was not because she fundamentally disliked makeup. It didn't disagree with her in any particular way. In fact, so far from having trouble with it, one could say she was quite skilled at its use. Why her aversion, then? It was because her face was *already* made up.

Several light stains could be seen on the damp cloth. The face everyone had taken to be heavily freckled was in fact the product of cosmetics.

CHAPTER 16

The Garden Party
(PART ONE)

With about an hour to go until the party started, Consort Gyokuyou and her ladies-in-waiting were passing the time in an open-air pavilion in the gardens. There was a lake hopping with all kinds of carp, and the trees were dropping the last of their fiery-red leaves.

"You really saved us."

The light of the sun was still plentiful, but the wind was cold and dry. Normally, the girls would have been standing there shaking, but with the warm stones under their clothes they found it wasn't so bad after all. Even Princess Lingli, whom they'd worried about, was curled up, cozy in her cradle, which was equipped with a heating stone of its own.

"Be sure to take out the stone under the princess periodically and change the wrapping. Otherwise, she might get burned. And take it easy on the candies; too many of them will make the inside of your mouth go numb." Maomao had several replacement stones waiting in a basket, along with the princess's diapers and a change of clothes. At a request to the eunuchs, the charcoal grill for heating the stones had already been moved to a discreet position behind the party venue.

"All right. But still . . ." Gyokuyou chuckled teasingly, and the other ladies-in-waiting also wore wry smiles. "You are *my* lady-in-waiting, remember." Gyokuyou pointed to the jade necklace.

"I am indeed, milady." Maomao decided to take her words at face value.

Gaoshun watched his master solicitously inquiring after the health of the Virtuous Consort. With his sublime smile and ambrosial voice, Jinshi was practically more beautiful than the consort herself, who was widely regarded to be exceptionally gorgeous even though still very young. Jinshi's current outfit was different from his usual plain official's garments only by virtue of some embroidery and some silver pins in his hair, yet he threatened to outshine the consort in all her finery. This could well have made him an object of resentment, but the overshadowed consort herself was looking at him starstruck, so perhaps there was no real problem after all.

His master was downright criminal, Gaoshun concluded.

After having visited with the other three consorts, finally Jinshi came to Gyokuyou. He found her in the open-air pavilion on the

The Garden Party (Part One)

far side of the lake. It was ostensibly his duty to divide his time equally among all four of the women, but of late it seemed he had been seeing quite a good deal of Gyokuyou. Perhaps it wasn't right to look askance at him for that; she was the emperor's favorite, after all. But there were clearly other reasons for his visits as well.

It seemed his old habit of playing endlessly with his toys had never been cured. *Troublesome*, Gaoshun thought with a shake of his head.

Jinshi bowed to the consort. He praised the beauty of her scarlet outfit. She certainly did look lovely in it, Gaoshun privately agreed. The foreign mystique and her natural allure combined to be practically palpable. Consort Gyokuyou was perhaps the only person in the rear palace who could truly compete with Jinshi for sheer elegant purity.

That was hardly to say the other women around were not beautiful, and indeed, each tried to emphasize her own charms. One of Jinshi's singular talents was his ability to speak directly to those charms. Everyone likes to hear their own best qualities praised. And Jinshi was very, very good at it.

He never lied, either. Although at times he refrained from telling the entire truth. He affected complete nonchalance, but the left corner of his mouth twitched ever so slightly upward. From long years of service to him, Gaoshun recognized this. It was the look of a child with his toys. *Troublesome.*

On the pretext of fawning over the young princess, Jinshi worked his way closer to a petite lady-in-waiting. The girl Gaoshun saw was a stranger. An unfamiliar lady-in-waiting, expressionless, but seemingly contemptuous of Jinshi.

"Good evening, Master Jinshi." Maomao was mindful not to let her thoughts (*Doesn't he have* anything *better to do?*) show on her face. Gaoshun was watching, so she wanted to remain calm if she could.

"Put on a touch of makeup, have we?" Jinshi asked indifferently.

"No, sir, I've not." She had put the slightest dab of red on her lips and at the corners of her eyes, hardly enough to consider makeup at all; otherwise, she was entirely natural. A few speckles remained faintly beside her nose, but they were hardly worth noticing.

"But your freckles are gone."

"Yes. I got rid of them."

The ones that remained were tattoos she had applied herself with a needle long ago. She hadn't pricked too deep; the diluted pigments would fade within a year. Even knowing they wouldn't last forever, her old man had been less than thrilled that she was doing essentially the same thing they did to criminals.

"You mean with makeup, yes?" Jinshi said probingly. He knitted his brow and squinted at Maomao.

"No. It was removing my makeup that got rid of them."

Hmm, maybe I should have just nodded along, she thought. But it was too late for Maomao to change answers now. And it would be annoying to have to explain.

"I don't understand what you're saying. It doesn't make any sense."

"Quite the contrary, sir. It makes perfect sense."

Nobody said makeup could only be used to make things more beautiful. Sometimes married women were known to use the stuff to make themselves less attractive. Maomao had been caking dry clay and pigments around her nose every day. Artfully combined with her tattooed freckles, they came to look like discolorations, or perhaps

The Garden Party (Part One)

birthmarks. And no one would have imagined she would do such a thing, so no one noticed. She was just another girl with freckles and splotches on her face. Homely, they called her. But that was another way of saying there was nothing special about her, that she didn't stand out from the crowd; she looked average.

Just a touch of red pigment could change that impression completely, make Maomao seem a different person altogether. Jinshi had his hands on his head as if he couldn't understand what he was hearing. "But why use makeup that way? To what purpose?"

"Sir, to prevent myself being dragged into some dark alley."

Even in the red-light district, there were some who were starved for women. They mostly lacked money, could be violent, and many of them had sexually transmitted diseases. The apothecary's shop was set up fronting the street in a part of one of the brothels, so it was sometimes mistaken for a display window that happened to have an unusual theme. There were many out there who enjoyed indulging their lusts. And Maomao, naturally, wanted to avoid them. A waifish runt of a girl, and with freckles to boot, seemed less likely to be targeted.

Jinshi listened to this with astonishment and what seemed to be mounting horror. "And were you ever . . . ?"

"A few tried." Maomao, taking his meaning, scowled at him. "But ultimately, it was the kidnappers who got me," she added spitefully.

Such people saw good-looking women as the greatest prizes they could send to the rear palace. It just so happened that Maomao had forgotten her makeup that day when she went into the woods to gather herbs. As a matter of fact, she had been looking for dyes to refresh her fading tattoos. It would seem she had been just that close to *not* being sold.

Jinshi again put his head in his hands. "I'm sorry. This is my failure as an overseer." It didn't appear to please him, as the one responsible for so much in the rear palace, to obtain women in this manner. Jinshi suddenly lacked his normal sparkle, a cloud seeming to hang over him.

"There's scant difference between being sold by kidnappers and being sold off to give a family one less mouth to feed, so I don't care."

The former was a crime, and the latter was legal. Though if the person who bought her from the kidnappers claimed not to have known how she had been obtained, they would likely go unpunished. Many women came to the rear palace through precisely this loophole. Their captors knew that if they sent enough women, enough different kinds, one might catch His Majesty's Imperial eye—and a portion of the resultant salary increase would go directly to the kidnappers' purse.

As for why Maomao continued to use her makeup here in the rear palace, it was the same reason she had pretended to be unable to write. At this point it no longer mattered, but she wasn't quite sure when would be the right time to suddenly appear with an unfreckled face, and the momentum had simply carried her along.

"You're not angry?" Jinshi looked puzzled.

"Of course I am. But it isn't your fault, Master Jinshi." Maomao understood that it was foolish to expect perfection from a country's administrators. One could try to protect against floods, so to speak, but some storm would always overwhelm the preparations.

"I see. You must pardon me." His voice was flat, almost affectless.

How unusually direct of him. Maomao was just about to look up when something jabbed her in the head. "That hurts, sir." This time she didn't hide her displeasure when she looked at Jinshi. She wanted to know what he had done.

The Garden Party (Part One)

"Does it? I give this to you." He wasn't wearing his usual saccharine smile but looked caught between melancholy and embarrassment. Maomao touched her hair, which was supposed to be unadorned, to feel something cold and metallic resting there.

"All right. I'll see you at the banquet," Jinshi said, departing the open-air pavilion with a wave over his shoulder.

He had put a man's silver hair stick in her hair. One of those he himself had been wearing, she presumed. It looked plain at first glance but was closely worked with delicate designs. It would probably fetch a tidy sum if she were to sell it.

"Wow, lucky you," Yinghua said, looking wistfully at the accessory. Maomao considered giving it to her, but as the other two ladies wore the same expression, she wasn't sure what to do. She was just holding it out to them when Hongniang grinned and pressed her hand away, shaking her head. The message seemed to be, don't be too quick to give away a gift received.

"So much for that promise. That didn't take long," Consort Gyokuyou said, almost pouting. The consort took the stick from Maomao and put it neatly in the young woman's hair. "I guess you're not just *my* lady-in-waiting anymore."

For better or for worse, Maomao was not well-versed in the manners and customs of the palace, especially those of its more august residents. She had no idea what the hair stick signified.

CHAPTER 17

The Garden Party
(PART TWO)

The party took place at a banquet area set up in the central gardens. Red carpets were rolled out through large open-air pavilions, and two long tables were placed end to end with the seats of honor at either end. The emperor himself occupied the central seat of honor, with seats for the empress dowager and the Imperial younger brother on either side of him. On the east side of the table were seated the Precious Consort and the Virtuous Consort, while on the west side were the Wise Consort and the Pure Consort. To Maomao, the seating arrangement looked deliberately designed to provoke dispute. It could only possibly fan the flames of hostility among His Majesty's "four ladies."

With the young prince deceased, the emperor's younger brother was now first in line for the succession. Although the Imperial younger brother was, like the ruler himself, the son of the empress dowager, it seemed he rarely saw the light of day. A seat of honor had been pro-

The Garden Party (Part Two)

vided for the prince, but in fact it was empty. He was frequently ill, rarely leaving his room and performing no official duties.

Everyone had a different explanation for this: that the emperor was quite fond of his substantially younger sibling and wanted to keep him calm for the sake of his health; that he wanted to keep the prince isolated and out of sight; or that the empress mother was overprotective and refused to allow the young man outside.

At any rate, none of it had anything to do with Maomao.

The food wouldn't be served until after noon; at the moment, the guests were enjoying musical performances and dances. Consort Gyokuyou was attended only by Hongniang; unless they had some particular business, her other ladies held station behind a curtain and awaited any instructions.

The empress dowager was currently rocking the princess in her arms. The woman exuded a class and unfading beauty that could not be ignored even with the four esteemed consorts around her. She appeared so young that, seated beside the emperor, she could easily have been taken for His Majesty's queen.

And the empress dowager was, in fact, relatively young. When Yinghua had told Maomao exactly how young—and when Maomao had done a little figuring from the current emperor's age to determine how old his mother must have been when she bore him—it was enough to make her profoundly suspicious toward the previous sovereign. There were those possessed of a special deviancy by which they favored very young girls—but how should one react when one's own ruler had possessed such a proclivity? In any event, the empress mother had held strong and given birth to the child, and for that at least, Maomao respected her.

As Maomao was having these thoughts, a gust of wind sprang up. She felt herself shiver. *They couldn't even bother to set up a tent for us?* she thought. The curtain she stood behind was only just enough to keep the attendants out of sight; it did little to block the wind. And if Maomao and the other ladies-in-waiting with their warm stones were feeling cold, how much worse must it be for the ladies of the other consorts? She could see them shivering furiously, and a few were turning pigeon-toed. She didn't think there would be any particular problem with going to use the toilet at that moment, but maybe there were certain pretenses that just had to be kept up with the other ladies watching.

It was a problem, the way these ladies-in-waiting felt compelled to play out proxy battles on behalf of their mistresses. And the head ladies-in-waiting, who might have been able to whip them into line, were busy attending the consorts. There was no one to stop the subordinate women.

At the moment, they were almost like two paintings, one of which could be entitled *Consort Gyokuyou's Forces Confront Those of Consort Lihua*, and the other of which could be called *The Forces of the Pure Consort Confront Those of the Virtuous Consort*. And let it be noted that "Gyokuyou's forces" consisted of just four women, less than half of those they were ranged against. The numbers were against them, but Yinghua was striving to make up the difference.

"What's that? *Plain?* What are you, dumb? Ladies-in-waiting exist for one reason—to serve their mistress. What good would it do them, preening and posturing?"

Apparently, there was an argument over their outfits. The ladies across from Maomao and Yinghua served Consort Lihua, and as such

The Garden Party (Part Two)

their ensembles were based on the color blue. The outfits were frilly and heavily accessorized, making them rather more conspicuous than Gyokuyou's retinue.

"You're the one who's dumb. If a lady doesn't look good, it reflects badly on her mistress. But what else would you expect from someone who'd hire such a clumsy oaf?" The girls from the Crystal Pavilion all set up a giggle.

Oops, I think I'm being made fun of. Maomao had the thought almost as if it were about someone else. No doubt she was the oaf in question. She was just as aware as anyone that she was hardly above average in any way by the standards of the rear palace.

The proud lady making these pronouncements was one of those who had defied Maomao before. She had force of personality, but without anything to ground her; she was constantly saying, "I'm going to tell my father!" To shut her up, Maomao had found her when she was alone once and pinned her against a wall, sliding a knee between the girl's thighs and tickling the nape of her neck with one finger. "Fine," she had said. "Let's just leave you too embarrassed to tell him anything." After that, the girl had kept her distance.

Guess the red-light district gave me a unique sense of humor.

At least one that didn't work with sheltered children of the nobility. Now the young woman always kept Maomao at arm's length, flinching away as if afraid of what might happen to her next. Too inexperienced with the ways of the world to take a joke for what it was.

"I can see she's not here. I guess you left her behind. Good choice. It would be humiliating for the consort to have such a hideous creature around. I'm sure she wouldn't even get a single decorative hair stick."

The serving woman had evidently completely missed Maomao.

That's not very nice. After we worked together for two months, too.

It was taking the best efforts of two other women to keep Yinghua from tackling the nasty attendant, and Maomao thought maybe it was time to put this little argument to rest. She went around behind Yinghua, holding up her hand to hide her nose, and looked at the young women in blue. One of them glanced at her suspiciously, realized who she was looking at, went pale, and started whispering to the other woman. With her hand in front of her nose, they realized it was Maomao even without her freckles.

Word worked its way along the chain of serving women like a whisper game until it reached the haughty lady at the front. The finger she had been pointing imperiously started to shake, and her mouth hung open. Her eyes met Maomao's.

Finally noticed me, huh? Maomao smiled her biggest smile, looking to Lihua's ladies-in-waiting like a wolf who had cornered her prey.

"Ah-ah-ah-ahem!" Apparently, the woman was so flabbergasted she could hardly think of anything to say.

"Yes? What?" Yinghua said, not knowing Maomao was standing behind her grinning. The suddenly meek-looking lady-in-waiting puzzled her.

"I-I-I think you've had enough for today. J-just be glad I'm letting you off." With that barely coherent parting shot, the lady bolted for the far end of the curtained area. There were plenty of open spaces, but she pointedly chose the one farthest away from Maomao and Gyokuyou's other women. Maomao looked at Yinghua and the others, who were staring open-mouthed. *Funny. It still hurts.*

Yinghua composed herself and then saw Maomao. "Bah, I always

The Garden Party (Part Two)

knew she was a witch. I'm sorry you had to hear that. What a thing to say about someone so sweet." Yinghua sounded downright apologetic.

"It doesn't bother me," Maomao said. "Anyway, don't you want to change your hand warmers?"

It really didn't bother Maomao, so it was no problem. But Yinghua wouldn't stop frowning and offering her looks of sympathy.

"No, it's all right. They're still warm. Still, I can't help wondering why that girl broke out shivering so suddenly." The other two ladies-in-waiting seemed to be asking the same question. The three of them from the Jade Pavilion were all devoted workers, but they shared a certain tendency to daydream, and it left them oblivious to some things. But Maomao somehow liked that about them, even if it could make them a little tricky to work with.

"Who knows? Maybe she had to go pick some flowers, if you know what I mean," Maomao said rather brazenly.

For those keeping track, Maomao's legend was growing: she was now a girl who had been abused by her father, then sold into the rear palace, made food taster like a disposable pawn, and after all that, she'd been compelled to spend two months enduring the slings and arrows of the residents of the Crystal Pavilion. She was, so it was held, so deeply mistrustful of men that she even felt the need to blemish her own face.

Inconveniently for Maomao, in other words, Yinghua and the others were just as imaginative as any girls their age. Even Jinshi's endless smiles were turned, in their minds, into looks of pity for the poor young thing. Maomao couldn't understand where they were getting that idea.

But as it would have been a great deal of trouble to try to set them straight, she let the story stand.

Meanwhile, another proxy battle was still going on. Seven on seven. One group of ladies-in-waiting in white, and the other in black. The first group were the women of Lishu, the Virtuous Consort, and the second served Ah-Duo, the Pure Consort.

"They don't exactly get along, either," Yinghua said. She was warming her hands over the brazier. She was also quietly roasting and eating some chestnuts Maomao had snuck in, but the women of the Crystal Pavilion were keeping their distance, and there was no one with enough of the moral high ground to chastise the two of them for it. "Lady Lishu is fourteen years old, and Lady Ah-Duo is thirty-five. Both consorts, but far enough apart in age to be mother and daughter. No wonder they don't see eye to eye."

"Yes, no wonder," said a reserved lady-in-waiting, Guiyuan. "With the Virtuous Consort so young and the Pure Consort so old, it must be a rather tricky relationship to navigate."

"And the Virtuous Consort is pretty much the mother-in-law of the Pure Consort," added the lanky lady-in-waiting Ailan with a nod. Both she and Guiyuan seemed less excitable than Yinghua, but all three of them were perfectly happy to gossip, as girls their age will.

"Mother-in-law?" Maomao asked, surprised. It didn't seem like an expression that was heard much around the rear palace.

"Oh, yes. The situation is a bit complicated . . ."

Lishu and Ah-Duo, Maomao was informed, had been the consorts of the former emperor and the young prince, respectively. When the

The Garden Party (Part Two)

former emperor had passed away, the Virtuous Consort had left the palace for the period of mourning. This was chiefly for show, however, and by abandoning the world—that is, becoming a nun—for a brief time, it was considered to be as if she had never served the previous emperor, and she then married the late ruler's son as his consort. It wasn't precisely aboveboard, but it was the sort of thing the powerful could get away with.

The last emperor died five years ago, Maomao reflected. At that time, the Virtuous Consort would have been nine years old. Even if the marriage was purely political, it was an unsettling thought. When she thought about how the empress dowager had entered the rear palace even younger, it was beyond unsettling; she felt the bile rise in her throat. It made the current emperor seem downright benign. All right, so he had a weakness for especially plump fruit, but he didn't share his father's deviancies.

He may be insatiable, but at least he doesn't go for . . . that. She pictured the thoroughly bearded ruler. One heard the most shocking things in passing conversation.

"That can't be true, can it? A mother-in-law at nine?" Ailan said disbelievingly. Thank goodness.

CHAPTER 18

The Garden Party
(PART THREE)

The first impression one had of Lishu, the Virtuous Consort, was that she was not very sensitive to the mood around her. The first part of the banquet had ended, and there was a break before the next part began. Maomao and Guiyuan went to see Princess Lingli. While Guiyuan was exchanging her hand warmer, which had gone cold, for a fresh one, Maomao took a quick look at the child.

Looks like she's in decent health.

Lingli, her face as red as an apple, had a healthy chubbiness that was a far cry from when Maomao had first seen her, and both her father, the emperor, and her grandmother, the empress dowager, doted on her.

Not sure she should be outside like this, though. It was especially unconscionable considering all the heads that would roll if the princess were to catch a cold on account of the elements. Just to be safe, they

The Garden Party (Part Three)

had engaged a craftsperson to create a crib with a sort of cover, not unlike a bird's nest.

Eh, she's cute. I guess that's a good enough reason.

A fearful thing, babies: this one could tug on even Maomao's heartstrings, and she had no special fondness for children. When Lingli began squirming to get out, Maomao packed her assiduously into her carrier and was just handing her to Hongniang when she heard a pronounced snort from behind her.

A young woman in elaborate peach-pink sleeves was looking at her. Several ladies-in-waiting were lined up behind her. She had a charmingly childish face herself, but at the moment her lips were pursed in obvious displeasure. Perhaps she was upset that Maomao had gone straight to the child without paying her respects to her.

Would this be the young mother-in-law, then? Maomao wondered. Hongniang and Guiyuan were bowing respectfully to her, so Maomao followed suit. Consort Lishu, still looking thoroughly put out, marched off with her ladies-in-waiting in her wake.

"Was that the Virtuous Consort?"

"That was her, all right. She stands out in a crowd."

"But it seems she can't read one."

Each of the emperor's "four ladies" was assigned a distinctive color palette of her own. Consort Gyokuyou's was ruby and jade, Lihua's ultramarine and crystal. To judge by the color of her attendants' robes, Ah-Duo, the Pure Consort, must have been given the color black. She lived in the Garnet Pavilion, suggesting the garnet was the gemstone with which she was associated.

If they're going by the five elements, you'd expect the last color to be white. The light-pink color worn by Consort Lishu seemed dangerously close to duplicating the red of Consort Gyokuyou. The two ladies were seated beside each other at the banquet, creating the impression that their colors clashed.

Actually . . . She realized the argument among the serving women that she had inadvertently eavesdropped on had been about roughly the same subject. One group had been scolding the other for wearing colors that weren't sufficiently distinguished from those of the mistress they accompanied.

"It makes you wish she'd grow up, doesn't it?" The way Hongniang sighed said it all.

Maomao took the cooled hand warmer and put it on the brazier they had waiting for just this purpose. She could see several ladies-in-waiting watching from a distance, so with Gyokuyou's blessing, she distributed a number of the warm stones. She was admittedly a little perplexed: these women were accustomed to a life of silk and gemstones, but some gently heated rocks could bring them genuine joy.

Sadly, the women of the Crystal Pavilion kept their distance from Maomao as if magnetically repelled. She could see them shivering—they should have just taken the hand warmers.

"Aren't you just a bit of a soft touch?" Yinghua asked, exasperated.

"Now that you mention it, perhaps." She had only expressed her feelings openly. *Come to think of it* . . .

It had become rather crowded behind the curtain since the break had started. It wasn't just ladies-in-waiting; military and civil officials were there, too. All of them carried accessories in at least one hand.

The Garden Party (Part Three)

Some spoke to the serving ladies one on one, while others were surrounded by a small crowd of women. Guiyuan and Ailan were talking to a military man Maomao didn't recognize.

"This is how they find the best girls hidden in our little garden of flowers," Yinghua explained to her. She gave a snort as if she were somehow above it all. What had her so worked up?

"Ah."

"They give them those accessories, as a symbol."

"Oh."

"Of course, it can sometimes mean something else . . ."

"Uh-huh."

Yinghua crossed her arms and pouted at Maomao's uncharacteristically uninterested responses. "*I said*, it can sometimes mean something else!"

"Yes, I heard you." She wasn't about to ask what that was supposed to mean.

"Fine, give *me* the hair stick," Yinghua said, pointing to the ornament Maomao had received from Jinshi.

"All right, but you have to do rock-paper-scissors for it with the other two girls," Maomao said as she flipped over the stones in the brazier. She didn't want this to turn into a fight. Besides, if Hongniang found out she had just given away the stick to the first person who asked, she'd probably be in for another smack on the back of the head. The chief lady-in-waiting had a quick hand.

For Maomao, who had every intention of getting back to her home after her two years of service were up, "making it in the world" held no attraction.

Besides, if he's going to think it gives him the right to push me around,

I would rather go back to serving in the Crystal Pavilion, Maomao thought with a look like she was observing a dead cicada.

That was when she heard a gentle voice: "Take this, young lady." An ornamental hair stick was presented to her. A small, light-pink coral decoration bobbed from it.

Maomao looked up to discover a virile-looking man giving her an ingratiating smile. He was still young and had no beard. He looked manly enough as far as it went, but his diligent smile aroused no feelings whatsoever in Maomao, who had an uncommonly strong resistance to such things.

The man, a military officer, saw she wasn't reacting the way he had expected, but he didn't withdraw the proffered gift. He was in a half-crouch, so his ankles were starting to shake.

At length, Maomao realized she was leaving this man in something of a dilemma. "Thank you." She took the hair stick, and the man looked as pleased as a puppy who'd satisfied its master. A mongrel puppy, Maomao thought.

"Well, ta-ta, then. Nice to meet you. Name's Lihaku, by the way."

If I ever thought I was going to see you again, I might try to remember that.

There were still a dozen hair sticks tucked in the belt of the big dog now waving to Maomao. Presumably he was passing them out to everyone so as not to embarrass any ladies-in-waiting by omission. Rather polite on his part.

I guess maybe I was unfair to him, Maomao thought, looking down at the coral ornament.

"Did you get one?" Guiyuan asked, coming over to her with the other girls. Each was clutching her loot.

"Yes . . . A participation prize," Maomao replied tonelessly. Maybe he was giving them to the girls who seemed to be standing around with no one to talk to.

"What a lonely way of looking at it," said a familiar, refined voice from behind her. Maomao turned and was confronted with that well-endowed consort, Lihua.

She's looking a little plumper. Still, though, not as robust as she had been before. The last of the shadows on her face, though, only cast her beauty into higher relief. She wore a dark navy skirt and a sky-blue overgarment with a blue shawl over her shoulders.

Might be a bit cold for her. So long as Maomao was a servant of Consort Gyokuyou, she couldn't directly help Lihua. After she had left the Crystal Pavilion, even updates on the consort's health came to her only via Jinshi's periodic remarks. Even if she had dared to try to visit the Crystal Pavilion herself, Lihua's ladies-in-waiting would have chased her away at the door.

Maomao bowed the way Hongniang had taught her. "It has been too long, milady."

"Yes, too long," Lihua said, touching Maomao's hair as Maomao looked up at her. She pierced something through it, just as Jinshi had done. It didn't hurt this time. It just felt like there was something stuck in a bundle of hair. "Well, take care," Lihua said, and moved elegantly away, chiding her ladies-in-waiting for their inability to hide their astonishment.

But the women of the Jade Pavilion were equally nettled. "Huh, can't guess what Lady Gyokuyou is going to make of *that*." Yinghua flicked the protruding hair stick with a look of annoyance.

On Maomao's head, a train of three quartz ornaments trembled.

The Garden Party (Part Three)

After noon, Maomao took Hongniang's place behind Consort Gyokuyou, for now it was time to eat. At Yinghua's insistence, Maomao had tucked the three hair sticks she'd received into her belt. The accessory Gyokuyou had given her was a necklace, so it would have been just as well for her to wear at least one of them in her hair, but whichever one she chose, it would have been perceived as a slight toward her other two benefactors. It was this constant need to be aware of how one's actions would impact others that made it so much work to be a lady-in-waiting.

Now that she had the opportunity to observe the banquet from the vantage point of one of the seats of honor, Maomao realized it was really quite an impressive production. Military officers lined the west side, civil officials the east. Only about two out of every ten of them were able to be seated at the long table; the others stood in a neat line. In one respect, they had it worse than the serving women working behind the scenes: they had to stand like that for hours on end.

Gaoshun was among those seated with the military officials. Maomao realized he was perhaps a more important man than she had given him credit for, but she was also surprised to see a eunuch take his place among the officialdom with such nonchalance. The big man from earlier was there, too. He was seated lower than Gaoshun, but considering his age, perhaps it only meant that he was just now starting to make his way in the world.

Jinshi, meanwhile, was nowhere to be seen. One would have thought someone so dazzling would stand out in a crowd. As there was not, however, any real need to look for him, Maomao focused on the job at hand.

Some wine came first as an aperitif. It was poured delicately from glass vessels into silver drinking cups. Maomao swirled the wine in the cup, taking her time, making sure there was no cloudiness. There would be dark patches if arsenic was present.

As she let the wine swirl gently, she gave it a good sniff, then took a sip. She already knew there was no poison in it, but if she didn't try the stuff, no one would believe she was doing her job properly. She swallowed, then rinsed her mouth out with clean water.

Hmm? Maomao suddenly seemed to be the center of attention. The other food tasters hadn't yet put the cups to their mouths. When they saw that Maomao had confirmed there was nothing dangerous, they hesitantly started taking sips.

Eh, understandable. Nobody wanted to die. And if one taster was willing to go first, it would be safest to wait for her and see what happened. *And if you were going to use poison at a banquet, a fast-acting one would be the only way to go.*

Maomao was probably the only one here who sometimes tried poisons for fun. She was, let us say, an exceptional personality.

If I had to go, I think I'd like it to be by blowfish toxin. The organs mixed into a nice soup . . .

The tingling of the tongue it caused—she couldn't get enough of it. How many times had she vomited and purged her stomach just so she could experience it? Maomao had exposed herself to a wide variety of different poisons in order to immunize herself to them, but blowfish was something more like a personal preference. She knew, incidentally, that blowfish toxin was not one to which the body could be inured, no matter how many times it was exposed.

As these thoughts ran through her head, Maomao's eyes met those of the lady-in-waiting who brought her the appetizer. The corners of

The Garden Party (Part Three)

Maomao's lips had turned up; it probably looked like she was grinning unpleasantly at the woman. Like she was a bit demented, perhaps. Maomao slapped herself on the cheeks, forcing herself to adopt her accustomed neutral expression.

The appetizer that was served was one of the emperor's favorites; it was a dish that appeared sometimes when he stayed the night. Apparently, the rear palace was handling the cuisine for this banquet. This dish was quite familiar. As the other tasters were all watching Maomao intently, she quickly brought her chopsticks to bear.

The dish was raw fish and vegetables seasoned with vinegar. His Majesty might be a bit oversexed, but his preferences in food tended toward the surprisingly healthful—thought the impressed taster.

They got it a little mixed up, Maomao thought as she noticed that the ingredients were different from usual. The dish was typically served with black carp, but today it featured jellyfish.

It was inconceivable that the chefs would make a mistake in the emperor's favorite recipe. If there had been a mix-up, it had to be that the meal prepared for one of the other consorts had come to Consort Gyokuyou instead. The culinary service *shang* at the rear palace was highly capable and would even prepare the same dish in distinct ways to please His Majesty and his various women. When Gyokuyou had been nursing, for example, they had served her an endless array of dishes that promoted good breastmilk.

When the food tasting was over and everyone was digging into their appetizers, Maomao saw something that, in her mind, strengthened her speculation that there had been a mistake in who was given what. Lishu, the oblivious consort, was gazing at her appetizer and looking a little pale.

I guess she doesn't like whatever's in it. But as this was the emperor's favorite dish, it would be unconscionable not to finish what she was served. She was bravely working her way through the food, a raw slice of blue-backed fish trembling in her chopsticks. Behind her, the lady-in-waiting who served as her food taster had her eyes closed. Her lips were quivering and appeared to be drawing themselves up into a slight arch.

She was laughing.

I sort of wish I hadn't seen that, Maomao thought, then turned to the next course.

If only it had been just a banquet, Lihaku thought. He didn't get along with these elite types who looked down on all and sundry from the lofty heights of the Imperial court. Where was the fun in having a party outside in the freezing cold, with the wind clawing at you at every moment?

A nice meal, that would have been fine. They should all imitate their ancestors, having a drink and a bit of meat in a peach garden with a few close friends.

But wherever there were nobles, there might be poison. Any ingredients, no matter how fine, no matter how exquisitely prepared, would have gone cold by the time the food tasters were done with them, and with the warmth went at least half the flavor.

He didn't blame the people who checked the food for poison, but just watching the way they had to force themselves to bring a mouthful to their lips, their faces pale the entire time, almost cost him his ap-

The Garden Party (Part Three)

petite. Today, as ever, he couldn't help feeling it was taking an inordinately long time.

But in reality, it seemed that wasn't what was happening. Normally, the food tasters would all glance uneasily at one another as they brought their utensils to their mouths. But today, there was a taster present who seemed downright eager. The petite lady-in-waiting who attended the Precious Consort took a mouthful of the aperitif from her silver cup without so much as glancing at the other women. She swallowed slowly, then washed her mouth out as if the entire thing was no big deal.

Lihaku thought she looked familiar—and then he remembered she was one of the women he had given a hair stick to earlier. She was not of any conspicuous beauty, neat and tidy but with no special distinctions. She was probably all but lost in the sea of serving women in the rear palace, many of whom were unmistakably gorgeous. And yet, the fixed expression on her face suggested a woman who could overpower others with a look.

His first impression was that she seemed rather detached, but no sooner had he judged her expressionless than she proved him wrong with a spontaneous, inexplicable grin—which vanished as suddenly as it had appeared. Now she looked rather displeased. In spite of all this, she continued to taste for poison with complete nonchalance. It was very strange. It was also the perfect way to pass the time, trying to guess what kind of face she would make next.

The young woman was given the soup and took a spoonful. She examined it critically, then slowly put a few drops on her tongue. Her eyes widened a little, then suddenly a rapturous smile spread across her face. There was a flush in her cheeks and her eyes began to water.

Her lips curved upward, revealing white teeth and a plump, almost alluring red tongue.

This was what made women so frightening. As she licked the last droplets off her lips, her grin was like ripe fruit, like that of the most accomplished courtesan. The food must have been truly delicious. What could be in it that it could transform a completely average girl into such an enchanting creature? Or perhaps it was the preparation, by the palace's inestimably talented chefs?

Lihaku swallowed heavily, and just then the young woman did something unbelievable. She took a handkerchief out of a pouch, put it to her lips, and spat out what she had just eaten.

"This is poisoned," the lady-in-waiting said, the flat expression once more on her face. Her voice held all the urgency of a bureaucrat reporting on some mundane matter, and then she vanished behind the ladies' curtain.

The banquet ended in utter chaos.

CHAPTER 19

After the Festivities

"A very energetic food taster you are."

Maomao had just washed her mouth out and was staring vacantly into the middle distance when a most unexpected, and altogether underemployed, eunuch appeared. She couldn't believe he had found her so far away from the banquet.

Not long before, Maomao had detected poison in the dish that was served just after the raw fish. She'd spat it out and retreated from the celebration.

I guess most ladies-in-waiting would be chastised for doing something like that.

She wished she could have been more discreet, but it simply wasn't possible. This poison was the first she'd had in so long, and it was inviting and delicious. She could practically have just swallowed it. But if a food taster eagerly swallowed whatever poison she came across, she wouldn't be able to do her job. Maomao had needed to remove herself from the situation before things got out of hand.

"Good day to you, Master Jinshi." She greeted him with her usual expressionless appearance, but she felt her cheeks weren't quite as stiff as usual; maybe a bit of the poison was still in her system. She resented that this might make it look like she was smiling at him.

"I daresay it's you who's having a good day." He grasped her by the arm. He looked, in fact, rather upset.

"May I ask what you're doing?"

"Taking you to see the doctor, obviously. It would be absurd for you to consume poison and simply walk away."

In actual fact, Maomao was the picture of health. As for the toxin in that dish—as long as she didn't actually swallow it, it could hardly hurt her. But what *would* it have done had she swallowed it instead of spitting it out? Curiosity coursed through her.

There was a good chance she would be starting to feel a tingle by now.

I shouldn't have spit it out. Maybe it wasn't too late to claim some of the leftover soup. She asked Jinshi if this might be feasible.

"What are you, stupid?" he said, scandalized.

"I would prefer to say I'm always eager to improve myself." Although she recognized that not everyone would endorse that sort of self-improvement.

In any event, Jinshi now had little of his characteristic glitter, even though he had replaced the stick in his hair, and he was wearing the same elegant clothes as earlier. Wait—was his collar ever so slightly askew? It was! So that was it—the scoundrel! He'd no doubt claimed he was cold as a pretext to do something smarmy.

After the Festivities

At the moment, there was no honey in his voice, and no lilting smile on his face.

Is that sparkle something he can turn on and off? Or was he simply tired after all that had happened? Maybe the reason for his absence from the banquet was because he had spent the entire time accosting—or being accosted by—ladies-in-waiting and civil officials and military men and eunuchs. Yes, that's what Maomao would go with. Talk about a man who kept busy.

I wouldn't want to be in his position.

Beautiful he may have been, but from where she was standing, he looked much more like the young age she suspected he was. Younger, perhaps. She would have to ask Gaoshun to make certain that from now on, when Jinshi visited her, it was only after he had been up to something indecent.

"Let me tell you something. You walked out of there looking so spry that one person actually ate the damn soup wondering if there was really poison in there!"

"Who would be that stupid?" There were many different kinds of poison. Some didn't manifest their effects for quite a while after they were consumed.

"A minister is feeling numbness. The place is in an uproar."

Ah, so the future of the nation was potentially at stake.

"I wish I'd known—we could have used this." She produced a cloth pouch from around her neck, something she'd hidden just under her chest padding. It contained an emetic she'd quietly concocted the previous night. "I made it so strong it'd make you cough up your stomach."

"That sounds like a poison itself," Jinshi said skeptically. "We have our own medical officer here. You can leave everything in his hands."

Suddenly Maomao thought of something and stopped in her tracks.

"What is it?" Jinshi asked.

"I have a request. There's someone I'd like to bring with us, if possible." There was a matter Maomao was desperate to clarify. And there was only one person who could help her do it.

"Who? Give me a name." Jinshi frowned.

"The Virtuous Consort, Lady Lishu. Would you call her?" Maomao replied, calm and confident.

When Lishu answered the summons, she gave Jinshi a smile as pleasant as springtime, while on Maomao she bestowed only a look of total contempt. Who *is* this? she seemed to want to know. She restlessly rubbed her left hand with her right. She was quite young, but she was still that creature called a woman.

They tried going to the medical office, but because all the puff-brained important types felt they had to be there, there was an impossible crowd, and Jinshi, Maomao, and Lishu were forced to go to an unused administrative office instead. It gave Maomao a chance to appreciate how the architecture differed between the rear palace and the outside. The room was unadorned but vast.

Consort Lishu wore something of a pout. Maomao requested Gaoshun to usher away most of Lishu's attendants, who had followed them in a gaggle, so that only one was left with the consort.

Maomao took an antitoxin to help cool her head. She would have been perfectly safe without it, but she felt like being sure, and anyway, she was intrigued to see how someone else had gone about making the drug. In this case, it caused her to vomit powerfully enough to bring up the entire contents of her stomach, a delightful emetic. Unlike the quack in the rear palace, the doctor of the main court was eminently compe-

After the Festivities

tent. Jinshi watched Maomao grin the entire time she retched as if he couldn't quite believe what he was seeing. She thought it was rather rude of him, though, to stare at a young lady while she was vomiting.

Now looking quite refreshed, Maomao bowed to Lishu. The consort regarded her with a squint.

"Pardon me," Maomao said, approaching Lishu. The consort reacted with astonishment when Maomao took her left hand, rolling back the long sleeve to reveal a pale arm. "I knew it," Maomao said. She saw exactly what she had expected: a red rash stippling the normally smooth, unblemished skin. "There was something in the fish course that you shouldn't have been eating."

Lishu refused to look at Maomao.

"What precisely do you mean by that?" Jinshi said, his arms crossed. The heavenly comportment had quietly returned, but he still wasn't smiling.

"Some people simply can't eat certain things. Not just fish. Some can't stomach eggs, or wheat, or dairy products. I myself have to avoid buckwheat." Jinshi and Gaoshun both looked amazed. This from the girl who casually ingested poison!

Leave me alone, Maomao implored them silently. She had tried to accustom herself to buckwheat, but it caused her bronchial tubes to contract and threatened her breathing. It also made her break out in a rash, but only once it was absorbed by her stomach, so it was hard to judge an appropriate portion, and the effects took a long time to subside. Eventually, she had given up trying to inure herself to the stuff. She still harbored hopes of making another attempt at it someday, but she wasn't going to do it here in the rear palace, where her only hope if something went wrong would lie with the quack doctor.

After the Festivities

"How did you know?" Lishu asked tremblingly.

"First, let me ask you a question. How is your stomach? You don't appear to have any nausea or cramps." Maomao then offered to prepare a purgative, but Consort Lishu shook her head vigorously. It was too humiliating to contemplate, right here in front of the one aristocrat with whom everyone seemed obsessed. It was Maomao's little way of getting back at Lishu for her contempt.

"In that case, please be seated." Gaoshun, more solicitous than he first appeared, pulled out a chair. Lishu sat down.

"The problem is that your meal was switched with Lady Gyokuyou's. The lady isn't picky about her food, so she largely eats the same things as His Majesty," Maomao said. But in this case, one or two of the ingredients had differed between their meals. "Mackerel and abalone—that's what you can't eat, isn't it?"

The consort nodded. The look of astonishment on the face of the lady attending Lishu wasn't lost on Maomao.

"Those who don't labor under such dietary restrictions don't always understand that this goes beyond preference," Maomao said. "In this case, the consequences seem to have been no worse than a rash, but sometimes such foods can cause difficulty breathing or even heart problems. I would go so far as to say that if someone were to *knowingly* give you food you can't eat, it would be tantamount to serving you poison." That word got an immediate reaction from the rest of the room. "I understand that under the circumstances you may have found it difficult to object, Consort, but you put yourself in tremendous danger." Maomao's gaze drifted between the lady and her attendant. "I urge you not to forget this lesson in the future." She was talking to both of them. After a beat, she added to Jinshi, "Please be sure her usual chef is aware as well."

Lishu and her attendant, however, still seemed uncomprehending. Maomao explained the danger at length to the lady-in-waiting and wrote down what to do in the event Lishu should have another reaction. The woman was pale, giving little, convulsive nods of her head.

So this is what it's like to threaten somebody.

The lady who had stayed with Lishu was her food taster. The one who had been laughing.

After Consort Lishu had withdrawn, Maomao sensed an almost viscous atmosphere behind her and finally felt a hand on her shoulder. She turned a cold look on the hand's owner; it would have been better had she looked at him the way she might look at an earthworm.

"I am but base and wish you would not touch me." In less elegant words: *Screw off.*

"You're the only one who says such things to me."

"I suppose everyone else is too considerate." Maomao edged away from Jinshi. She sighed as if she had heartburn and looked for Gaoshun in hopes that he might serve as her tonic, but, ever loyal to his master, he looked back with an expression that said: *Please, just put up with him.*

"Well, I must return and report to Lady Gyokuyou," Maomao said.

"Tell me why you asked the consort's food taster to come here with us," Jinshi said, suddenly springing on the heart of the matter. This was why it was so hard to deal with him.

After the Festivities

"I'm sure I don't know what you mean," Maomao said expressionlessly.

"You think the one who set out the meals made the mistake, then?"

"I wouldn't know." She was going to play dumb to the bitter end.

"Then answer me this, at least. Was the Virtuous Consort being deliberately targeted?"

"If there's no poison in any of the other bowls . . ."

Then it would have to be deliberate.

Maomao left the room as Jinshi lapsed into thought. Once she was safely outside, she slumped against the wall and let out a long breath.

CHAPTER 20

Fingers

Upon returning to the Jade Pavilion, Maomao found herself subjected to scrupulous nursing. She was changed into fresh clothes and thrown into bed, not in the cramped room she usually occupied, but in a much larger spare room made up with a nicer bed. After a bit of rest on this new silk bedding, Maomao thought of the straw mattress on which she usually slept and felt like she had ascended from a bog into the clouds.

"I've taken medicine, and there's nothing wrong with me physically," she protested. By *medicine* she meant the emetic, but there was no need to say that.

"Don't be ridiculous. You should have *seen* the minister who ate that food. I don't care if you did get the stuff out of your system, there's no way you're fine and dandy," Yinghua said, pressing a damp cloth to Maomao's forehead with concern.

Stupid, stupid minister, Maomao thought. She wondered if he had really managed to get it all out with the first medication he was given, but her curiosity wasn't going to win her freedom here. She resigned herself to this fact and closed her eyes.

It was an agonizingly long day.

Maomao must have been more tired than she thought, because it was almost noon when she woke up. That wasn't good for a lady-in-waiting. She hopped out of bed and changed, then went looking for Hongniang.

No, wait. First...

Maomao went back to her own room to find the face powder she always used. Not the whitening powder everyone else was so concerned with, but the stuff that created the freckles on her face. Using a polished sheet of bronze as a mirror, she tapped the spots around her tattoos with her fingertip, paying special attention to the ones on her nose.

I'm absolutely not going out without my makeup again. It was just too much trouble to explain. It crossed Maomao's mind that she could just pretend she had used makeup to hide her "freckles," but the idea only embarrassed her. She would probably be expected to react like a blushing virgin every time somebody mentioned it.

Maomao's stomach was rumbling, so she had one of the leftover mooncakes for a snack. She would have liked to wipe down her body, but she didn't have the time. She made a beeline for where the others were working.

Hongniang was with Consort Gyokuyou, watching over Princess Lingli. She hardly looked away from the rather mobile young lady, moving her so that she stayed on the carpet, or supporting chairs so they wouldn't fall as the princess used them to try to stand up. She seemed quite precocious.

"My sincere apologies for oversleeping," Maomao said with a bow.

"Oversleeping? You should have taken the day off." Gyokuyou put a hand to Maomao's cheek, looking worried.

"Hardly, milady. If you have need of me, please call," Maomao said—but she knew full well that she was rarely given any serious work to do and would probably be left alone.

"Your freckles . . ." Gyokuyou said, fixing immediately on the one thing Maomao least wanted her to notice.

"I feel much better with them. If milady doesn't mind."

"Yes, of course," Gyokuyou said, letting the matter go much more readily than Maomao had expected. Maomao gave her a probing look, but Gyokuyou said: "Absolutely everyone wanted to know *who* that lady-in-waiting of mine was. I thought the questions would never end!"

"My apologies."

Maomao suspected people didn't look favorably on a serving girl who declared the presence of poison and then simply left a banquet of her own volition. Privately, she had even fretted over whether she would be punished for it, and she was relieved to discover no reprimand was forthcoming.

"At least with those freckles, people won't recognize you right away. That might be for the best."

Maomao had thought she'd been more subtle than that, but maybe she was wrong. Where had her mistake been?

"Oh, and something else. Gaoshun came by this morning looking for you. Will you see him? He looked like he had time on his hands, so I set him to weeding outside."

Weeding?

True, it was the emperor's favorite consort dispensing the task, but then, Gaoshun was no serving girl. Or perhaps he had taken on the job voluntarily. Maomao had the impression Gaoshun ranked reasonably high in the hierarchy, but he also seemed something of a soft touch. She could see any number of ladies-in-waiting falling hard for him. She especially had the sense that Hongniang's eyes lit up when Gaoshun was around. The chief lady-in-waiting was thirty or so, and despite her good looks, her considerable competence had the side effect of scaring off potential suitors.

"Might we borrow the sitting room?" Maomao asked.

"You may. I'll have him summoned immediately," Gyokuyou said, taking the princess from Hongniang, who left to go call Gaoshun. Maomao had been just about to follow her, but Gyokuyou stopped her with a hand, and directed her to the sitting room instead.

"Master Jinshi sends this, with his regards," Gaoshun said promptly when he entered the room. He placed a cloth-wrapped package on the table. Maomao opened it to discover a silver bowl full of soup. Not the stuff Maomao had sampled, but the dish from which Consort Gyokuyou had been about to eat. He had refused her yesterday, but in the end, had been kind enough to provide it. He was being polite, but this was also, Maomao surmised, an order to investigate.

"Please don't eat it," Gaoshun said with a distinct look of concern.

"Perish the thought," Maomao replied. *But only because silver promotes rotting.* Oxidized food was never tasty.

Gaoshun didn't seem to realize she had her own reason for not drinking the soup. He watched her doubtfully. Maomao stared at the bowl, careful not to touch it directly. And she was staring at the *bowl*, not at the contents.

"Learning anything?" Gaoshun asked her.

"Did you touch this with your bare hands?"

"No. I only took out some of the contents with a spoon to ascertain whether they were in fact poisonous."

Then he had wrapped it in a cloth to bring to Maomao, apparently leery of touching a bowl full of poison.

That caused Maomao to lick her lips in anticipation. "All right. Wait here a moment." She left the sitting room and went to the kitchen, rifling through the shelves looking for something. Then she went back to the room in which she'd been sleeping earlier. She ducked her head toward the fancy bed, splitting the cloth at the seams and pulling out some of what was inside before going back to where Gaoshun was waiting. To his eyes, she was simply carrying some white powder in one hand and soft-looking padding in the other.

Maomao balled up the padding and dusted the powder—flour—on it. Then she tapped it gently against the silver bowl. Gaoshun peered at her curiously. "What's this?" he asked, observing the marks that appeared on the bowl.

"Traces of human touch."

Human fingers easily left prints on metal. Particularly silver. When she was young, Maomao's father had daubed dyes on vessels she wasn't supposed to touch, to stop her from getting into mischief. Her little trick with the flour just now was a stroke of inspiration born of that old memory, and even she was surprised how well it had worked. If the

Fingers

flour had been a little finer, the prints might even have been easier to make out.

"Silver vessels are always wiped down before use. They would be worthless if they were cloudy, after all."

Several different sets of prints were evident on the bowl. From their position and size, it was possible to guess how the bowl had been held.

Even if the exact patterns of the prints aren't quite visible.

"This bowl has been touched . . ." Maomao said, but then she stopped.

Gaoshun was too perceptive to miss the way she came up short. "Yes? What's wrong?"

"Nothing." There was no point clumsily trying to keep secrets from Gaoshun. Even if it would render her little charade of the day before meaningless. Maomao let out a small sigh. "This bowl has been touched by four people in all, I would guess." She pointed to the differing patterns in the white dust, careful not to touch the surface herself. "One doesn't touch the bowl while polishing it, so we can presume the prints belong to the person who doled out the soup, the one who served it, the Virtuous Consort's food taster, and one more unidentified person."

Gaoshun turned an intense look upon her. "Why the food taster?"

Maomao wanted this to end quietly, but it would all depend on how this taciturn man reacted. "It's simple. Because I suspect the food taster deliberately switched the bowls." She knew perfectly well what her mistress could and could not eat and had changed the bowls on purpose. With malice aforethought. Maomao set the bowl down, an unpleasant look flashing across her face. "It's a form of bullying."

"Bullying," Gaoshun repeated as if he couldn't quite believe it. And who could blame him? For a lady-in-waiting to do such a thing to a high-ranking consort was unthinkable. Impossible.

"I see you aren't certain," Maomao said. If Gaoshun didn't appear to wish to know, Maomao was not inclined to tell him. She didn't like to speak from assumptions, after all. But she might have to, if she was to explain why the fingerprints of the lady-in-waiting were on this bowl. Maomao decided it would be better to give her honest opinion than to make any half-baked attempts to throw Gaoshun off the scent.

"Would you let me in on what you're thinking?" Gaoshun asked, his arms crossed as he studied her.

"Very well, sir. Please understand that this is ultimately just speculation on my part."

"That's fine."

To begin with, consider the unusual situation of Consort Lishu. She had become the concubine of the previous emperor while still very young, and soon found herself becoming a nun when he died. Many women, especially the rich ones, were taught that it was their wifely duty to commit themselves totally, body and spirit, to their husbands. Though she may have understood the political reasoning, Lishu must have found it appallingly unvirtuous to be married as a consort to the son of her former partner.

"Did you see what Consort Lishu was wearing at the garden party?" Maomao asked. The Virtuous Consort had been attired in a gaudy pink dress that seemed well above her station.

Gaoshun said nothing, suggesting her reputation was poor in the circles he ran in.

Fingers

"It was . . . somewhat gauche, shall we say?" Maomao offered. But Consort Lishu's attendants, for their part, had all been wearing clothes that were mostly white. "In any normal situation, the ladies-in-waiting would have collectively convinced their mistress to wear something more prudent, or else they would have coordinated their outfits with hers. Instead, what they did made Consort Lishu look like a clown."

A lady-in-waiting was there to support her mistress. This was something Hongniang had drilled into Consort Gyokuyou's other women. Yinghua had said something similar during the banquet. Something about wearing subdued clothing to make their mistress stand out all the more. With that in mind, the argument with Consort Lishu's ladies-in-waiting about clothing took on a new aspect.

The Pure Consort's ladies-in-waiting were reprimanding them for their unconscionable behavior.

The callow Lishu was at the mercy of her serving women, who must have flattered her and insisted the pink dress would look good on her. There was no doubt in Maomao's mind. In the rear palace, all around were enemies; the only people one could trust were one's ladies-in-waiting. And these had betrayed that trust to humiliate their mistress.

"And you believe they further switched the food purely in order to make Consort Lishu's life more difficult?" Gaoshun said tentatively.

"Yes. Though funnily enough, it saved her."

Poison came in many varieties. Some were quite strong but showed no immediate effects. In other words, had the bowls not been switched, Lishu's food taster would still have shown no ill effects, and the consort would probably have drunk the soup, presuming all was well.

I think that's enough speculation for today. Maomao picked up the bowl again and pointed to the rim. "I suspect these are the fingerprints of whoever put the poison in here. Perhaps they pinched the rim of the bowl while they did so."

One must never touch the rim of a food vessel—something else Hongniang had taught them. One's fingers must not dirty anything that might be touched by the lips of some noble person.

"That's my view of what happened," Maomao said.

Gaoshun rubbed his chin and gazed at the bowl. "May I ask you one thing?"

"Yes, sir?" Maomao passed the vessel, still cradled in its cloth, back to Gaoshun.

"Why did you attempt to cover for that woman?" In contrast to Maomao's strained expression, Gaoshun appeared downright curious.

"Compared to a consort," Maomao said, "the life of a lady-in-waiting is all too cheap." Particularly that of a food taster.

Gaoshun nodded easily as if he understood what she was saying. "I'll make sure Master Jinshi understands the situation."

"My thanks." Maomao politely watched Gaoshun leave—and then she slumped into a chair. "Right. Right. I'll have to thank her."

Since she was kind enough to change them, after all.

Maomao really ought to have drunk it, she thought.

"Such is how matters stand, sir," Gaoshun said, concluding his report on what he had learned at the Jade Pavilion. Jinshi, who had been too busy to go himself, ran a hand through his hair thoughtfully. Papers were piled on his desk, and his chop was in his hand. In the whole

Fingers

administrative office, large but barren, only he and Gaoshun were present.

"I never cease to be impressed by what a fine talker you are," Jinshi said.

"If you say so, sir," his ever-intense aide said curtly.

"Whatever the case, it was clearly an inside job."

"The circumstances would seem to suggest so," Gaoshun said, furrowing his eyebrows. He always got right to the point.

Jinshi's head hurt. He wanted to stop thinking. Among other aggravations, he'd had no time to sleep since the day before, nor even to change his clothes. It was enough to make him want to throw a temper tantrum.

"Your, ahem, expression is betraying you, sir."

Jinshi's usual sweet smile was gone. His sullen countenance honestly looked more appropriate for a man of his youth. And Gaoshun seemed to read him like a book.

"No one else is here. Does it really matter?" His minder was always so strict.

"I am here."

"You don't count."

"Yes, I do."

Jinshi had hoped the joke would get him out of this, but Gaoshun, serious and diligent, never did have a sense of humor at the right times. What a burden it was to have someone minding your every move from the day you were born.

"You're still wearing your hair stick," Gaoshun said, pointing to his head.

"Oh. Crap." Jinshi didn't usually talk that way. "It was fairly well hidden. I doubt anyone noticed." Jinshi pulled out the stick to reveal an accessory of considerable craftsmanship. It was carved in the shape of the mythical *qilin*, a sort of scaly cross between a deer and a horse. It was said to be the chief of the sacred beasts, and the right to wear its likeness was conferred only upon those of considerable rank.

"Here. Keep it somewhere safe." Jinshi tossed the stick nonchalantly to Gaoshun.

"Be careful with that. It's immensely important."

"I understand."

"You certainly don't."

And then, having gotten in the last word, the man who had been responsible for Jinshi for well-nigh sixteen years left the office. Jinshi, still comporting himself like a child, laid down across the desk. He had so much work to do. He needed to hurry up and make some free time for himself.

"All right, let's get to it." He gave a great stretch and picked up his brush. In order to have too much time on his hands, first he had to finish his work.

CHAPTER 21

Lihaku

The attempted poisoning, it seemed, was a much bigger deal than Maomao had given it credit for. Xiaolan hounded her about it relentlessly. A spot behind the laundry shed had become the serving girls' favorite spot to gossip; now Maomao and Xiaolan sat there on wooden boxes, eating skewers of candied hawthorn berries, a treat Xiaolan seemed to especially love.

She would never believe I was right in the middle of it all.

Xiaolan looked younger than her years as she wolfed down the sweets, kicking her dangling legs. She was another one who had been sold into the rear palace, but this poor farmer's daughter seemed to be enjoying her new life. Cheerful and talkative, she seemed less despondent that her parents had sold her into servitude than she was glad to have enough to eat.

"The one who ate the poison—it was one of the ladies-in-waiting where you work, wasn't it, Maomao?"

"Yes, it was," she said. She wasn't lying. She just wasn't quite telling the truth.

"I don't know much about it. You think she's okay?"

"I think she's fine." Maomao wasn't sure exactly what kind of "okay" Xiaolan had in mind, but an affirmative answer seemed in order. Awfully uncomfortable with the conversation, Maomao dodged a few more questions before Xiaolan pursed her lips and gave up. She sat there holding a skewer with just one berry left on it. To Maomao, it looked like an ornamental hair stick with a decoration of bloodred coral.

"Fine. Did you get any hair sticks?" Xiaolan ventured.

"I guess." Four, in fact, including the one given out of obligation. And counting the necklace from Consort Gyokuyou. (Why not?)

"Huh! So, you can get out of here, then." Xiaolan gave a carefree smile.

Hmm? This piqued Maomao's interest. "What did you say?"

"What do you mean, what did I say? You aren't leaving?"

Yinghua had been emphatic about the same thing. Maomao had all but ignored her. Now she realized she'd made a mistake. She held her head in her hands and fell into self-recrimination.

"Whazza matter?" Xiaolan asked, looking at Maomao with concern.

"Tell me more about that."

Realizing that Maomao suddenly, and finally, seemed interested in something she was saying, Xiaolan puffed out her chest. "You got it!" And then the voluble young woman told Maomao everything she knew about how the hair sticks were used.

Lihaku

The summons came for Lihaku just as he finished training. Mopping away sweat, he tossed his sword, the blade cracked, to a nearby subordinate. The practice grounds smelled of sweat and carried the warmth of exertion in the air.

A spindly military officer handed Lihaku a wooden writing strip and a woman's ornamental hair stick. The accessory, decorated with pink coral, was just one of several he'd passed out recently. He'd assumed the women would understand he was giving them the ornaments out of obligation, not in seriousness, but apparently at least one of them hadn't. He wouldn't want to embarrass her, but it could be problematic for him if she were really in earnest. But then again, if she was beautiful, it would be a shame not to at least meet her. Idly mulling over how he would let her down gently, Lihaku looked at the writing strip. It said: *Jade Pavilion—Maomao.*

He'd given a hair stick to only one of the women from the Jade Pavilion, that cold-eyed lady-in-waiting. Lihaku stroked his chin thoughtfully and went to change his clothes.

Men were typically forbidden from entering the rear palace. That of course applied to Lihaku, who still had all his various parts. He didn't expect to serve in the rear palace; indeed, he was quite concerned what it would mean if he did so.

Terrifying though the place could be, however, with special permission women could be called from its precincts. The means—one of several possible—was a hair stick like this. Lihaku waited in the guardhouse by the central gate for the young woman to be brought to him. In the somewhat cramped space were chairs and desks for two people, and eunuchs standing, one before the door on either side.

Through the door from the rear palace side appeared a petite young woman. Freckles surrounded her nose. Hers was the rare plain face in a place populated by exquisite beauties.

"And who are you?" Lihaku growled.

"I'm often asked that," the girl replied indifferently, hiding her nose behind the palm of her hand. Suddenly he recognized her. It was the very woman who had called him here.

"Anyone ever tell you that you look very different with makeup on?"

"Often." The young woman didn't appear put off by this remark, but candidly acknowledged the fact.

Lihaku understood, intellectually, that this was her, the lady-in-waiting, the food taster. But in his mind, he just couldn't reconcile the freckled face with the alluring courtesan's smile. It was the strangest thing.

"Listen, you understand what it means to call me out here like this, don't you?" Lihaku crossed his arms, then crossed his legs for good measure. Not the least bit intimidated by this display from the bulky army officer, however, the petite young woman said, "I wish to go back to my family." She sounded completely emotionless as she said it.

Lihaku scratched his head. "And you think I'm going to help?"

"Yes. I've heard that if you'll vouch for me, I might be able to procure a temporary leave of absence."

This girl said the darndest things. He wondered if she actually understood what the hair sticks were *really* for. But as it happened, the girl, Maomao, evidently wanted to use him to get back to her home. She wasn't just fishing for a nice officer for herself. Was she bold, or reckless?

Lihaku rested his chin on his hands and snorted. He didn't care if she thought it was rude. This was how he was going to be. "So, what? I should just play along with you?" Lihaku was known for his decency and goodness of heart, but when he glared, he could still manage to look suitably intimidating. When he gave lazy subordinates a dressing-down, even those who'd had nothing to do with it felt compelled to apologize. And yet, this Maomao didn't so much as furrow an eyebrow. She simply looked at him without emotion.

"Not exactly. I believe I have a way of showing my gratitude." She placed a bundle of writing strips on the desk. It appeared to be a letter of introduction.

"*Meimei, Pairin, Joka.*" They were women's names. In fact, Lihaku had heard of them. Many men had.

"Perhaps a flower-viewing excursion at the Verdigris House."

They were names of courtesans of the highest class, women with whom one could spend a year's wages in silver in a single night. The women named in the letter were collectively known as the Three Princesses, and they were the most popular ladies of all.

"If you have any concerns, you need only show them this," Maomao said, and the slightest of smiles played across her lips.

"This has to be a joke."

"I assure you, it's quite serious."

Lihaku could hardly believe it. For a mere lady-in-waiting to have connections with courtesans even the most highly ranked officers had trouble gaining an audience with was almost unthinkable. What was going on here? Lihaku tugged at his own hair, completely at a loss, and the young woman sighed and stood up.

"What?" Lihaku asked.

"I can see you don't believe me. My apologies for wasting your time." Maomao quietly withdrew something from the neck of her uniform. Two things, in fact. Hair sticks: one in quartz, the other, silver. The implication was clear: she had other options. "Again, I'm sorry. I'll ask someone else."

"N-now hold on just a second." Lihaku slapped his hand down over the bundle of wood strips before Maomao could take it off the table.

She gazed at him, expressionless. "Is something the matter?" She looked him straight in the eye, meeting the gaze that could overpower experienced men of war. And Lihaku had to admit she'd bested him.

"Are you sure about this, Lady Gyokuyou?" Hongniang watched Maomao through a crack in the door. Her color seemed healthier than usual; she appeared almost cheerful as she packed up her things. The strange thing was, Maomao herself seemed to think she looked perfectly normal.

"It's only three days," the consort replied.

"Yes, ma'am, but . . ." Hongniang picked up the little princess, who was clasping at her skirts to be held. "I'm *certain* she doesn't actually understand."

"Yes, I'm sure you're right."

The other ladies-in-waiting had showered Maomao with congratulations, but she didn't seem to grasp exactly why. She'd just blithely promised to bring them souvenirs.

Gyokuyou stood at the window, gazing out. "Really, the one I feel most sorry for of all is . . . well." She let out a long breath, but then a mischievous smile appeared on her face. "It is very amusing, though." She spoke in a whisper, but the words didn't escape Hongniang.

The head lady-in-waiting worried: it seemed to her that there would be another argument.

Having finally finished his work and become a man of leisure again, Jinshi at last visited the Jade Pavilion, only to discover that he had missed Maomao by a single day.

CHAPTER 22

Homecoming

The red-light district to which Maomao had been so eager to return was not, in fact, that far away. The rear palace was the size of a small city itself, but it was situated within the nation's capital. The red-light district sat on the opposite side of the metropolis from the palace complex, but if one could only get past the high walls and deep moats of the Imperial residence, it was within walking distance.

We hardly needed to go to the trouble of getting a carriage, Maomao thought. Beside her, the hulking man called Lihaku sat whistling a tune, holding the horse's reins in his hands. His high spirits could be attributed to the fact that he now realized Maomao's story had been true. The prospect of meeting the most famous courtesans in the land would put any man in a good mood.

Courtesans, it should be said, were not to be simply lumped together with common prostitutes. Some of them sold their bodies, yes, but others sold purely their accomplishments. They didn't take enough customers to be "popular" in the crass sense. Indeed, this helped drive up their perceived value. To share even a cup of tea with one of them could take a substantial amount of silver—let alone a night! These revered women became idols of a sort, objects of the common people's admiration. Some city girls, taken by the idea of becoming one of these enchantresses themselves, came knocking on the gate of the red-light district, though only a scant handful would ever actually achieve that exalted status.

The Verdigris House was among the most venerable of the establishments in the capital's pleasure quarter; even the least notable of its ladies were courtesans of the middle rank. The most notable were among the most famous women in the district. And some of those were women Maomao thought of almost as sisters.

Familiar scenery came into view as the carriage clattered along. There was a street stall selling the meat skewers she had longed to eat, the aroma wafting to her as they drove past. The branches of willow trees drooped over a canal, and she heard the voice of someone selling firewood. Children ran by, each carrying a pinwheel.

They passed under an ornate gate, and then a world painted in a riot of colors spread out before them. It was still midday, and there weren't many people about; a few idle ladies of the night waved from the second floors of their establishments.

Finally, the carriage stopped in front of a building whose entry was noticeably larger than that of many others. Maomao hopped out and jogged over to a slim old woman who stood smoking a pipe by the entrance. "Hey, Grams. Haven't seen you in a while."

Long ago she had been a lady said to possess tears of pearl, but now her tears had dried up like faded leaves. She'd refused offers to buy her

Homecoming

out of bondage, instead remaining as the years passed, until now she was an old hand feared by all and sundry. Time was cruel indeed.

"A while, indeed, you ignorant brat." A shock ran through Maomao's solar plexus. She felt the bile rise in her throat, a bitter taste welling up in her mouth. And strangely, even this she registered only as familiar, nostalgic. How many times in the past had she been induced in this way to vomit out poisons of which she had ingested too much?

Lihaku was at a loss as to what exactly was going on, but, being a fundamentally decent person, he rubbed Maomao gently on the back. *Who the hell is this woman?* his expression seemed to ask. Maomao scuffed some dust over the sodden ground with her foot. Lihaku looked at her with concern.

"Huh. So this is your so-called customer, eh?" The madam gave Lihaku an appraising look. The carriage, meanwhile, was entrusted to the establishment's menservants. "Good, strong body. Manly features. An up-and-comer, from what I hear."

"Grams, I don't think you usually say that right in front of the person you're talking about."

The madam pretended not to hear, but called for the apprentice, a prostitute-in-training, sweeping in front of the gate. "Go call Pairin. I think she's lazing about somewhere today."

"Pairin . . ." Lihaku swallowed heavily. Pairin was one of those famed courtesans; it was said her specialty was exquisite dancing. For the sake of Lihaku's reputation, we should add that what he felt was not simple lust for a female companion, but sincere appreciation for a woman of genuine talents. To meet this idol who seemed to live above the clouds, even simply to take tea with her, was a great honor.

Pairin? I mean . . . Yeah, maybe . . . Pairin could do extremely fine work for those who were to her liking.

"Master Lihaku," Maomao said, giving the big but currently vacant-eyed man beside her a jab. "How confident are you in your biceps?"

"Not quite sure what you mean, but I like to think I've honed my body as well as any man."

"Is that so? Best of luck, then."

Lihaku gave her a final, puzzled tilt of the head as the young apprentice led him away. As for Maomao, she was thankful to Lihaku for bringing her here and wanted to provide him with something that would adequately express her gratitude. And a night's dream could provide a lifetime's memory.

"Now, Maomao." The owner of the hoarse voice wore a terrible smile. "Not a word for ten freakin' months?"

"What was I supposed to do? I was serving in the rear palace." At least she'd sent a wood strip explaining the general situation.

"You owe me big. You know I never take first-time customers."

"Believe me, I know." Maomao pulled a pouch out of her bag. It contained half her earnings from the rear palace to date—she'd specially asked for an advance on her salary.

"Huh," the woman sniffed, peering into the pouch. "Not nearly enough."

"I admit I didn't expect you to actually produce Pairin." She'd thought the money would cover a night's dalliance with a highly ranked courtesan. Besides, the likes of Lihaku would probably have been satisfied even to get a glimpse of the Three Princesses. "At least pretend it'll cover a cup of tea together. Please, for me?"

Homecoming

"Dumbass. A muscle-brained bozo like that? Pairin'll bite, and you know it."

Yeah, I might have guessed. The most esteemed courtesans didn't sell their bodies, but that didn't mean they couldn't fall in love. Such was the way of things. "Let's just say it's out of my hands . . ."

"Never! It's going on your tab."

"There's no way I can pay that much!" *Don't think even the rest of my salary would make up the difference. No way . . .*

Maomao was deep in thought. The woman was clearly messing with her. Not that that was anything new.

"Bah, worst comes to worst, you can pay off your debt with your body. I know His Majesty's your only customer in that big, fancy palace of yours, but it's the same idea. And don't worry about all those scars. We get certain types who like that sort of thing."

For lo these many years, the madam had persisted in trying to get Maomao to become a courtesan. Having spent her entire life in the red-light district, the woman didn't think of a courtesan's lot as an unhappy one.

"I still have a year left on my contract."

"Then spend it scaring me up more customers. Not old farts, either. Young bucks like your friend today that we can squeeze something out of."

Aha. So she does think there's profit to be had.

The only thing the old woman ever thought about was where the money was. Maomao had no intention of ever selling herself, so she would have to begin supplying a steady stream of "sacrifices" to the madam. Anyone who seemed feasible.

Wonder if I could get away with sending eunuchs . . . Jinshi's face drifted through her mind, but Maomao dismissed the idea. The courtesans might get so serious about him that they'd bring the whole establishment to its knees. Wouldn't want that. But then again, she would feel bad sending Gaoshun or the quack doctor. She didn't want to be the reason they ended up wrung out by the old lady. Now Maomao was really regretting that there were so few good ways to meet men in the rear palace.

"Maomao, your old man ought to be at home. Scamper along and see him."

"Yeah, thanks."

Think as she might, she couldn't resolve the issue here and now. Maomao ducked down a side path beside the Verdigris House.

Just a single street farther along, the red-light district became a much more lonely place—tumbledown shacks that passed for shops or houses, beggars waiting for someone to throw some small change into the broken teacups they held, and nightwalkers with visible scars from syphilis.

One of these ragged buildings was Maomao's home. It was a cramped house with a dirt floor. Within, a figure knelt on a rush mat, bent over a mortar and pestle, working the device industriously. It was a man with deep wrinkles on his face and a gentle appearance; there was an almost grandmotherly aspect to him.

"Hey, Pops. I'm back."

"Ah, took you a while," her father said, greeting her the same way he always had, as if nothing had happened. Then he went to prepare

Homecoming

tea with an unsteady gait. He poured it into a battered teacup, which Maomao received gratefully. Even though it was made from tired leaves, the tea was warm and relaxed her.

Maomao started to talk about all that had happened to her, one thing after another, and her father listened with only the occasional *hmm* or *huh*. For dinner, they had congee thickened with herbs and potatoes, and then Maomao went straight to bed. A bath could wait until the next day, she decided, when she could borrow some nice, hot water from the Verdigris House.

She curled up on her simple bedding, a mat laid out on the dirt floor. Her father pulled a kimono over her, then stoked the fire in the oven to ensure it wouldn't go out.

"The rear palace . . . That's karma, I suppose," her father whispered, but the words didn't reach Maomao; she was already asleep.

CHAPTER 23

Wheat Stalks

Oh yeah...
　　The crowing of the rooster woke Maomao up, and she shuffled outside her dilapidated house. There was a small chicken coop in the back and a shed for farm implements, along with a wooden crate. From the fact that the hoe was missing, she gathered her father was in the field. He kept one in a grove just outside the red-light district.

　　He knows that's not good for his legs. Her father was getting on in years, and she wished he would stop with the difficult physical labor, but he showed no sign of doing so. He liked to make his medicines from herbs he had grown himself. Hence, a motley collection of strange plants sprouted around their house.

　　Maomao plucked a leaf here and there, checking how the plants were doing. She glanced at the discreet wooden crate. It bore a sign with characters in brushwork, reading: *HANDS OFF.* Maomao swallowed at that. She nudged the lid back and peeked in, although it did

Wheat Stalks

her heart rate no favors. If she remembered correctly, the crate contained various ingredients left to stew in wine. She seemed to recall the ingredients being very lively and difficult to catch.

After a moment, Maomao put the lid back just the way it had been. It seemed people were heeding the sign. Ever the careful thinker, her father had put just one thing inside the box. That was a wise choice. Several together might eat each other and become toxic.

All right, anyway . . . Her thoughts were interrupted by a noisy pounding at the door. Scratching her head lazily, Maomao went around the front of the house. "You're gonna break it," she said to the panicked-looking girl who had been slamming her fist against the unsteady door. She wasn't from the Verdigris House. She was a servant-apprentice at another of the nearby brothels who occasionally came to Maomao's pharmacy.

"What's up? If you're looking for my dad, he's out." Maomao was in the middle of a yawn when the girl grabbed her hand and veritably dragged her away.

The apprentice brought Maomao to a middling brothel not far from the Verdigris House. It wasn't a big place, but it boasted decent quality. Maomao recalled there were several courtesans here, with some excellent patrons. But what did the servant girl want, bringing her here?

Maomao tried to straighten her frazzled hair and brush the wrinkles out of her clothes. She hadn't changed into her sleepwear the night before, which was starting to seem like it might be a good thing. But she'd been planning to get hot water from the Verdigris House . . .

"Sis, I brought the apothecary!" the girl called as they went through the back door of the brothel and headed for one of the rooms. There, Maomao discovered a cluster of women, wearing no makeup and looking fatigued, gathered around something she couldn't see. When she got closer, she found a man and a woman lying on a bed, sharing a pillow, spittle dribbling out of their mouths. There appeared to be traces of vomit on the bedding.

A pipe lay on the floor nearby, and tobacco leaves were scattered around. She saw some pieces of straw on the ground as well, and a shattered glass vessel nearby. The contents had spilled, staining the pillow. The air was filled with a very distinctive aroma. Two wine bottles were likewise part of the chaos, also tipped over and spilled. The two differently colored stains on the pillow looked almost like some strange kind of art.

Confronted with this scene, Maomao's eyes snapped open, and sleep left her. She pried open the man's and woman's eyes, looking into them; she checked their pulses and stuck a finger in their mouths. She wasn't the first, it seemed, as the fingers of one of the courtesans were filthy with sick.

The man wasn't breathing; Maomao pressed on his solar plexus in an effort to disgorge the contents of his stomach. There was a *hrrk*, and spit came pouring out of his mouth. She grabbed at the sheets to wipe the inside of his mouth. Finally, she slid him around and breathed into his mouth.

Seeing this, one of the courtesans tried to imitate what Maomao had done for the woman. Unlike the man, she was still breathing, so she was easily induced to vomit. The courtesan made to offer her some water, but Maomao shouted: "Don't let her drink that! Charcoal—we need charcoal!" The startled courtesan spilled the water in her surprise but then rushed off down the hallway.

Maomao repeated the process with the man several more times, pressing on his chest to induce vomiting, then breathing for him. When only stomach acid began to come up, he finally started to breathe on his own.

Maomao, exhausted by this point, took the water that was offered to her and rinsed out her mouth before spitting it out the nearby window.

First damn thing in the morning. She hadn't even eaten breakfast, and now she felt like she wanted to go back to bed. But she shook her head to stave off the sensation and called the servant girl. "Bring my father here. He's probably in the field by the south wall. Give this to him; he'll know what it means." She had a wooden writing slip brought and scrawled a few characters on it, then gave it to the girl. The child looked conflicted, but she took it and left. Maomao took another mouthful of water, drinking it down this time, and then she began powdering the charcoal that had been brought.

Stupid, annoying, troublesome thing to do, she thought, scowling at the tobacco leaves and then heaving a sigh.

About half an hour later, an elderly man with bad legs arrived, led by the servant girl. *Took her long enough,* Maomao thought, but she showed her father the carefully pulverized charcoal. He added dried leaves from a few different varieties of herbs, then gave the concoction to the man and woman to drink.

"I guess you did a passable job dealing with this," he said, then picked up one of the pieces of straw from the floor and studied one end of it intently.

"Just passable?" Maomao watched her father—old but by no means soft—work. He picked up a shard of the glass on the floor and some of the tobacco leaves. Finally, he examined some of the vomit, the first stuff that had come out before Maomao had arrived.

She studied him as he went. If she had a habit of observing her surroundings closely, she had surely gotten it from him. This man—her adoptive father, a master apothecary—could discern two or three new things from just one new fact.

"What poison did you take this to be?" her father said. His tone implied he was giving her some sort of lesson. Maomao picked up one of the tobacco leaves herself and showed it to him. A wide smile crossed his wrinkled face as if to say, *Yes, that's right.* "It appears you didn't let them drink any water?"

"That'd be counterproductive, wouldn't it?"

Her father responded with an ambiguous gesture that seemed to be both a nod and a shake of the head at the same time. "Depends. Stomach acid can help prevent the absorption of poison. In those cases, giving the patient water is counterproductive. But if the agent was dissolved in water to begin with, then diluting it is sometimes the best choice." He explained everything slowly, carefully, as though instructing a child. Indeed, it might have been her father's very presence that prevented Maomao from considering herself more of an apothecary in her own right. And perhaps he caused her to see the rear palace's doctor as more of a quack than he deserved.

When Maomao observed that the vomit contained no traces of tobacco leaves, she realized the method her father was prescribing was

Wheat Stalks

probably the right one. It wasn't that she might never have noticed the absence of the leaves, but it remained that she *had* overlooked it. Maybe she'd been sleepier than she realized.

While she tried to make herself remember this course of treatment, the apprentice girl tugged on her sleeve, saying, "This way." Was it just Maomao's imagination, or did the girl look sullen somehow? In any case, Maomao allowed herself to be shown to a room where tea had been prepared.

"You must pardon all the trouble," said a woman portioning out a treat of sweet red beans. She looked like she was no longer practicing the profession; Maomao guessed she was the madam of this particular house. Clearly she didn't share quite the same miserly streak as the madam of the Verdigris House; *she* would never have given tea and sweets to a mere apothecary ("Customers only!").

"We only did our job, ma'am." Maomao would be happy enough if they could just get paid. Her father, sitting beside her in a jovial mood, was apt to forget about that part, so Maomao had to make sure she got the money.

The woman squinted, looking into the next room. The courtesan who had been sick was asleep now, and the male customer was sleeping in another room. The woman's face darkened noticeably.

An attempted lovers' suicide, maybe? It wasn't that unusual in the red-light district. When a man without means met a woman with too much time left on her contract, it was always the first damn thing they thought of. They would whisper sweet nothings about meeting each other in the next life, when there was no proof such a thing even existed.

Maomao took a bit of the red-bean treat and chewed thoughtfully. The tea was lukewarm, with a wheat stalk lounging on one side.

You know, I saw a couple of those back in that room, Maomao reflected. Stems of wheat were hollow on the inside; this one was intended to serve as a straw. Brothels here hated for lipstick to get on the drinkware, and it was customary to use wheat stalks for drinking.

God, but a little friendship between men and women could be complicated. The man in that room had looked awfully well-to-do. Like a playboy, certainly, but he'd been wearing a robe backed with fine silk. He had a charming face, too: the sort of person an inexperienced young woman might easily be drawn in by. Maomao knew her father would scold her for letting prejudice like this into her thinking, but this just didn't look to her like a lady of the night who took poison in despair over her lack of a future. *She didn't look like someone who felt cornered enough to want to die.*

Once Maomao got an idea into her head, she couldn't let it go until she had followed it through. It was just how she was. Once Maomao was sure her father had gotten the money from the madam, she said, "I'm going to go check on the patient," and she left the room.

The man was in worse shape than the courtesan. When Maomao headed for his room on the far side of the building, she noticed that the door was slightly ajar. And through the small crack, she saw something very strange.

It was the servant girl, the disconsolate child who had brought her here—and she was raising a knife over her head.

"Hey! What are you doing?!" Maomao said as she hurried into the room and took the knife from the child.

"Don't you stop me! He deserves to die!" The girl launched herself

Wheat Stalks

at Maomao, trying to get the knife back. Maomao was so small herself that even a child might have overpowered her if desperate enough. Left with no other option, Maomao clouted the girl on the head, and while she was reeling from the blow, slapped her hard across the cheek. The girl fell back from the impact. She began to cry, huge, wracking sobs, her nose leaking copious amounts of snot.

Maomao was just registering her own disbelief when another courtesan, alerted by the noise, came into the room. "Wh-what in the world is happening here?!" She quickly seemed to grasp the answer to her own question, however, and Maomao was hustled away to another room, much to the detriment of her investigation.

The man at the center of this attempted lovers' suicide, it transpired, was already a notoriously problematic customer. He was the third son of a wealthy merchant family, and he had a history of using his handsome looks and silver tongue to get into a courtesan's good graces, stringing her along with vague promises of buying out her contract, before casting her aside when he tired of her. At least one woman had subsequently despaired of her life and killed herself. This wasn't his first encounter with near-fatal resentment, either; other women, enraged by his philandering, had attempted to stab him or even poison him. As the son of his father's favorite concubine, though, Daddy always managed to buy the boy's way out of trouble, and it left him a rotten, spoiled child. Recently he had even prevailed upon his father to have bodyguards see him safely to the brothels.

"This girl's older sister worked at another shop," explained a courtesan as she stroked the child, who continued to cry. The servant girl's sister had been one of those the man had loved and left. The last word the girl had gotten from her sister was a letter joyfully communicating that she was to be bought out of her contract. And the next thing the child heard of her was that she had killed herself. How must she have felt?

"She became close to one of the girls here . . . The one you saved from poisoning today." The woman looked at Maomao apologetically.

Look the other way—is that what she's asking me to do? The woman's hope, it seemed, was to share this sorry tale in order to earn Maomao's sympathy and keep her mouth shut. Thankfully, the commotion hadn't reached the room where her father and the madam were. If Maomao chose not to say anything, the child would most likely go unpunished. *What a pain.*

Personally, she felt that if a customer was known to be that much trouble, they should have just banned him, but apparently it was the unfortunate courtesan herself who had invited him in. If it got out that there had been an attempted double suicide, this establishment would have quite a headache to deal with. Part of why everyone seemed so grateful to Maomao and her father was that as repugnant as he might be, the man in question was still the son of an important family, and she had saved him from dying.

Which, to the little servant girl, must have felt like an unbearable injustice.

Can't say I blame her, Maomao thought. She'd happened to be at home today, but for the past many months, Maomao hadn't been in the red-light district. It was plausible to suspect that this little girl, who did the shopping and other errands for her house, would have been

Wheat Stalks

aware of when Maomao's father was and wasn't home. Besides, for an emergency like this, one would normally go to the doctor, not the apothecary.

Had the child deliberately chosen a moment when the apothecary would be out? It implied an intimidating quickness of mind for one so young. That might also have explained why she had been so slow bringing Maomao's father. It was a testament to how much she hated this man.

Finally, Maomao said simply: "I understand," and went back to her father.

"Quite a welcome home, this," her father said lightly. He and Maomao were heading back to their little shack, having spent most of the morning on the incident. Maomao relieved her father of the coin purse, double-checked the contents, then gave it back to him. The amount suggested there was a bit of hush money included. The notorious customer was in stable condition, but this was probably the last time he would be allowed around here. Not just this brothel, but the entire red-light district. Word traveled fast in a place like this.

When they got home, Maomao settled in a creaking chair and kicked out her legs. She never had gotten that hot water. She was lucky it wasn't the sweating season, but thanks to all that rushing around she was perspiring anyway, and it felt icky.

Almost as uncomfortable was this business about the double suicide. Something about it nagged at her. The man in question had been such a lowlife that even the apprentice girl hated him, and from what the others had said, it sounded like the person he most looked out for was himself. Would a man like that get sucked into some overheated display of love like a double suicide?

Did the courtesan poison him, then?

Maybe he hadn't *chosen* to commit suicide. But Maomao quickly gave up the idea. There'd already been at least one attempt to poison the man; he wouldn't be too quick to eat anything a courtesan offered him. Maomao crossed her arms and grunted to herself. Her father watched her as he crushed some herbs in a mortar. After a beat he said, "Don't say anything based on an assumption."

For him to say that suggested he already had an inkling as to the truth of the incident. Maomao looked at him ruefully, then slumped against the table. She tried to bring to mind everything that had been at the scene of the incident. Had she missed something?

There was a man and woman, collapsed. The scattered tobacco leaves, the glass vessel with its . . .

Now Maomao registered that unless she was remembering wrongly, there had been only one glass vessel at the scene. And the wheat stalks. Two different colors of alcohol.

Without a word, Maomao got up and stood in front of the water jug. She ladled up some of the contents, then put them back. Her father watched her do this several times, before he sighed and put the powdered ingredients into a container. Then he rose and shuffled over to stand in front of her. "It's over now," he said. "It's done." He mussed her hair fondly.

"I'm aware of that," Maomao said, putting the ladle back in the jug one more time and then leaving the house.

Wheat Stalks

Not suicide. Murder, Maomao thought. And it was the courtesan, she believed, who had tried to kill the man. The playboy son, the smooth talker, the lover-and-leaver of so many women. The very courtesan whom the man had been courting, the most recent subject of his amorous advances, might be the one who had attempted to kill him.

Maomao felt she could safely suppose that the philanderer had, as usual, plied this woman with promises to buy her out of her contract. Unlike Maomao, many people seemed to believe that love could change a person. And when enough people repeated an idea enough times, somewhere along the line it became the truth.

Very well. How, then, had the courtesan managed to poison the vigilant man? It was simple: just show him that there was no poison present. The courtesan would have taken a drink of the wine first, just the sort of thing Maomao did in her job. When the man saw that the woman was perfectly fine, he would drink the same stuff. That was why there had been only one container.

That, however, raised the possibility that the woman would succumb to the poison first, and the man wouldn't drink the tainted wine. Some poisons, like the one Maomao had discovered at the banquet, were slow-acting, and there was probably one of those present, too: in this case the agent was most likely the tobacco. It had a stimulant effect when chewed and was spat out quickly.

If the courtesan was a talented actress and could consume the poison without being discovered, well and good, but Maomao suspected she'd had help. She'd drunk the wine through a straw made from a wheat stalk. It was a perfectly normal thing to do and wouldn't have aroused the man's suspicion.

How had this enabled her to avoid the poison? Maomao thought it had something to do with the wine. There had been two different types. Two colors of wine in a single, transparent glass vessel. Though they might not be as immiscible as oil and water, two types of wine would have slightly different densities. If you poured a lighter wine on top of a heavier one carefully enough, two layers would form. And how pretty that would be, a dual-colored wine in a glass container. A lovely little trick to delight a favored guest. And meanwhile, the courtesan would use her straw to drink only from the lower layer, while the man, without a straw, drank from the top.

Once the woman was sure the man had collapsed, she would drink a bit of the poisoned wine herself. Not enough to die, just enough to present a convincing illusion. The tobacco leaves scattered around would help hide the smell, and make people think that was what they had used to do the deed. If the courtesan died herself, it would all have been for naught. She had worked very hard to make sure the man succumbed and she survived. Which presumably also explained why she had chosen to do this first thing in the morning.

There was even someone to conveniently discover the situation for her.

Maomao arrived at the brothel from that morning. She went around back, to the room where the poisoned courtesan had been put to get some rest. She found the exhausted-looking woman leaning against a railing and gazing up at the sky. Apparently, she was up and about. She was humming a children's song, and an ephemeral smile floated across her face. Ephemeral and yet, Maomao thought, somehow dauntless.

"Sis, what are you doing?" a servant girl—not the child from that morning—called when she saw the courtesan leaning on the railing. She dragged the woman back into her room and closed the window.

The behavior of the first servant girl, the one who had tried to stab the man, struck Maomao as odd for someone whose beloved "sister" was at risk of dying of poison. She'd deliberately gone to the apothecary and not the doctor, in hopes of being too late to save the man. And she'd taken her time summoning Maomao's father, too. Wasn't she worried about the courtesan at all? Or did she not believe a second person so close to her could die as well? Was Maomao overthinking things—or did it almost seem the girl had known all along that the courtesan would make it through?

Then there was the other courtesan, who had so emotionally described the woman's plight to Maomao. And the uncommonly generous madam. The more she thought about it, the stranger everything seemed.

No assumptions, huh?

Maomao looked slowly from the newly closed window up to the sky. She was finally back in the red-light district for which she had pined all those months in the rear palace, but deep down they were the same place. Both were gardens and cages. Everyone in them was trapped, being poisoned by the atmosphere. The courtesans absorbed the toxins around them, until they became a sweet poison themselves. With the playboy son alive, it was hard to say what would happen to his would-be killer. He might suspect an attempted poisoning. But then again, it might go the other way around: the brothel might accuse *him* of having ruined an important product of theirs, and squeeze something out of him that way.

I guess it doesn't matter which, Maomao thought. It had nothing to do with her. If you felt personally involved in everything that happened in this place, you would never survive.

Maomao gave the back of her head a tired scratch and decided to go over to the Verdigris House. She was going to get that hot water. She set off at a slow trot.

CHAPTER 24

A Misunderstanding

Maomao's three days at home went by in a flash. It hurt to have to leave after becoming reacquainted with so many familiar faces, but she couldn't just abandon her work at the rear palace. Not least because of the trouble it would cause for Lihaku, who had vouched for her. The final push came from the madam of the Verdigris House, who was even now trying to pick the perfect sadist to make Maomao's first customer.

I'll just pretend I had a very pleasant dream. When she saw the slick Pairin and Lihaku, who resembled a pile of melting honey, Maomao reflected that maybe she had paid too rich a reward. The next place Lihaku would visit for pleasure was set in stone. Having tasted the nectar of heaven, he could never again be satisfied with the tepid offerings of earth. Maomao felt a little bit bad for him. She was sure the madam would take him for all he was worth.

But that wasn't Maomao's problem.

And so she returned to the Jade Pavilion, bearing gifts, only to discover a nymphlike young man who seemed quite on edge. She could detect something toxic just the far side of his delicate smile. Why did he seem to be glaring at her?

His personality aside, he certainly was beautiful. The glare he fixed on her was a little intimidating. Maomao ducked her head, hoping to avoid the trouble of dealing with him, and tried to make a beeline for her room, but he got a solid grip on her shoulder. She felt his nails dig into her flesh.

"I'll be waiting in the sitting area," he said, his voice like honey in her ear. Wolfsbane honey, that was. Poisonous. Behind him, Gaoshun was urging Maomao with his eyes not to fight it. She saw Gyokuyou, too, whose eyes were sparkling even though she seemed a bit troubled. Finally, there was Hongniang, looking at Maomao with what she took to be reproach, and the other three ladies-in-waiting, looking on more with curiosity than concern. She expected to be well and truly interrogated after this was over.

Whatever this is.

Maomao set down her baggage, changed into her uniform, and went to the sitting area.

"You asked for me, sir?"

Jinshi was alone in the room. He was dressed in a simple official's uniform, but he wore it well. He was seated in a chair with his legs crossed, resting his elbows on the table in front of him. And to Maomao's eyes, he appeared to be in a worse mood than usual. Maybe

A Misunderstanding

it was just her imagination. She hoped it was just her imagination. Yes, that's what she would go with: it was her imagination.

Jinshi's customary sedative, Gaoshun, was nowhere to be seen. Neither was Consort Gyokuyou.

And that made the situation unbearable for Maomao.

"I see you had a little visit home," Jinshi began.

"Yes, sir."

"And how was it?"

"Everyone seemed in good health and good spirits. That's what matters."

"Oh, indeed?"

"Yes, sir."

Jinshi said nothing further, so neither did Maomao. It was clear they weren't going to have much of a conversation at this rate.

Finally, Jinshi prodded, "This Lihaku. What kind of a man is he?"

"Sir. He vouched for me to leave the palace."

How does Jinshi know his name? Maomao wondered.

Lihaku would yet become a regular customer. A major source of revenue. A very important person indeed.

"Do you know what it means? Do you *understand*?" Jinshi said, the irritation plain in his voice. There was none of his usual sweetness.

"Of course. One must be a high official of impeccable background in order to vouch for another."

Jinshi looked absolutely taxed by this response, as if enervated by the statement of the obvious.

"Did he give you a hair stick?"

"Me and quite a few others. He was passing them out to every girl in sight—apparently he felt obliged to do so." For all his intimidating look, Lihaku could actually be quite generous. The design of his accessory was clean and simple, but the workmanship was solid, and it was overall a quite lovely piece. If Maomao ever lacked money, she could probably sell it for a decent price.

"You're telling me I lost out to *that*? That I was bested by a bauble some hack felt *obliged* to give you?"

Wow, I've never heard him talk like that, Maomao thought, puzzled by Jinshi's unfamiliar tone. Clearly, something was wrong.

"I gave you a hair stick, too, as I recall," Jinshi went on, "but I didn't see hide or damned hair of you when you needed someone to *vouch* for you!" He looked positively sullen. His alluring smile had been replaced by the pout of a petulant boy, and suddenly he looked hardly older than Maomao. Perhaps younger, even. Maomao marveled that a single change of facial expression could alter how a person looked so drastically.

This much she understood: Jinshi was displeased that she had leaned on Lihaku for help rather than coming to him. Maomao couldn't say it made sense to her. Why should he want one more thing on his to-do list? Wouldn't his life be easier without? Or was it precisely having so much time on his hands that made Jinshi so eager to get involved even in things that might mean inconvenience for him?

"My sincere apologies," Maomao said. "I couldn't think of compensation that would be worthy of you, Master Jinshi."

Would've been rude to give a eunuch an invitation to a brothel, right?

Maybe if it had been one of those innocuous places where the ladies only served tea and played music for the entertainment of the guests. But Maomao knew full well that wasn't all that happened at

A Misunderstanding

the Verdigris House. She balked at the idea of inviting a man who was no longer a man to come there.

What was more, she had to consider who Jinshi was. Maomao could all too easily imagine the average courtesan falling completely under his spell. She was sure she would have caught hell from the madam for introducing him to her ladies.

"Compensation? What's that supposed to mean? Did you pay this Lihaku?" He looked deeply disturbed; a touch of insecurity was now added to his overall ill humor.

"Yes. I offered him the pleasure of a night's dream."

And I don't think he'll be back to reality for a while, she added privately. A man like Lihaku might be a lion with his troops, but he was probably a kitten in the hands of Pairin. And folk belief held that a cat well cared for might bring its master luck . . . or money.

Maomao looked at Jinshi and realized the blood had drained from his face. His hand, clutching a teacup, was shaking.

Maybe he's feeling cold. Maomao turned to heap a few more pieces of charcoal on the brazier and fanned the flames gently. "He seemed entirely pleased," she reported. "It makes me feel all the hard work I did for him was worth it."

And now I'll have to work hard to find more new customers. Maomao clenched her fist to demonstrate her private determination. From behind her, she heard the sound of a teacup shattering.

"Whatever are you doing?" she asked. Bits of ceramic were scattered on the floor. Jinshi was standing there, his face absolutely pale. Tea stained his neat uniform. "Oh, I'll grab something to wipe up with," Maomao said, but when she opened the door, she discovered Consort Gyokuyou, clutching her stomach with laughter. Gaoshun was there, too, seeming exhausted. Finally, there was Hongniang, who looked at Maomao with an expression of pure exasperation: she didn't need to say anything more. Maomao looked at them, baffled. Without a word, Hongniang walked over to her and smacked her on the back of the head. The chief lady-in-waiting was quick on the draw. Maomao rubbed her head, still not understanding quite what was going on, but she headed for the kitchen to get a rag just the same.

"And how long can we expect you to sulk?" Gaoshun asked, thinking what a great deal of trouble this was going to be. Even after they got back to his office, Jinshi refused to do anything but lie slumped across his desk. Gaoshun heaved a sigh. "Must I remind you that you *are* supposed to be at work?" The desk, so recently and with such effort cleared off, was already piled with new papers to attend to.

"I know that."

I hate work. This person, Jinshi, would never have actually given voice to such a childish response. He wouldn't become too attached to his toys.

After Jinshi's conversation with Maomao, Gaoshun had painstakingly extracted a clarification from Consort Gyokuyou. The "payment" for Maomao's guarantor had consisted of a meeting with a "star" courtesan, she said. It had never occurred to Gaoshun that a girl like Maomao might have such connections.

So what, exactly, had his master been imagining? Ah, the terrors of youth, the withered thirty-something mused.

Jinshi had calmed down considerably since then, but his bad mood

remained. He had powered through his work and rushed off to find Maomao, only to discover she'd gone back to her home with a man he didn't know. It must have hit him like a bolt from the blue.

That was too bad, Gaoshun thought, but he couldn't spend all his time soothing the tantrums of an overgrown child.

At length, Jinshi started putting his chop to the accumulated papers. If, at a glance, he judged a paper was one he couldn't approve, he set it to one side on his desk. No sooner had he gone through the pile than an under-official arrived with a new armload.

Jinshi could stand to ponder some of the papers just a little longer, Gaoshun thought, watching his master work. Many of them were proposals from officials whose ideas would benefit no one but themselves. Gaoshun lamented that the young master's workload should increase for such a sordid reason.

Before he knew it, the sun was going down, and Gaoshun lit the lamp.

"Pardon me, sirs."

Gaoshun saw a subordinate coming and moved to intercept him. "We're done working for the day," he said. "Perhaps you'd be so kind as to come by tomorrow."

"Oh, it's not a business matter, sir," the man said with a hurried wave of his hand. "In fact . . ."

And then, furrowing his brow, the messenger related a most urgent situation.

CHAPTER 25

Wine

"What terrible news," Consort Gyokuyou said, her face darkening. Standing before her, Jinshi's heavenly countenance was likewise troubled.

I guess some bigwig is dead. Maomao was there, too, but she was simply present, feeling none of the emotion of the moment. It might have seemed cold, but she wasn't sentimental enough to muster any sympathy for someone whose name she had never heard and whose face she had never seen. The deceased had been more than fifty years of age, anyway, and the cause of death was drinking too much. You reap what you sow; that was all there was to it.

Or it should have been.

Even after completing her food-tasting duties, Maomao couldn't leave the room. Jinshi had apparently sent Hongniang on some kind of errand, and as a consequence, Maomao had to stay instead. Even a eunuch couldn't be alone with a royal consort; a lady-in-waiting had to be present. The salient point was that Jinshi had charged Hongniang, and not her minion, Maomao, with the task.

And that means he's plotting something, Maomao thought. And she was right.

"Do you think the cause of death was truly too much wine?" Jinshi inquired, and his lovely gaze was focused not on the consort, but just over her shoulder—in other words, on Maomao.

There were a number of ways to die of drink. Even Maomao, who enjoyed her alcohol, understood it became a poison if one drank too much. Any medicine did if the dosage was too large. Chronic drinking could induce dysfunction of the liver. Too much at one time could cause death on the spot. In this case, it was the latter: an overabundance of drink at a party among compatriots. Allegedly, the victim had partaken liberally from a generous jug.

"That certainly would kill you," Maomao remarked flippantly as they came to the guardhouse by the main gate. It was the same place she had met Lihaku. Still a simple room with only the barest furnishings, but today tea and snacks were provided, and a brazier was lit to ward off the cold.

"But it was half as much as usual," Jinshi said. (Half as much wine as usual, presumably.) Gaoshun took something from a serving girl who appeared from outside the rear palace. The girl said nothing, only bowed her head and withdrew.

"Frankly, I can't bring myself to believe he died of drink," Jinshi said. "Not Kounen."

Kounen was the name of the dead man. He had been a splendid

Wine

warrior who drank wine by the jugful, and from what Jinshi and Gyokuyou said, he was not half bad as a person, either.

Gaoshun placed the object he'd received from the serving girl on the table. It was a gourd flask. Gaoshun poured from it into a small drinking cup.

"What's this?" Maomao asked.

"The same wine that was served at the party," Jinshi informed her. "We took it from one of the other jugs that was present. The one Kounen was drinking from had been overturned and all the contents spilled out."

"So we'll never know if that jug had poison in it." After all, poison would be the next obvious culprit, if it wasn't the wine proper that had killed him.

"Quite right." Jinshi obviously knew how unrealistic his hopes were, bringing Maomao this alcohol to examine. The fact that he did so anyway—that he clearly wanted closure on this matter—made her curious. Did he owe the dead man a favor? *He just needs to turn that stupid charm back on,* Maomao thought. Lately Jinshi had looked so much more childish to her; she couldn't help it. Honestly, it was easier on her when he huffed and puffed and ordered her around.

Now she brought the wine to her lips and lapped at it gently with her tongue.

Hello, what's this? The wine tasted both sweet and sour at once. It was as if it had started out sweet, and then someone had added a pinch of salt. *It's like cooking wine.*

"A most unusual flavor," she commented, looking intently at Jinshi.

"Yes. It was Kounen's personal preference. He had quite the sweet tooth. He enjoyed a sweet wine and would only take sweet snacks with it." Jinshi almost seemed in a rapture as he described the deceased. Kounen could be presented with the finest smoked meats, or luxurious rock salt, but he wouldn't touch them, according to Jinshi. "Way back when, he used to enjoy more savory foods, but then . . . One day, out of the blue, he completely reversed himself. So much so that almost all his meals became exclusively sweet." The hint of a smile, genuinely spontaneous, it seemed, drifted across Jinshi's face.

"Sounds like he was flirting with diabetes," Maomao said, unsparingly presenting her opinion.

"Don't sully my memories with bleak reality, if you please," Jinshi said ruefully.

So, a man who likes savory foods suddenly prefers sweet ones instead, Maomao thought as she drained her cup and poured more alcohol from the gourd. She drank it down and repeated the process. Jinshi and Gaoshun were watching her closely, but she ignored them. When the gourd was about half empty, she finally spoke: "The snacks served with the alcohol at this party. Was there salt involved?"

"Yes. Rock salt, mooncakes, and cured meat were served. Shall we prepare some of the same for you?"

"No, thank you. I'll be done drinking this stuff by the time it's ready."

If they were going to offer me snacks, I wish they'd done it sooner. A good, salty meat would have complemented the wine perfectly.

"That's not exactly what I was thinking," Jinshi said, annoyed. Maomao poured herself more wine. She paid no heed to Jinshi's transparent disbelief that she was going to resume drinking. The chance for a tipple was such a rare one, outside the occasional mouthful she tasted for poison, and she was going to take advantage of it.

Wine

Maomao drank the gourd dry, to the last drop. She was tempted to let out a big, boozy whoop of satisfaction, but considering the presence of nobility, decided to refrain.

"Do you have the actual jug Master Kounen was drinking from?"

"Yes, although it's in pieces."

"That's fine. Let me see it. Oh, also . . . there's something I'd like you to check into for me," Maomao informed them.

The next day, Jinshi summoned Maomao once again. They came to the same room as before. Jinshi's customary place of business seemed to be the office of the Matron of the Serving Women, but her quarters had been quite busy recently with women coming and going. The offices of the other two service divisions were much the same. Maybe it had something to do with the approaching end of the year.

I knew it, Maomao thought as she reviewed the paper summarizing the results of the investigation she'd requested. She looked at the shard of pottery that had likewise been brought to her, where it sat on the wrapping cloth that had been used to transport it. There were whitish grains stuck to it. She picked up the shard and licked it.

"Are you sure it's safe to be doing that?" Jinshi reached out as if he might stop her, but Maomao shook her head. "It's not poisonous. There's not enough of it for that."

Her words sounded portentous, but clearly puzzled Jinshi and Gaoshun. Maomao went over to the brazier with the paper wrapper that had held the report and started it burning. Then she held the shard of the jug near the flame. The color of the fire changed.

"Salt?" Jinshi asked, peering at the flames. He had evidently learned his lesson from the last time she'd shown him this trick.

"That's right. Apparently, there was so much of it in this jug that even after the liquid evaporated, grains of it remained." There had been salt in the wine Maomao had tasted, as well. Not something added during the production process, but more like the sort of stuff that might be served as a snack—it had simply been thrown into the wine. If the attendees at the party generally preferred more savory flavors, then wine that was too sweet wouldn't be to their liking. Everyone knew how you could dust salt around the rim of a cup, but to have put the stuff directly into the wine—someone must have been either very drunk or a complete culinary ignoramus. A pinch of salt was one thing and would have been fine, but the jug Kounen had drunk from had contained copious amounts.

"Salt is essential to human survival, but too much of it is toxic," Maomao said. In that respect, it was like wine: too much at once could be fatal. When she considered the amount of wine Kounen had drunk and the quantity of salt dissolved in it, it seemed a possible cause of death.

"But that doesn't make any sense," Jinshi said. "No one could fail to notice they were drinking something that salty."

"I believe at least one person could." Maomao turned the report toward them. It contained details of Kounen's personal habits. "You told me, Master Jinshi, that one day Master Kounen spontaneously went from preferring salty foods to preferring sweet ones, yes?"

"Yes, that's right," Jinshi said. "Wait, you can't mean—"

"Yes. I think perhaps he stopped tasting saltiness."

Wine

This man Kounen had been a capable bureaucrat, diligent and dedicated to his work. His self-control, bordering on stoicism, was evident even from the somewhat superficial report. After the deaths of his wife and child in a plague some years ago, it said, he had lived for his work. Wine and sweet treats were his only pleasures.

"There are some illnesses that can rob a person of the sense of taste. They're said to be caused by imbalances in diet, or sometimes stress."

The more straitlaced a person was, the more repressed their spirit could become. And the burden created by that condition could lead to illness.

"All right. Who put the salt in the wine, then?"

Maomao cocked her head. "It's not my job to figure that out."

Armed with the facts that the other jugs had been salted as well, and that Kounen was a very serious person, she suspected Jinshi could work out the rest. Not everyone liked a diligent worker. They might decide to play a little prank on him while he was drunk. And when they saw he hadn't even noticed their joke, they might decide to lean into it until he did. Sometimes the alcohol takes over, so to speak—but would the perpetrators ever have expected this result?

Cowards, running away like they did.

Maomao had pulled up short of spelling it all out, though she could have. She was no more eager than anyone else to be the proximate cause of somebody's brutal punishment. Even though with all the clues she'd given Jinshi, it was as good as if she'd told him herself.

Jinshi said something to Gaoshun, who subsequently left the room. Jinshi gazed after him for a moment. Careful observation revealed a small, tasseled ornament mounted with an obsidian on his belt.

Is that a mourning emblem? And was it deliberate that he had made it so inconspicuous?

"My apologies. I appreciate your help," Jinshi said, turning that transcendent smile on her.

"Not at all." Maomao was keenly curious what the connection had been between Jinshi and Kounen, but she held herself back from prying. *If it turned out to be something indecent, I might be sorry I asked.* After all, one could never be certain who was related to whom and in what way. Instead, she tried a less loaded question. "Was he really such an outstanding person?"

"Indeed. He was quite good to me once, when I was small."

Jinshi didn't elaborate but closed his eyes. He seemed to be thinking back into the distant past, and it made him look just like an ordinary young man. It was an effect Maomao rarely saw from his preternaturally beautiful face.

Huh. I guess he's human after all. It was too easy, with Jinshi's unearthly beauty, to forget that he was born of woman just like anyone else; it might have been easier to believe sometimes that he was the thousand-year-old spirit of a peach. Of late, Maomao had increasingly found herself oddly unsure how to feel about this man, Jinshi.

After he had stood silently for some moments, Jinshi seemed to recall something; he reached under the table and produced an object.

"A gourd?" Maomao asked.

He had come up with a gourd of substantial size. She could hear a splashing sound from whatever was inside it.

"Mm-hmm. Not the stuff from yesterday, though," he said. Then he handed the gourd to Maomao. "It's yours, with my thanks."

Wine

She pulled out the stopper and caught the rich aroma of spirits. *Ah!* "Just try to drink it discreetly."

"Thank you very much," Maomao said with uncommon earnestness.

So, he does know how to be thoughtful, when he wants to be.

Shortly thereafter, she was confronted with the saccharine face. She glanced at it reflexively. Yes, it was still the same eunuch.

"I can't say you *look* very grateful at the moment," Jinshi said.

"Is that so, sir? Well, perhaps you should worry less about my expression and more about the work you have to do now." For some reason, she thought she saw a tremor run through Jinshi. So, she was right: he had shirked his business to come talk to her.

It's one thing to have too much time on your hands. But to actively ignore your job?

"Perhaps you should go take care of it before the tasks pile up too much." Maomao conveniently ignored the fact that she hardly did any work herself.

Jinshi blinked, and for a second he looked pained, but then a thought seemed to occur to him. A nasty, mischievous grin came across his face. "Oh, I'm working quite diligently," he said.

"In what way, sir?"

Jinshi stroked his chin thoughtfully. "One of the legal proposals that came across my desk suggested that in order to keep young people from drowning themselves in drink, there should be an age limit on the drinking of wine."

Maomao looked at him, open-mouthed.

"It recommended drinking be forbidden before twenty-one years of age." His grin got even nastier.

"Master Jinshi, I beseech you not to pass such a law."

"I'm afraid it's not up to me alone," he said, his smile like a blossoming flower as he observed the misery on Maomao's face.

Her lip curled down. She did the only thing she could do and looked at him like an overturned beetle.

CHAPTER 26

Two 'Cides to Every Story

Gaoshun placed a lacquered box on the desk and took out a scroll from inside. "The report you requested has finally arrived." Nearly two months had passed since Jinshi's instruction to find any serving woman who had sustained a burn.

"That took too long," Jinshi said, looking up sharply.

"My apologies." Gaoshun made no effort to add any excuse. It was a matter of principle with him not to do so.

"So, who is she?"

"Sir. Surprisingly highly placed." He unrolled the scroll on Jinshi's desk. "Fengming, of the Garnet Pavilion. Chief lady-in-waiting to the Pure Consort."

Jinshi let his chin rest on his hands, his eyes cold as he scanned the paper.

"Oh, young miss! Come with me, won't you, please?" When Maomao arrived to help with medical matters, this was the first thing out of the mouth of the layabout—ahem, the doctor. A eunuch was nearby, apparently with a message; he had evidently come to summon the physician.

"What on earth has you so upset?" Maomao asked, smelling trouble. The quack was practically quaking as he begged for her help, though, so she obliged and went with him. They soon found themselves at the guard post by the north gate. Several eunuchs were standing and looking at something, surrounded by a gaggle of serving women.

"We're lucky it's winter," Maomao said, utterly calm in the face of what she found.

A rush mat concealed a woman, her face bluish and pale. Her hair was stuck to her cheeks and face, her lips blue-black. Her spirit no longer resided in this world.

The body was uncommonly neat for a drowning victim, but it still wasn't exactly pleasant to look at. It really was a good thing it was a cold time of year. Typically, it would fall to the physician to inspect the corpse, but at present he was cowering behind Maomao like a little girl. A quack, indeed.

The dead woman had apparently been found that morning, floating in the outer moat. From her appearance, it was clear she was a servant of the rear palace. Hence why the quack doctor had been summoned; the business of the rear palace was to be taken care of by the inhabitants of the rear palace.

"Young lady, perhaps you could . . . look at her for me?" the doctor implored, his loach mustache quivering, but Maomao was unmoved. Who did he think she was?

"No, I couldn't. I've been instructed never to touch a dead body."

Two 'Cides to Every Story

"What a strangely specific instruction." The needling comment came from an all-too-familiar, heavenly voice. The girls gave the by-now customary squeals. It was almost as if they were watching a stage show.

"Good day to you, Master Jinshi." *As if it could be good with a dead body lying right there* . . . Maomao, as ever, regarded the handsome youth, totally unimpressed. Gaoshun was behind him, as usual, conducting his standard business of beseeching Maomao with his eyes to be courteous.

"Well, Doctor? Might we trouble you to take a proper look?"

"Very well . . ." The quack flushed and moved to examine the corpse without much conviction. First, visibly trembling, he pulled away the rush mat, provoking some screams from the assembled women.

The deceased was a tall woman, wearing hard wooden clogs. One of them had come off, exposing a bandaged foot. Her fingers were red, the nails cruelly damaged. Her uniform was that of the Food Service.

"*You* don't seem too bothered by this," Jinshi remarked to Maomao.

"I'm used to it."

Beautiful as the pleasure district might appear, one step into its back alleys and hidden corners could reveal a world of lawlessness. It wasn't so uncommon to discover the body of a young woman, raped, beaten, and left for dead. It was easy to see the women of the pleasure district as being trapped in a cage, but by the same token one could say they were protected from its dangers. Brothels treated their courtesans as merchandise, yes. And one wanted merchandise to last a long time and not be damaged.

"I'll be very interested in your perspective—later."

"Certainly, sir."

She doubted she could be of much help, but she didn't deny him. It would have been impolite.

It must have been so cold. When the doctor had finished his examination, Maomao delicately covered the body with the mat once again. As if it made any difference now.

Maomao found herself escorted into the guard post by the central gate. The matron's office must have been busy again. She presumed Jinshi didn't want to have this conversation in the Jade Pavilion. It wasn't appropriate for the ears of a child.

I think it's about time he got his own damn place. Maomao nodded politely at the eunuchs standing before the door.

"The guards are of the opinion that it was suicide," Jinshi informed her. The woman had ostensibly climbed up on the wall, then flung herself into the moat. She was, as her outfit had suggested, one of the lower-ranking women of the Food Service; she had been accounted for at work until yesterday. In other words, she had died sometime the previous night.

"I don't know whether it was suicide," Maomao said. "I do know that she didn't do it alone."

"And how is that?" Jinshi asked, looking regal as he sat in his chair. He was like a different person from the childish youth he sometimes showed her.

"Because there was no ladder by the wall."

"That's true enough."

"Do you think it would be possible to scale that wall with a grappling hook?"

Two 'Cides to Every Story

"I very much doubt it. No?" he asked probingly. It was truly frustrating, dealing with him. She wanted to tell him off for asking questions he already knew the answers to, but Gaoshun was watching, so she refrained.

"There *is* a way to reach the top without any tools, but I don't believe that woman could have managed it."

"Is there? What way would that be?"

After the commotion surrounding the "ghost" of Princess Fuyou, Maomao had wracked her brains trying to understand how the woman had gotten up on the outer wall. It wasn't a place one simply clambered up to.

When Maomao got a question into her head, she gnawed at it until she had the answer, so she had spent a great deal of time contemplating the walls. What she had discovered was a series of projections at one corner where the walls met. A brick jutting out slightly here and there. They could conceivably serve as footholds—if one were, say, a talented dancer like Princess Fuyou. Maomao speculated that the protruding bricks had been used by the builders when they were constructing the wall.

"It would be difficult for most women. Especially one who'd had her feet bound."

Sometimes a girl's feet were wrapped in bandages and shoved into tiny wooden shoes. The bones were crushed, her feet then bound with strips of cloth and constrained in wooden clogs. All this was done on account of a standard by which the smaller a foot was, the more beautiful. Not every woman was subject to the practice, but one sometimes saw it in the rear palace.

"You're suggesting it was homicide?"

"I'm not suggesting anything. But I do believe she was alive when she fell into the moat." The red fingertips implied the woman had scratched desperately at the walls around the moat. Down there in the cold water. Maomao didn't want to think about it.

"Couldn't you have a closer look?" There was the honeyed smile, impossible to refuse. Yet, unfortunately, refuse she must: she couldn't do what she couldn't do.

"A master apothecary instructed me never to touch a dead body."

"For what reason? Some simple-minded fear of impurity?" Jinshi seemed to be implying that apothecaries interacted with the sick and injured all the time, and contact with corpses could hardly be unusual for them.

Maomao's riposte was to state the reason plainly: "Because human beings can likewise become medicinal ingredients."

No telling how far your curiosity goes, her father had said. *If you must do it, well . . . leave it till last.* He'd claimed that if she ever handled a dead body, she might well turn into a grave robber. It wasn't the nicest thing he'd ever said. Maomao privately felt that she had more sense than that, but she had nonetheless somehow managed to respect his stricture thus far.

Jinshi and Gaoshun, jaws slightly agape, looked at each other and nodded in understanding. Gaoshun turned a pitying gaze on Maomao. She thought that was terribly rude but forced her fist not to tremble.

In any event . . .

Did she kill herself, or did someone else do it? Maomao had never once thought of ending her own life, and she had no interest in being murdered, either. If she were to die, it would mean she could no longer test medicines or experiment with poisons. So, if she had to go, she wanted it to be while she was trying out some heretofore unexplored toxin.

I wonder which one would be best...

Jinshi was looking at her. "What are you thinking?"

"Sir. I was meditating on which poison would be best to die by."

She was just being honest, but Jinshi frowned. "Are you of a mind to die?"

"Not in the slightest."

Jinshi shook his head as if to say she wasn't making any sense. Well, she didn't have to make sense to him. "No one knows the day or the hour of their death," she said.

"True enough." A hint of sorrow passed over Jinshi's face. Perhaps he was thinking of Kounen.

"Master Jinshi."

"Yes, what?" He looked at her skeptically.

"If, perchance, I must be put to death someday, may I humbly request that it be done by poison?"

Jinshi put his hand to his forehead and sighed. "And why would you ask *me* that?"

"If I should ever commit an offense that warrants such punishment, it would be you who handed down judgment, would it not?"

Jinshi studied her for a moment. He seemed in an ill temper, though she wasn't sure why. Indeed, he almost seemed to be glaring at her. Gaoshun was looking increasingly anxious behind him.

Hmm, perhaps I just committed the offense.

"Pardon me, sir, I've overstepped myself. Strangulation or beheading would be equally acceptable."

Two 'Cides to Every Story

"I don't follow," Jinshi said, visibly passing from anger to exasperation.

"Because I'm a commoner, sir," Maomao said. Commoners couldn't contradict nobles. It wasn't a matter of right or wrong; that was simply how the world worked. True, the way the world worked was sometimes turned on its head, but she didn't think there would be many who would be pleased with a revolution at this particular moment. The rulership in this day and age simply wasn't that bad. "My head might be chopped off for the slightest mistake."

"I wouldn't do that." Jinshi watched her, unsettled.

Maomao shook her head. "It's not a question of whether you would. But whether you could." Jinshi had the right and authority to dispose of Maomao's life, but Maomao didn't have the same right. That was all there was to it.

Jinshi's face was impassive. Was he upset? It was hard to tell. He might have been mulling something over. Maomao had no special need to know. It simply looked to her as if many different thoughts were running through his head.

I guess what I said bothered him.

Neither Jinshi nor Gaoshun said anything further, and Maomao, with nothing more to do, bowed and left.

A rumor reached her sometime later that the dead woman had been present at the scene of the attempted poisoning not long before. She said as much in a note that had been discovered. The case was closed, ruled a suicide.

CHAPTER 27

Honey
(PART ONE)

Holding tea parties was legitimate business for the consorts. Gyokuyou had them seemingly every day. Some were held at the Jade Pavilion, while other times she was called to the residence of another consort.

Excellent chance to sound each other out and play politics, Maomao thought. She wasn't a big fan of the tea parties herself. The subjects of conversation were mostly limited to makeup and trends in fashion. Boring talk interspersed with probing questions: a veritable microcosm of the rear palace. *They look pretty comfortable with all of it . . . Guess that's what makes them consorts.*

Gyokuyou was talking to a middle-ranked consort who also came from the west. Their shared homeland seemed to be spurring real conversation between them. Maomao didn't know the details, but it seemed the main subject had to do with future relations with Gyokuyou's family.

Gyokuyou was a cheerful and engaging talker, and many consorts would tell her little secrets before they knew what they were doing. One of Gyokuyou's jobs was to write these things down. Consort Gyokuyou's home was a parched land—but it also sat at a nexus of trade, and the ability to read both people and the shifting of the times was paramount. In addition to what she earned as a consort, she helped her family by communicating tidbits of information to them.

She was up awful late last night, but she doesn't look tired at all. The emperor was visiting his beloved Gyokuyou once every three days, or even more often. Ostensibly, it was to see his daughter, who was starting to grab on to things and pull herself up to standing, but needless to say, admiring the princess was not the only thing he did on his visits. Maomao was aware that the emperor no more neglected his daily than his nightly business, suggesting a man of tremendous energies. From the perspective of helping the country to prosper, it was a praiseworthy thing.

At the conclusion of the tea party, Maomao received a bevy of tea candies from Yinghua. She was willing to eat some of them, but it was really too much for her to handle alone, so she made her customary visit to Xiaolan. Xiaolan's stories weren't always articulate, or even completely coherent, but she obligingly shared her latest crop of rumors with Maomao. Today she had talk about the serving woman who had killed herself, the attempted poisoning, and for some reason, something about the Pure Consort.

"They can talk about the emperor's 'four favored ladies' all they want, but there's no getting around the fact that she's getting older."

Consort Gyokuyou was nineteen, Lihua was twenty-three, and Lishu just fourteen. But the Pure Consort Ah-Duo was fully thirty-five, a year older than His Majesty. It might still be possible for her to bear a child, but under the system operating in the rear palace, she could soon expect to be moved aside in a process they sometimes called "being slid from one pillow to another." In other words, Ah-Duo could not hope to become a mother of the nation.

Talk was already going around about her possible demotion and who might be elevated to the rank of high consort in her place. Such chatter was nothing new, but because Ah-Duo had been the emperor's consort since before his accession, and because she had in fact borne him a son at one time, the talk had rarely gained much traction.

Mother of a dead little prince, Maomao thought. It was the same fate Lihua had to look forward to if she didn't become pregnant with another child for His Majesty. And she wasn't really alone: Consort Gyokuyou couldn't assume she would hold pride of place in the Imperial affections forever.

For every beautiful blossom faded in time. The blossoms of the rear palace had to bear fruit, or they were worthless. As familiar as this logic was to Maomao by now, it never ceased to remind her that the palace was also a prison.

She brushed a few stray crumbs of mooncake from her skirt and looked up at the overcast sky.

Gyokuyou's partner for today's tea party was somewhat unusual. It was Consort Lishu, another of the four favored ladies. It was uncommon for consorts of the same rank to hold parties for each other; still more so when it came to the highest-ranked women.

The nervousness was clear on Lishu's childlike face. She was attended by four ladies-in-waiting, including the notorious food taster. Apparently, the woman hadn't been punished as severely as Maomao had feared she might be.

It was cold out, so the tea party was being held indoors. Some eunuchs were put to work setting up chaise longues for the ladies-in-waiting in the sitting room. The table had a mother-of-pearl inlay, and the curtain was changed for a new one with elaborate embroidery. To be perfectly blunt, they hardly put this much care into receiving the emperor himself—but it was the way of women to want to put their best foot forward for their peers.

Makeup was likewise applied with gusto, and Maomao was summarily deprived of her freckles. The girls accented the corners of their eyes with red lines. It was a level of makeup men might have considered ostentatious, but that didn't matter; here, the gaudier of the two parties would be the victor.

In their conversation, Consort Gyokuyou seemed to do all the talking, while Lishu nodded along meekly. Perhaps that was just what came of the difference in their ages. Behind Lishu, her attendants seemed less interested in their lady than in the accoutrements of the Jade Pavilion, glancing this way and that at the ornaments and furnishings. Only the food taster stood dutifully behind Consort Lishu, across from Maomao, eyeing her erstwhile tormentor watchfully.

What's the story, here? First the women from the Crystal Pavilion, now this girl. Maomao wished people would stop treating her like some sort of monster. She wasn't a stray dog, and she wouldn't bite.

Offhand, they look like perfectly ordinary ladies-in-waiting, Maomao thought. She'd once told Gaoshun that they bullied their consort. It might be a little awkward if the allegation turned out not to be true, but she would have been just as glad to be wrong.

Compared with the few, the proud ladies-in-waiting of the Jade Pavilion, Lishu's women seemed a bit slow to act, but they did their jobs. At least, such as they were: since Gyokuyou was the hostess of today's tea party, they didn't have that much to do.

Ailan appeared with a ceramic jar and hot water.

"Are you partial to sweet things? It's so cold today, I thought this might be comforting," Gyokuyou said.

"I like sweets," Lishu answered. It seemed to make her feel a little more at ease.

Inside the jar was citrus rind that had been boiled in honey. It would warm the body and soothe the throat and could even help prevent colds. Maomao had made it herself. Gyokuyou seemed to like it and had frequently served it at her tea parties lately.

Hmm? Despite her pronouncement that she liked sweets, Consort Lishu suddenly looked distinctly uncomfortable. The food taster likewise seemed as if she wanted to object to what was being poured into her lady's drinking cup. *Can't take honey, either?* Maomao thought.

None of the other ladies-in-waiting lolling about seemed prepared to say anything. They just looked at Lishu in annoyance. *Get over it,* they seemed to be saying. They still thought it was just childish pickiness.

Maomao gave a little sigh and whispered in Consort Gyokuyou's ear. Her eyes widened slightly, and she called Ailan over. "I'm terribly

Honey (Part One)

sorry, but it seems this needs to steep a little longer. I'll serve something else. Do you take ginger tea?"

"Yes. Thank you, ma'am," Lishu said, sounding a little more upbeat. Changing teas had evidently been the right move.

As Maomao glanced up, she saw Lishu's ladies-in-waiting. She almost thought they looked disappointed. The impression only lasted for a second, and then it was gone.

Come evening, that loveliest of eunuchs appeared, as ever, nymph-like smile in front, Gaoshun behind. Maomao had the feeling lately that there were more furrows in Gaoshun's brow than before. Perhaps he had new troubles to contend with.

"I hear you had a tea party with Consort Lishu," Jinshi said.

"Yes, and it was lovely."

Jinshi made regular rounds of the emperor's most prominent consorts, almost as if it was his business to keep things together in the rear palace. He seemed to sense something unusual in the day's get-together and so felt compelled to involve himself. Maomao tried to make her exit before she got sucked into anything, but naturally, he stopped her.

"Would you be so kind as to let go of me?"

"I wasn't done talking." When the sublime young man turned his gaze on her, Maomao could only drop her own eyes to the ground. She was sure she was looking at him as if he were a dead fish. Not a pretty fish, either. Probably one of those bottom-feeding ones.

"Ah, such friends you are," Gyokuyou said, laughing merrily. A little *too* merrily.

Maomao found herself replying, "Lady Gyokuyou, a bit of acupressure around the eyes may help prevent wrinkles."

Oops. Can't be talking like that. She had to be careful not to be rude to anyone but Jinshi. *Er . . . Guess that's not such a great idea, either.* She'd already upset him just the other day. Too many little missteps like that, and she might find herself out of the eunuch's good graces, and perhaps meeting a prompt end by strangulation directly after that.

"Have you heard that the serving woman who killed herself is allegedly the perpetrator of the poisoning the other day?"

Maomao nodded—for it seemed by Jinshi's tone that he was asking her and not Gyokuyou. As for the consort, she seemed to sense that this conversation would best be held in private and left the room. Maomao, Jinshi, and Gaoshun were left alone.

"Do you really believe the culprit committed suicide?"

"That's not for me to determine." To turn a lie into fact was the prerogative of the powerful. She didn't know who had made the determination, but she suspected Jinshi was connected somehow.

"Would a mere serving woman have reason to poison the food of the Virtuous Consort?"

"I'm afraid I wouldn't know."

Jinshi smiled, a seductive look he could use expertly to manipulate people. Unfortunately for him, it didn't work on Maomao. She was sure he knew he didn't have to leer at her to get what he wanted; he simply needed to give her an order. She wouldn't refuse.

"Perhaps I could dispatch you to help in the Garnet Pavilion, starting tomorrow?"

What purpose did the question mark serve? Maomao gave the only possible answer: "As you wish."

Honey (Part One)

A house, they say, comes to reflect its master. Just so, Consort Gyokuyou's Jade Pavilion was homey, while Lihua's Crystal Pavilion was elegant and refined. And the Garnet Pavilion, where Ah-Duo lived, was eminently practical. Nowhere in the decor was there anything unnecessary; there was a conspicuous lack of interest in extraneous ornamentation, which itself achieved a kind of sublime refinement.

It spoke directly to who the mistress of the house was. Every bit of waste had been stripped away from her body, which boasted neither flowery excess nor ample abundance nor charming loveliness. What was left, though, was a stark, neutral beauty.

Is she really thirty-five? If Ah-Duo had put on an official uniform, one could have mistaken her for some up-and-coming civil servant. Here in the rear palace, where there were nothing but women and eunuchs, she must have been the apple of many an eye. She was attractive in a way that was very similar to Jinshi—and then again, different. Maomao hadn't seen exactly what Ah-Duo had been wearing at the banquet, but now she had shed any skirt or wide sleeves in favor of what looked almost like riding clothes.

Maomao was being shown around the residence along with two other serving women. Ah-Duo's head lady-in-waiting, Fengming, was a plump, garrulous beauty who delivered fluent exposition as they trotted through the household.

"I'm sorry, having you brought here on such short notice," she said. The chief lady-in-waiting of one of the emperor's four favored ladies was likely to be a woman of no mean station herself, and Fengming's willingness to engage the lesser women was endearing.

Wonder if she's the daughter of a merchant family or something, Maomao thought. She and the others had been summoned to help with the great spate of cleaning that marked the turn of every year. There weren't enough hands at the Garnet Pavilion to do it alone. *And is she injured?* Maomao wondered, glimpsing a bandage around Fengming's left arm. Maomao's left arm was likewise bandaged. She was tired of people looking at her with alarm every time they saw her scars.

The women let the eunuchs handle the physical labor, while they passed the day airing out the furniture and scrolls to protect them from bugs. And there were so many of each in the Garnet Pavilion, many more than in Consort Gyokuyou's residence. Such was the quantity Ah-Duo had accumulated over her residence in the rear palace, the longest of any of the consorts.

Maomao didn't go back to the Jade Pavilion that evening but slept alongside the other two serving women in a large room at the Garnet Pavilion. To ward off the cold, Maomao was given an animal-fur blanket that was indeed very warm.

I haven't been told what to do exactly. Maomao concentrated on cleaning, just like Fengming said. The plump lady-in-waiting was generous with her praise, making it that much harder to slack off. Maomao started to suspect Fengming was in fact a dexterous user of people.

Fengming seemed like the type of woman people had in mind when they talked about a good wife who did her chores with a glad heart. She had been with Ah-Duo for the consort's entire time in the rear palace, meaning she was well past the usual age of marriage, and even Maomao found herself thinking that was something of a shame. She knew that as head lady-in-waiting, Fengming could earn more than many unskilled men, but she wondered if it had really never occurred to her to find a husband. Wasn't that something most people thought about? Maomao knew the other three ladies in the Jade Pavilion talked about it often. They had no intention of leaving Consort Gyokuyou's side for some time yet, but still they dreamed of a dashing princeling appearing for them. "Dreams are free, so have your fill," Hongniang would say with a smile. Maomao found the remark strangely frightening.

First time in a while I feel like I've actually worked, she thought. Then she curled up, just like her namesake, the cat, and was soon asleep.

Is the mastermind behind that poisoning attempt really here? Maomao wondered. The ladies-in-waiting at the Jade Pavilion were extremely hard workers, but even by that standard, Maomao had to admit that the women at the Garnet Pavilion were no slouches, either. All of them adored Consort Ah-Duo and wanted to do their best work for her.

This was as true of their leader, Fengming, as it was of anyone. She never let herself be constrained by her station; if she saw a speck of dust, she would grab a cloth and wipe it away herself. She hardly seemed like the chief lady-in-waiting to a highly ranked consort. Even the industrious Hongniang would leave such tasks to the other women.

I wish those proud peacocks at the Crystal Pavilion could see this.

Consort Lihua, it seemed, simply wasn't lucky in serving women. Maybe the reason she had so many of them was because each one did so little work. They were excellent talkers, but nothing more, and therein lay the problem. Then again, taking such problems in hand was one of the challenges of holding a high rank.

Powerful loyalty, though, could bring its own troubles. It could motivate someone to attempt poisoning, for example. Some high official was trying to get his own daughter into the rear palace, leading to the prospective disenfranchisement of one of the four foremost consorts. If anyone was apt to be demoted, it was Ah-Duo—but what if one of the other consorts' places were suddenly vacant?

Gyokuyou and Lihua were more or less secure, but presumably the emperor didn't visit Consort Lishu. Maomao suspected that was one of the reasons her ladies-in-waiting took her so lightly. *His Majesty doesn't like them so . . . scrawny.* Maybe it was a reaction against his father's preference for extremely young girls: the current ruler was only aroused if a woman had enough meat on her bones. Every consort he visited, not least Gyokuyou and Lihua, possessed a certain voluptuousness.

As such, Lishu had yet to fulfill her duty as a consort. Maybe that was just as well for someone so young. She was technically of marriageable age, yes, but a pregnancy at fourteen could put considerable strain on her body come childbirth. Even back at the Verdigris House, girls didn't graduate from apprenticeship until fifteen. And until then, they didn't take customers. It ultimately made them better courtesans who lasted longer.

Maomao preferred not to think too hard about the former emperor's predilections. If one did a little math involving the respective ages of the current emperor and his mother, one arrived at a most unsettling number.

In any event, if someone wanted to get one of the four ladies out of the picture, Consort Lishu would be a logical choice.

Maomao let her thoughts wander as she organized a kitchen shelf, upon which was a line of small jars. A sweet aroma tickled her nose. "What should we do with these?" Maomao, picking up one of the jars, said to a lady-in-waiting who was cleaning the kitchen with her. The two serving girls who had accompanied Maomao the day before were cleaning the bath and the living area, respectively.

"Oh, those. Dust the shelf and then put them back the way they were."

Honey (Part One)

"Are these all honey?"

"Mm-hmm. Lady Fengming's family are beekeepers."

"Ah."

Honey was a luxury item. A person would be lucky to have even one variety, let alone a whole shelf full—but that explained it. Maomao peeked into several of the jars and saw honeys of different colors: amber, dark red, and even brown. They came from different flowers and had different flavors. Come to think of it, she'd thought the candles they'd used for illumination the night before had a sweet scent. They must have been beeswax.

Hmm . . . Something nagged at her, something to do with honey. The subject had come up recently, she was sure.

"When you're done there, would you dust the second-floor railing? It always gets missed when we're cleaning."

"Of course." Maomao put the honey back in its place and went up to the second floor with her rag. *Honey. Honey . . .* As she carefully dusted each post of the railing, she turned the word over in her mind, trying to remember what it represented.

Well, now. From the second floor, she could see outside clearly. Including some figures among the shadows of the trees. They evidently thought they were hidden, but they were obviously observing the Garnet Pavilion.

Is that Consort Lishu? The young consort was there, with only one attendant, her food taster. None of this was making sense to Maomao. Her memory went back to the tea party, and Lishu's unaccountable aversion to honey.

Honey . . .

She just couldn't let the thought go.

Maomao appropriated the Jade Pavilion's reception area to report to Jinshi about what had transpired at the Garnet Pavilion.

"All of which is to say, I have no idea." What she didn't know, she didn't know. Maomao refused to underestimate herself, but by the same token, she wouldn't oversell her abilities, either. She was perfectly frank with the gorgeous eunuch. She'd told him all she'd come up with after three days in the Garnet Pavilion.

Jinshi reclined on a chaise longue, looking elegant as he sipped a fragrant tea from some other land. It had a sweet aroma; the concoction involved lemons and honey.

"I see. Yes, of course."

"Indeed, sir."

Maomao was just as happy that, of late, the gorgeous eunuch appeared a little less sparkly than before, but it seemed to her that his tone had grown somewhat glib. Perhaps it was that the sweetness was gone from his voice, and he gave the impression of a young man, almost a boy. Maomao didn't know what he wanted from her, but she was always and ever nothing more than an ordinary apothecary. She had no interest in playing spy.

"Let's try a different question, then. Hypothetically, if, by some special means, there were someone who was communicating with outside parties, who do you suppose that would be?"

Again with the roundabout interrogation. I wish he would just say what he means. Maomao didn't like to speak without proof. She had always been taught not to work based on assumptions. Now she closed her eyes and let out a deep breath. If she couldn't calm herself a little, she might just look at the entrancing young man as if he were a flattened toad. Gaoshun was, as ever, silently urging restraint with his eyes.

Honey (Part One)

"This is purely a possibility, but *if* there were such a person, I think perhaps it would be Lady Fengming, the chief lady-in-waiting."

"You have any proof?"

"She had a bandage wrapped around her left arm. I walked in while she was changing it once and caught a glimpse of some burns."

Maomao had previously dealt with an incident involving writing strips impregnated with various chemicals. She'd thought at the time that if the chemicals meant anything at all, they might represent some kind of code, but she had kept that to herself. Based on the fact that the outfit holding the writing strips had been scorched, it was a short leap to imagining the person who had once worn the outfit had a burn on their arm. She was confident Jinshi had investigated the possibility. It was probably what had led him to try to make Maomao his eyes and ears.

Maomao thought, quite honestly, that the serene chief lady-in-waiting hadn't looked like the type to try such a thing, but she had to admit this was only her subjective opinion. And one had to look objectively at things, or one would never arrive at the truth.

"Mm-hmm. Passing marks for you." Jinshi suddenly let his eyes fall on a small jar on the table. Then he glanced at Maomao, and that nectared smile appeared. She was sure she could see something sinister just behind it. Maomao felt all her hair stand on end. She did not like where this appeared to be going, not one bit.

Jinshi picked up the jar and came toward her. "Such a smart girl deserves a reward."

"I couldn't."

"You could. And you should!"

"I'm quite happy without a reward. Give it to someone else." Maomao fixed Jinshi with her most withering look in an attempt to dissuade him, but he didn't so much as flinch. Was this a little punishment for hurting his feelings the other day? Unfortunately for them both, Maomao still had no idea why Jinshi had been so upset.

The eunuch came closer. Maomao backed away a half step and found herself up against the wall. She looked to Gaoshun for help, but the reticent aide was sitting by the window, idly watching birds flying through the sky. The obviously artificial nature of the pose made him look most disagreeable.

I'll have to sneak him a laxative later.

Jinshi, still wearing a smile that would have melted anyone else, stuck his fingers into the jar. They emerged dripping with honey. This little prank, Maomao felt, was going too far.

"Don't you like sweet things?"

"I prefer spicy flavors."

"But you *can* stomach them, can't you?"

Jinshi showed no sign of relenting; his fingers crept toward Maomao's mouth. This must be how he always comported himself, she thought. But beauty didn't give you license to do whatever you wanted.

The eunuch was studying Maomao's piercing glare with a look of rapture.

That's right . . . I forgot he's one of those *types.* She tried giving him a crushing look, as if he were a small, brown rat, but it was having the opposite of the effect she wanted.

Should she take this as an order and simply let him stuff the honey in her mouth? Or should she try to salvage what remained of her pride by finding some way to escape?

I could live with it if it were at least wolfsbane honey, she thought.

Honey from a poisonous flower would at least have the virtue of being, well, poisonous.

Suddenly, something came together in Maomao's mind. She wanted to take a moment, tease out the threads of the thought, but with the pervert about to stick his hand into her mouth, she couldn't think anything at all. Just as the fingers were about to touch her lips, she heard a voice.

"What are you doing to my attendant?" It was Consort Gyokuyou, standing there and looking very displeased. Hongniang was with her, her head in her hands.

CHAPTER 28

Honey
(PART TWO)

"I grant Master Jinshi's joke went a little too far, but it really was just a bit of mischief. Perhaps you might find it in your heart to forgive him?" Gaoshun was showing Maomao to the Diamond Pavilion, where Consort Lishu lived. His master had already been roundly excoriated at the Jade Pavilion for the incident in question.

"Very well. If you'll lick it off in the future, Master Gaoshun, I don't foresee any problems."

"L-lick it . . ." Gaoshun looked conflicted. His proclivities seemed to be, if you will, quite modest, and he was not inclined to lick anything off the hands of another man, not even Jinshi.

"If you take my point, then that's enough." Maomao, lips pursed, proceeded ahead at a brisk trot.

The man was an unrepentant pervert. Such a pretty face for such a repugnant personality. Maomao was sure he'd entrapped countless

Honey (Part Two)

others with just the same trick. Shameless, that was the only word for it. If he hadn't been so damned important, she would have seriously considered kicking him between the legs. She was somewhat mollified by the thought that you couldn't kick what wasn't there.

At length, they arrived at the Diamond Pavilion, a brand-new building planted with auspicious *nantian* bamboo.

Consort Lishu greeted them wearing a cherry-pink outfit, her hair held back by a hair stick decorated with flower ornaments. Maomao thought the girlish ensemble suited her better than the elaborate getup from the garden party.

Once Consort Gyokuyou had gotten involved, Maomao had requested an audience with Consort Lishu, in hopes of getting closure about something that had been nagging at her.

Lishu didn't bother to hide her disappointment when she saw Jinshi wasn't with them. It was somewhat hard to blame her—he at least had that pretty face, after all.

"May I inquire what it is you wished to ask of me?" Lishu reclined on a chaise longue, hiding her mouth behind a folding fan made of peafowl feathers. She lacked the authority and presence of the other consorts; in fact, she almost seemed nervous. She was still so young. Yes, she was beautiful—they didn't call her the "lovely princess" for nothing—but she had yet to come into her womanliness. Indeed, she was even flatter than Maomao, who was as scrawny as a chicken.

Two ladies-in-waiting stood apathetically behind the consort. Lishu at first regarded the unfamiliar freckled woman with annoyance, but then she looked closer and appeared to realize Maomao was one of the ladies-in-waiting who had been at the garden party. Her eyes widened and her disposition seemed to improve somewhat.

"Do you dislike honey, ma'am?" It would have been just as well for Maomao to start with some pleasantries or idle chatter, but it would have been tiresome, so she dispensed with them.

Lishu's eyes widened further. "How did you know?"

"It was clear on your face." *Anyone with eyes could have seen it,* Maomao thought. Consort Lishu appeared more and more amazed. Maomao had rarely met anyone so easy to read. She went on, "Have you ever been sick to your stomach on account of honey?" Consort Lishu appeared yet more astounded. Maomao took that as a yes. "It's not uncommon for a person who has experienced food poisoning to become averse to the food that did it to them."

This time, Lishu shook her head. "That's not it. I don't remember it. I was only a baby at the time." As an infant, Lishu had nearly died because of some honey. She found it hard to eat now because for her entire life, her nursemaids and ladies-in-waiting had told her to avoid it.

"Listen, you little tart," a woman said nastily. "How dare you march in here and start interrogating Lady Lishu?"

You're one to talk, Maomao thought. The woman had been at the tea party; she was one of those who hadn't made the slightest attempt to aid her honey-hating mistress. *Don't act like you're her friend now.*

The ladies-in-waiting seemed to have a simple con going: they treated visitors like villains, pretending to stand up for Consort Lishu. The guileless young woman came to believe there were enemies all around her. Her attendants assured her that they—and they alone—were her allies, and thus isolated her. Then the consort had no choice

Honey (Part Two)

but to rely on her ladies. It was a vicious cycle. And so long as the consort didn't realize that it all came out of her ladies' malice, no one would ever figure it out. The women had simply made the mistake of getting overconfident at the garden party.

"I'm here on Master Jinshi's orders. If you have some kind of problem with me, I'd advise you to take it up with him personally." Maomao would borrow the menace of the tiger, so to speak, and give the women something to think about at the same time. Surely she could at least be allowed that.

The attendants' faces were burning, and Maomao was most amused to ponder what pretext they would use to get close to the perverted eunuch.

"One more thing," Maomao said, remaining carefully expressionless as she returned her gaze to Lishu. "Are you acquainted with the chief lady-in-waiting of the Garnet Pavilion?"

The consort's shocked look was all the answer she needed.

"There's something I'd like you to look for," Maomao had said to him, and that was what led to Gaoshun's presence in the court archives.

Maomao, a serving lady in the rear palace, was, in principle, not permitted to leave her place of service. But she seemed to have discovered something—what could it be? The depth of her thinking and her cool head didn't seem like those of a girl only seventeen years of age. One could even feel that such an ability to think rationally and solve problems was a shameful waste in a girl child. (Though some with certain proclivities might disagree.)

Such an easy pawn to use. If only he would simply do it. She would go along with it, though perhaps with a token objection or two.

Who was "he"? Who else? Gaoshun's master, who was not as mature as he first appeared.

"I've been remiss," Gaoshun mumbled. Perhaps he should have stopped his master before that joke went so far. But what would he have done? He would have stopped Jinshi, and then . . . what?

When he recalled Maomao's baleful look, he worried she might yet have something in store for him later. Gaoshun touched his hairline. He was just starting to fret about it.

Maomao sat on the bed in her room, flipping the pages of a book. The cramped space contained a brazier and a mortar and pestle for making medicine, while some dried herbs hung along the wall. Some of the tools she had wheedled from Gaoshun, others she had "borrowed" from the medical office.

"Sixteen years ago, huh . . . ?" *About the same time the emperor's younger brother was born.*

Maomao was holding a stitched bound book, the volume Gaoshun had procured for her. It chronicled events in the rear palace.

The current emperor had produced a single child when he was still heir apparent. Its mother had been the then-prince's milk-sibling, the later Pure Consort. But the child had died before it was weaned, and the prince produced no further progeny until after his father had died and the Imperial harem had been reestablished.

He only had the one consort during his entire princedom. She found it

Honey (Part Two)

strange. Knowing that horny old man, she would have expected him to take a whole crowd of concubines. She almost couldn't believe he had been faithful to one woman for more than ten years. It only went to show that you couldn't rely on rumors and hearsay. Best to check the records for yourself.

Sixteen years ago.

A child dead in infancy.

And . . .

"The court doctor, Luomen, banished." Maomao knew that name. The feeling that washed over her wasn't surprise so much as a sense that some pieces had fallen into place. On some level, she'd suspected something like this must be the case. Maomao made frequent use of the various herbs that grew around the rear palace. They weren't there naturally—someone, she always assumed, had planted them. She knew one person who cultivated a panoply of herbs around his house.

"I wonder what my old man is up to . . ." She thought of her father, who limped as he walked like an old woman. A practitioner as skilled and knowledgeable as he was wasted languishing in a pleasure district.

Indeed, Maomao's mentor in medicaments was a former palace eunuch, missing the bone in one of his knees.

CHAPTER 29

Honey
(PART THREE)

"A letter from Consort Gyokuyou?"

"Yes. I was told to deliver it personally."

"I'm afraid Lady Ah-Duo is attending tea right now..." Fengming, Ah-Duo's pudgy chief lady-in-waiting, regarded Maomao apologetically.

Maomao opened the small wooden box she was carrying. Normally it might have contained a slip of paper, but this one held a small jar with a single red trumpet of a flower within. A familiar, sweet aroma drifted from it. Maomao saw Fengming wince; she must have recognized the blossom.

So I was right? Maomao slid the jar aside, revealing a scrap of paper on which was written a list of specific words she suspected Fengming knew perfectly well.

"I would like to speak with you if I may, Lady Fengming," Maomao said.

Honey (Part Three)

"Very well," Fengming replied.

I like the sharp ones, Maomao thought. *Makes things so much quicker.* Fengming, her face taut, ushered Maomao into the Garnet Pavilion.

Fengming's personal chambers were laid out on much the same plan as Hongniang's, but everything she owned was crammed into one corner. It seemed she was all packed.

Yep. That tallies. Maomao and Fengming sat facing each other across a round table. Fengming served warming ginger tea, and a caddy on the table contained hard buns of bread. Fruit honeys were slathered all over them.

"Now, whatever is the matter?" Fengming asked. "We're quite finished cleaning, if that's what you're here for." Her voice was gentle, but it had a searching quality. She knew why Maomao had come, but she wasn't going to be the one to start the conversation.

"When will you be moving, if I may ask?" Maomao said, indicating the belongings in the corner.

"You're very perceptive." Fengming's voice immediately turned cold.

The "spring cleaning" had been only a pretext. In order that a new consort might be in place by the time people made their formal new year's greetings, Ah-Duo was going to have to leave the Garnet Pavilion. Consorts who would not or could not bear children had no place in the rear palace. Not even if they had been the emperor's companion for many years. All the more so if they lacked any powerful backer at court to secure their status, as Ah-Duo did.

To this point, the fact that Ah-Duo was the monarch's milk-sibling, a bond closer than that with one's own biological parents, had protected her. Perhaps if at least the prince she'd borne had lived, she might have been able to hold her head up.

I have a guess about her. Consort Ah-Duo had the handsome beauty of a young man; there was hardly a hint of womanliness about her. If a woman could become a eunuch, she might look something like Ah-Duo. Maomao hated to say anything based on an assumption—but when it was an obvious fact, sometimes that was all you could do.

"Consort Ah-Duo is no longer able to bear children, is she?"

Fengming said nothing, but her silence was as good as confirmation. Her face grew harder and harder.

"Something happened during the delivery, didn't it?" Maomao prodded.

"That has nothing to do with you." The middle-aged lady-in-waiting narrowed her eyes. They held no hint of the tender, considerate woman Maomao had met before, but burned with a deep hostility.

"In fact, it does. For the attending physician at the birth was my adoptive father." Maomao delivered this fact dispassionately. Fengming got to her feet.

The medical staff at the rear palace was continually shorthanded, so much so that even the quack who filled the position at the moment could hold on to his job. The reason was simple: a man who possessed that unique skill—well-developed medical knowledge—had no need to become a eunuch. It had probably been easy enough to foist the job on her socially inept old man.

"Consort Ah-Duo's misfortune was that the birth of her child coincided with that of the Imperial younger brother. Weigh the two in the scales of this court, and your lady's delivery was clearly deemed the less important."

The baby survived the difficult delivery, but Ah-Duo lost her womb. Then the child died young. Some speculated that Ah-Duo's infant had

Honey (Part Three)

been lost to the same toxic makeup that had killed Consort Lihua's prince, but Maomao thought differently. The mother of a young prince, like Ah-Duo, would never have been allowed the deadly face powder on Maomao's father's watch.

"Do you feel at all responsible for what happened, Lady Fengming? When Consort Ah-Duo was indisposed after the birth, I believe it was you who cared for the infant in her place . . ."

"Well," Fengming said slowly. "You've got it all figured out, haven't you? Even though you're the daughter of the worthless quack who couldn't help Lady Ah-Duo."

"Yes. Even so." Blame in medicine couldn't be dismissed with a helpless shrug: something else her father had said. He would have readily accepted abuse like "quack." "You know that *quack* prevented your mistress from using face powder with white lead in it. And you were too smart to have given the child something so deadly." Maomao opened the small jar in the letter case. Honey glistened inside. Maomao put the red flower from the jar into her mouth.

It carried the sweetness of the honey. She plucked off the blossom, playing with it in her fingers. "There are many varieties of poisonous plants. Wolfsbane and azalea, for example. And the toxins carry over to honey made from them, as well."

"I'm aware of that."

"I should think so." A family of beekeepers could certainly be expected to understand such things. And if a toxin would cause serious poisoning in an adult, think what it would do to a child. "But you didn't realize that honey could contain poison that *only* affected children."

It wasn't an assumption. It was fact. It was rare, but some such toxins existed—agents that were only poisonous to children, with their lower levels of resistance.

"You tasted it and were fine, so you assumed he would be, too. Yet the stuff you gave to the boy to help him grow was doing exactly the opposite, and you never knew it."

And then, Ah-Duo's child had perished. Cause of death unknown.

Luomen—Maomao's father and the chief physician at the time—was blamed for this tremendous failure, in addition to the trouble during the birth. For these he was banished, and he was further punished with mutilation: they removed the bones of one knee.

"The last thing you wanted was for your mistress to find out—for Consort Ah-Duo to know." To discover that Fengming was the reason the one child her mistress would ever have was dead. "So you tried to get Consort Lishu out of the picture."

During the reign of the prior emperor, Lishu had apparently been quite close to Ah-Duo, and Ah-Duo, it was said, had seemingly taken a great liking to her. Was it possible Ah-Duo had been staying close to the young consort in hopes that the emperor would not consummate their relationship?

A child separated from her parents, and a grown woman who could never give birth: a sort of symbiosis emerged between them. But one day, abruptly, Consort Ah-Duo ceased admitting Lishu. The young consort came repeatedly to visit her, but each time, Fengming chased her away. Then the former emperor died, and Consort Lishu took vows.

"Consort Lishu told you, didn't she? That the honey could be poisonous." And if Lishu had continued her frequent visits, she might have eventually let the fact slip to Ah-Duo. Ah-Duo was clever enough that it might be all she needed to put the pieces together. That, Fengming was desperate to avoid.

After the emperor's death, however, with Lishu safely in a nunnery, Fengming had thought she would never see the girl again—until she reappeared at the rear palace, still a high consort. And now a threat to Ah-Duo. Yet the girl almost seemed to make a show of coming to visit Ah-Duo, like a child eager for her mother. So sheltered, Lishu was. So blind to the world around her. So Fengming decided to get rid of her.

Across from Maomao there was no trace of the calm, caring chief lady-in-waiting. Fengming's gaze was as cold as ice. "What do you want?"

"Nothing," Maomao said, although she felt a tingling on the back of her neck. The knife they had used to cut the buns earlier was on the shelf behind her. It was only a simple cleaver, but it was more than enough to threaten the petite Maomao. It was easily within Fengming's reach.

"Anything at all," Fengming ventured, almost sweetly.

"You know perfectly well, milady, that such an offer is meaningless."

Fengming's lips curved vacantly at that. It didn't even rise to the level of a polite smile, but there was something deep within the expression—what?

"Say . . . Do you know what matters most to the person who matters most to you?" Fengming said to Maomao, the whisper of a smile still on her face. Maomao shook her head. She was ignorant of what was most important. Be it things or people.

"Well, I took it away," Fengming said. "Stole the child she cherished more than a jewel." From the moment Fengming had entered Ah-Duo's service, she had known she would serve no one else in her life. The consort had a firmness of will uncommon in a woman and could bring to bear the same look as the heir himself when she spoke, and Fengming respected her to no end. The consort was like a thunderbolt to Fengming, who had spent her whole life doing just as her parents told her. She smiled as she told the story.

"Lady Ah-Duo said something to me, back then. She said her son had only followed the will of heaven. That it wasn't something for us to be disturbed over." It was impossible to know if a child would survive to the age of seven. The slightest illness could kill them seemingly on the spot. Fengming continued, "And yet I could hear Lady Ah-Duo crying every night."

The woman looked slowly at the ground. A sort of moan escaped her. The immovable chief lady-in-waiting was gone. In her place there was only a woman wracked with regret.

How must she have felt as she served Consort Ah-Duo these sixteen years? Devoting herself entirely to her lady, with no thought of a spouse or partner? Maomao could not imagine. Not Fengming's emotions, not what it would feel like to cherish another person to that degree. Thus, she truly didn't know what it was she wanted.

Would Fengming accept what Maomao was about to propose? No doubt Jinshi had been informed of Maomao's recent interest in the archives. She didn't think she could hide anything from the eunuch who all but ran the rear palace. She had managed to keep the truth to herself in the matter of Princess Fuyou, but she didn't think she could throw him off the trail this time.

Nor did she want to.

When he heard what Maomao had to say, Jinshi would have Fengming arrested. She would certainly not escape the ultimate punishment,

Honey (Part Three)

no matter what else happened or who appealed on her behalf. The truth would come to light after sixteen years. Things had been set in motion, and even if Maomao were to vanish here and now, sooner or later, Fengming would be found out. The chief lady-in-waiting was too smart not to realize that.

There was only one thing Maomao could do for her. Fengming couldn't hope for a reduction in her punishment, nor for the intercession of Consort Ah-Duo. But her two motives could be reduced to one. She could continue to hide her motivation from Consort Ah-Duo.

Maomao knew what a terrible thing she was suggesting to Fengming. It amounted to asking another woman to die. But it was the only thing she could think of. The only thing a young woman with no particular influence or authority could offer.

"The outcome will be the same. But if you can accept that . . ."

If Fengming could accept that, she would do as Maomao urged her.

So tired . . .

Maomao returned to her chamber at the Jade Pavilion and collapsed onto her hard bed. Her clothes were soaked with sweat—sweat that had poured off of her at the moment of highest tension, reeking of fear. She wanted a bath.

Thinking she could at least change, she pulled off her outer garments, revealing a large cloth wrapped from her chest all the way down to her stomach. It held several layers of oil paper in place.

"Glad I didn't need it," she said to herself. *Getting stabbed still would have hurt.*

Maomao stripped off the oil paper and found herself a fresh outfit.

Jinshi could only contemplate the fact in amazement. Who would have imagined that the attempted poisoning of Consort Lishu would end with the culprit's suicide?

Jinshi was in the sitting area of the Jade Pavilion, describing this outcome to a reticent lady-in-waiting. He had already informed Consort Gyokuyou.

"And so Fengming is dead, by her own hand," he said.

"How lucky for all of us," the lady-in-waiting replied with no special show of emotion.

Jinshi rested his elbows on the table. Gaoshun looked like he wanted to object, but Jinshi ignored him. Manners be damned. "Are you sure you don't know anything about this?" he said. He sometimes had an inescapable feeling that this young lady was up to something.

"I can tell you what I *don't* know—what you're talking about."

"I'm given to understand you kept Gaoshun quite busy gathering books."

"Yes. All for nothing, I'm afraid."

She sounded so nonchalant he almost thought she was making fun of him. Then again, what else was new? It was possible she was carrying a bit of a grudge from his joke the other day—he *had* gone a bit overboard. But for the most part, this seemed normal. She was giving him her standard looking-at-filth glare. It went beyond rudeness to achieve a purity all its own.

"The motive, as you guessed, was to help Consort Ah-Duo retain her seat among the four ladies."

"Is that so?" Maomao looked at him with total disinterest.

Honey (Part Three)

"I'm sorry to have to tell you that Consort Ah-Duo will indeed be demoted from her place as a high consort. She's to leave the rear palace and live at the South Palace."

"Retribution for the attempted poisoning?" Maomao asked. The cat had finally started to take an interest in the ball of string.

"No, the move was already settled. His Majesty's decision." The emperor's long affection for Ah-Duo must have been what allowed her to remain in an Imperial residence, rather than being sent back to her home and family.

Maomao's uncharacteristic show of interest promptly led Jinshi to get carried away. He stood and took a step forward, whereupon she tensed and took a half step back. So, he was right; she hadn't quite gotten over his little japes. Naturally, Gaoshun watched them both with exasperation.

It would do Jinshi no good if Maomao got too tense. He sat back down. The petite serving woman bowed her head and made to leave the room, but then she stopped. A branch of red, trumpet-shaped flowers decorated the room.

"Hongniang put them there earlier," Jinshi informed her.

"Indeed," Maomao said. "What a great burst of blooms." She took one of the blossoms, broke off the stem, and put it in her mouth. Jinshi, perplexed, approached slowly and did the same. "It's sweet."

"Yes. And poisonous."

Jinshi spat out the stem and covered his mouth as Gaoshun rushed to get water.

"Don't worry," Maomao said. "It won't kill you."

Then the strange girl licked her lips, which carried the hint of a sweet smile of her own.

CHAPTER 30

Ah-Duo

It was pure coincidence that Maomao sneaked out of the Jade Pavilion on that particular night: she couldn't sleep.

The next day, the Pure Consort would depart the rear palace.

Maomao wandered aimlessly around the grounds. The palace was already firmly in the grip of winter cold, and she wore two cotton overgarments against the chill. One thing hadn't changed in the rear palace: promiscuity was alive and well, and one had to be careful not to look too closely among the bushes or into the shadows. For those who burned with passion, the winter chill presented no obstacle.

Maomao glanced up and saw the half-moon hanging in the sky. A memory of Princess Fuyou danced through her head, and Maomao decided that since she was out here anyway, maybe she would climb up on the wall. She would have liked to "share a drink with the moon," as the old poets put it. But as there was no alcohol in the Jade Pavilion, she regretfully gave up the idea. She should have saved some of the stuff

Ah-Duo

Jinshi had given her. Maomao suddenly craved some snake wine—it had been so long since she'd had any—but then she remembered what had happened the other day, and shook her head, realizing it wasn't worth it.

Using the protruding bricks in the corner of the outer wall as footholds, Maomao pulled herself up to the top. She had to mind her skirt, lest she tear it.

A proverb had it that only two things liked high places—idiots and smoke—but Maomao had to confess, it felt good to be up above it all. The moon and a sprinkling of stars shone down upon the Imperial city. The lights she could see in the distance must have been the pleasure district. She was sure that the flowers and the bees had begun their nightly communion there by now.

Maomao had no particular business up there on the wall. She simply sat on the edge, kicking her legs and looking up at the sky.

"Well, well. Someone got here before me?" The voice was neither high nor low. Maomao turned to discover a handsome young man in long pants. No—it looked like a young man, but it was Consort Ah-Duo. She'd tied her hair in a ponytail that cascaded down her back, and a large gourd-flask was suspended from her shoulder. There was a touch of red in her cheeks, and she was dressed relatively lightly. Her footing was sure, but it seemed she'd had a bit to drink.

"Don't mind me, milady. I'll be leaving presently," Maomao said.

"There's no rush. Share a cup with me?"

Presented with a drinking cup, Maomao could find no reason to refuse. She might normally have declined on the grounds that she was Consort Gyokuyou's serving woman, but Maomao wasn't so vulgar as to refuse a last drink with Consort Ah-Duo on her last night in the rear palace. (Perfectly logical, you see: she *certainly* wasn't simply tempted by the opportunity for some wine.)

Maomao held the cup in both hands; it was full of a cloudy drink. The wine had a strongly sweet taste, without much of the acid sting of alcohol. She didn't say anything, just lapped at the cup of wine. Ah-Duo showed no compunction in drinking directly out of the gourd.

"Thinking I seem a little mannish?"

"Thinking that's how you seem to be acting."

"Hah, a straight shooter. I like that." Ah-Duo raised one knee, bracing her chin on her hand. Her sharp nose and the long eyebrows that fringed her eyes looked somehow familiar to Maomao. They reminded her of someone she knew, she thought, but her mind was a little cloudy, like the drink. "Ever since my son slipped away from me, I've been His Majesty's friend. Or maybe I should say, gone back to being."

She stood by him as a friend, without having to act like a consort. Someone who had known him since they nursed together. She'd never imagined she would be chosen as a consort. She was his first partner, yes, but only, she'd assumed, as his guide. One might almost say a mentor. Then, because of His Majesty's fondness for her, she'd remained a consort for more than ten years, though she'd been only ornamental. She'd wished he would hurry up and hand her off to someone. Why had he clung to her so?

Ah-Duo continued ruminating to herself. She would likely have gone on whether or not Maomao was there, whether or not anyone was there. This consort would be gone tomorrow. Whatever rumors might spread in the rear palace would no longer be any concern of hers.

Maomao only listened in silence.

When she had finally finished speaking, the consort got to her feet and turned the gourd upside down, emptying its contents over the wall, into the moat beyond. She seemed to be offering the libation as a parting gift, and Maomao thought of the serving woman who had killed herself some days before.

"It must have been so cold, in the water."

"Yes, ma'am."

"She must have suffered."

"Yes, ma'am."

"How stupid."

After a beat, Maomao said, "You may be right."

"Everyone, so stupid."

"You may be right."

She understood, dimly. The serving woman *had* been a suicide. And Ah-Duo knew it. Perhaps she had known the woman who killed herself.

Maybe "everyone" who was stupid included Fengming. She might have had a hand in the woman's death.

There was the serving woman, sunk in the freezing water so that suspicion might not fall on Consort Ah-Duo.

There was Fengming, who had hung herself to keep a secret that must never be known.

There were all those who had given their lives for Ah-Duo, literally or figuratively, whether she wished it or not.

What a tremendous waste.

Ah-Duo had the personality and the mettle to rule people. If she could have been by the emperor's side, not as his consort, but in another form, perhaps politics would have gone more smoothly. Perhaps.

Maomao let the thoughts drift through her mind, though there was no point to them now, as she gazed up at the stars.

Ah-Duo climbed back down the wall first, and Maomao, starting to feel properly chilly, was just doing the same when she was stopped by a voice.

"What are you doing?"

Startled, Maomao lost her footing and slipped from halfway down the wall, landing hard on her back and behind.

"Who the hell was that?" she grumbled to herself.

"Well, pardon me," the voice hissed, now right in her ear. She turned in surprise to see Jinshi, looking less than pleased.

"Master Jinshi. What are you doing here?"

"You took the words right out of my mouth."

Maomao realized she hadn't felt any pain when she landed. There had been an impact, true, but no sense of having hit the ground. This was one mystery that wasn't hard to solve: she had fallen right on top of Jinshi.

Whoops! Maomao made to get up again, but she couldn't move. She was held fast.

"Master Jinshi, perhaps you could let go of me?" she said, trying to sound polite, but Jinshi's arms remained resolutely wrapped around her midriff. "Master Jinshi . . ."

He stubbornly ignored her. Maomao squirmed a little, turning to get a look at his face, and she discovered there was a flush in his cheeks. She could smell alcohol on his breath. "Have you been drinking?"

"I was socializing. Didn't have a choice," Jinshi said, and looked up at the sky. The winter air was crisp and clear, making the light of the stars seem even brighter.

Socializing. Right. Maomao looked suspiciously at him. "Socializing" in the rear palace could mean some very shady things. It could be argued that the emperor still gave the place's inhabitants a bit too much freedom, even if many of them were missing some very important parts.

"I said, let go of me."

"Don't wanna. I'm cold." For all his beauty, the eunuch sounded downright petulant. Well, of course he was cold; he wasn't wearing so much as a light jacket. Maomao wondered where Gaoshun was.

"I'm sure you are, so you'd better get back to your room before you catch a cold." She didn't care whether the room he went back to was his own quarters or the chambers of whoever had shared the wine with him.

Jinshi, though, pressed his forehead against Maomao's neck, almost nuzzling her. "Dammit . . . Asking me in to drink, getting me all soused up. Then it's 'I think I'll step out for a while.' Sure! Off you go! To . . . to who knows where! Dammit. Then you're back, but now you're 'feeling much better'! And chasing me out, too! Damn it all!"

Maomao discovered she was impressed to realize that there was anyone in the rear palace with the nerve to treat Jinshi that way. But that was neither here nor there. *I'm so not interested in having to hang out with a drunk person.* They always got clingy like this, that was the problem. *Actually, hold on . . .*

It finally sank in that Maomao was in her current situation because she'd come falling down on Jinshi from above. He'd had the good grace to break her fall, even if he hadn't known he was doing it. Even if it was the alcohol that had left him lying among the weeds at that particular moment. Maybe it *was* a little rude, Maomao reflected, to immediately start giving orders without even a word of thanks to someone who had just saved you from a nasty fall. But then, she couldn't just lie there, either.

"Master Jinsh—" Her latest attempt to free herself was interrupted by a feeling of something dropping onto her neck. The warm feeling ran down her back.

"Just a moment longer," Jinshi said, hugging her tighter. "Help me warm myself just a little bit."

Maomao sighed: his voice sounded nothing like it ordinarily did. Then she looked up at the sky and started counting the gleaming stars one by one.

A great crowd gathered at the main gate the next day. The rear palace's longest-serving consort was, in contrast to the night before, dressed in a wide-sleeved jacket and skirt that hardly suited her. Some of the women standing around clutched handkerchiefs. The handsome, boyish consort had been something of an idol to many of the young ladies.

Jinshi stood in front of Ah-Duo. One might have worried about them after all the drinking the night before, but neither showed any sign of a hangover. She gave him something: a headdress, the symbol of the Pure Consort. Before long, it would pass to another woman.

They could stand to trade outfits. The celestial beauty and the handsome woman. In principle, they could hardly have been more different, and yet oddly, they seemed to share much. *So that's it,* Maomao thought. The night before, she'd thought Ah-Duo resembled somebody, but hadn't been able to think of who. It must have been Jinshi.

Ah-Duo

What would have happened if Consort Ah-Duo had been in Jinshi's position?

But it was a silly question. Not worth thinking about. Ah-Duo in no way appeared like a pitiful reject being chased out of the rear palace. She walked with her head high and her chest out; one could even say she had the triumphant look of a woman who had done her duty.

How could she look so proud? How, when she had never done the one thing a consort must do? Maomao suddenly found herself in the grip of an absurd possibility. Ah-Duo's words from the night before came back to her: *"Ever since my son slipped away from me..."*

Now Maomao thought: *Slipped away? Not... died?*

One could very nearly take the consort to mean her son was still alive. Ah-Duo had lost the ability to bear children because her delivery had come at the same time as that of the empress dowager. The Imperial younger brother and the consort's child were uncle and nephew, and they'd been born at almost the exact same time. It was possible they had practically looked like twins.

What if they were switched?

Even as she was giving birth, Consort Ah-Duo would have known with absolute certainty which of the two infants would be the more diligently raised, the more treasured. The best possible patronage for a child would never come from Ah-Duo, the daughter of a wet nurse. But from an empress dowager...

It couldn't have been easy for Ah-Duo, whose recovery after the birth had been slow, to be sure what was right. But if, by making the switch, her own son might be saved—it would be understandable if she wished for such a thing.

And if it came to light later? If the true Imperial younger brother was already dead by then? Then it would make sense why Maomao's father had been not only banished but mutilated as well. Because he had failed to notice that the infants had been switched. It would explain why His Majesty's younger brother led such a constrained life. And why the otherwise chaste Ah-Duo had remained so long in the rear palace.

Bah. This is ridiculous. Maomao shook her head. An outrageous fantasy. A leap even her fellow ladies-in-waiting at the Jade Pavilion wouldn't make.

No point in staying here, Maomao thought. She was just about to head back to the Jade Pavilion when she saw someone coming her direction in a rush. It was the sweet-looking young consort, Lishu. She showed no sign of having noticed Maomao, but veritably ran toward the main gate. Her food taster trailed behind her, gasping for breath. Her other ladies-in-waiting came behind them, not running at all, and in fact looking thoroughly annoyed by the entire scene.

Some people never change. Well, I guess at least one *of them has.* It wasn't like Maomao would or could do anything about it. Someone who couldn't take her own people in hand was someone who wouldn't survive in this garden of women.

But now she wasn't alone. That, at least, was heartening.

Consort Lishu appeared before Consort Ah-Duo, her arms and legs moving awkwardly together, almost mechanically. She was tripping on the hem of her own dress, and presently tumbled headlong to the ground. As the crowd attempted to suppress its laughter, and Consort Lishu lay there looking like she might cry, Ah-Duo took out a handkerchief and gently helped the young woman wipe the dirt off her face.

In that moment, the face of the handsome young consort was that of a loving mother.

CHAPTER 31

Dismissal

"What am I going to do?" Jinshi gazed mournfully at the paper. "What do you wish to do?" his taciturn aide asked, likewise looking at the document. The situation was enough to make any man despair. "This is a list of names," Gaoshun observed. "Fengming's family, and their known associates."

Fengming was already dead, and her clan and family relations would be spared total annihilation, but her relatives were to be subject to the confiscation of all their assets and would each be punished with mutilation, though to varying degrees of severity.

Jinshi could be grateful, at least, that there had been no sign of any instructions from Consort Ah-Duo. Fengming was to be held to have acted alone.

Among the associates were a number of clients who engaged her family's services. Jinshi had always taken the clan to be simple apiarists, but they seemed to have their hands in quite a few cookie jars.

"Eighty of their girls serve at the rear palace," Gaoshun remarked.

"Eighty out of two thousand. A respectable ratio."

"I should say so," Gaoshun said, watching his master furrow his brow. "Shall they be discharged?"

"Can that be done?"

"If you wish it."

If he wished it. Whatever Jinshi told him, Gaoshun would see done. Whether it was right or not. Just or not.

Jinshi sighed, a long, slow exhalation of breath. He recognized at least one of the names on the list of associates. The purchasers of a kidnapped apothecary's daughter.

"What to do about this . . ." he mused. All he had to do was choose. But he sat in fear of how *she* would look at him, depending on what he decided to do. It was so simple to give an order. But how would she take it, if it was contrary to what she wanted?

Maomao saw the divide between herself and Jinshi as that between a commoner and a noble. No matter how distasteful the command, he suspected she would ultimately accept it. But he saw it making the gulf between them that much wider.

But—send her away? He waffled. She wasn't here voluntarily, that much was true. Yet could he end her service at his own whim? And what if the ever-perceptive girl caught a whiff of it?

"Master Jinshi," Gaoshun said, as Jinshi turned the questions over and over in his mind. "Was she not a very fortuitous pawn?"

His aide's words were coldly rational. Jinshi ran a hand across his brow.

Dismissal

"A mass dismissal?"

"Yep," Xiaolan said, munching on a dried persimmon. Maomao had helped herself to a few persimmons from the fruit orchard, then discreetly hung them under the eaves of the Jade Pavilion to dry. If anyone had noticed, she would have been in a spot of trouble. In fact, she actually was: there was no way Hongniang would fail to notice the fruit. Gaoshun had arrived at just the right moment to save her skin. When Hongniang discovered that he was quite fond of persimmons, she said she would let it go "this one time," with a conspiratorial wink.

"I guess it's like, you know how sometimes they slaughter everyone related to a case like this? All the girls from all the merchant houses they had dealings with are going to have to quit. That's what I heard."

Xiaolan's explanation left something to be desired, but Maomao nodded. *Not sure I like where this is going. Got a bad feeling about it,* she thought. And her bad feelings had an unfortunate tendency to be accurate.

Maomao's nominal family had a business and sometimes engaged in commerce. Fengming's family were beekeepers, so there could well be a connection between them.

It'd be tough on me if they fired me now, Maomao thought. Besides, she was starting to like her life here. True, there was no question she would be happy to be able to go home to the pleasure district, but as soon as she got there, she would wind up in the clutches of the old madam, a woman who wouldn't let the smallest coin go unnoticed. Maomao still hadn't sent her any customers since Lihaku's visit. A fact that would not have escaped her calculating mind.

She really will start selling me this time.

Maomao said goodbye to Xiaolan, then set off to find a person she would normally have had no interest whatsoever in seeing.

"How unusual. And breathing so hard," the gorgeous eunuch said lightly. They were by the main gate of the rear palace, where Maomao had only arrived after visiting the residences of all four of the favored consorts. She struggled to muster a biting riposte, but Jinshi said, "Calm down. You're bright red." On the nymphlike face was a shadow of alarm.

"I-I h-have to . . . to talk to you," Maomao managed between gasps. Jinshi almost seemed to smile, and yet, for some reason she couldn't guess, there was a hint of melancholy in the expression, too.

"Very well. Let's speak inside."

She felt a little bad for the Matron of the Serving Women, who (for the first time in a while) was forced to wait outside while Maomao and Jinshi used her office. Maomao gave the woman a polite bow as she passed; it seemed she had been terribly busy of late handling Ah-Duo's departure. By the time Maomao got inside, Jinshi was already sitting in a chair, eyeing a piece of paper on the desk. "I presume you wanted to ask me about the mass dismissal taking place."

"Yes, sir. What's to happen to me?"

Instead of answering, Jinshi showed her the paper. It was of excellent material—and among the names on it was Maomao's.

"So I'm to be let go."

What do I do? she thought. She could hardly insist they keep her on. She was all too keenly aware that she was only an ordinary serving woman. She studiously maintained a neutral expression, wary lest her face should seem to show any hint of flattery. The result, though, was

Dismissal

that she looked at Jinshi exactly as she always did: as though staring at a caterpillar.

"What do *you* want to do?" Jinshi's voice was devoid of its usual honeyed tone. Indeed, he nearly seemed like a pleading child himself. In fact, he sounded just like he had the night before Consort Ah-Duo left. His face, though, remained frozen, grave.

"I'm only a servant. At a word, I can be put to menial labor, cooking. Even tasting food for poison."

She was only telling the truth. If she was ordered to do something, she would do it, so long as it was within her power, and she liked to think she would do it well. She wouldn't complain, even if she had to take a bit of a pay cut. If it put some distance between her and having to sell her body, she would do whatever it took to wrangle some new customers.

So please, just don't cut me loose . . .

Maomao felt she had said, as clearly as she possibly could: *Let me stay.* But the young man's expression remained unmoved; he offered only a small exhalation, his eyes flitting away for the barest second.

"Very well," he said. "I'll make sure you receive adequate compensation." The young man's voice was cold, and he looked down at the desk so she couldn't read his expression.

The negotiations had failed.

How many days now, Gaoshun wondered with a sigh, had his master been cagey and withdrawn? It wasn't interfering with his work, but when they got back to his room, he would only sit in a corner brooding, and Gaoshun was frankly getting a little tired of it. Jinshi was casting a cloud over the entire place. The boy with the enchanting smile and the captivating voice was not there.

Maomao had left the week after receiving official notice of her dismissal. She had never been unduly warm, but she was also never rude, and she had gone from place to place in the rear palace to formally thank all her various acquaintances and benefactors.

Consort Gyokuyou had been openly opposed to Maomao's dismissal, but when she heard that the decision came from Jinshi, she didn't continue to push the matter. She did, though, leave him with a parting shot: "Don't come crying to me if you find out you wish you hadn't done this."

"Are you certain you shouldn't have stopped her, sir?"

"Don't say a word."

Gaoshun crossed his arms, frowning. A memory from the past came back to him. How much strife there had been when the young man lost a favorite toy. How Gaoshun had suffered to give him something newer, and more enticing still!

Perhaps he shouldn't think of her as a toy. Perhaps Jinshi had chosen not to stop her as his way of refusing to treat her as an object. What point would it serve, then, to find some other remarkable lady?

It all portended a great deal of trouble.

"If no substitute will do, the only recourse is to the original," Gaoshun murmured, so quietly that Jinshi didn't hear him. One person in particular flashed through his mind. A military officer well acquainted with the girl's family. "A great deal of trouble though it is." The long-suffering Gaoshun scratched the back of his neck.

EPILOGUE

The Eunuch and the Courtesan

"Time to work. Get going." The old madam hustled Maomao into a rather distinguished-looking carriage. This evening's job was apparently a banquet for some noble. Maomao could only sigh as they arrived at a large mansion in the north of the capital. She was just one of a number of people accompanying her "sisters" to the banquet. Everyone was dressed in gorgeous clothing and done up with ostentatious makeup. When she contemplated the fact that she was made up to look just like them, Maomao felt oddly queasy.

Their party was ushered down a long hallway, up a spiral staircase, and into a large room. Lanterns hung from the ceiling, and festive red tassels dangled everywhere. *Someone has money to burn*, Maomao thought.

Five people sat in a row in the room. They were younger than she'd expected. Pairin licked her lips when she saw the young men in the flickering lamplight. She was rewarded with a gentle jab in the side from Joka. When she wanted to, Maomao's sexy "sister" could be very quick about things, enough to make even the madam throw up her hands.

Wish he'd made these introductions sooner! The men at this banquet were supposedly high officials from the palace; Lihaku had been the go-between. And with him involved, at least a portion of the profits should go to paying off Maomao's debts. If nothing else, she'd been given a substantial amount of severance pay, more than she'd counted on, so she'd escaped being forced to sell her body, but the madam still put her on odd jobs like this.

Old hag. The way she clucked when she heard . . . The old lady really seemed to want to make Maomao a courtesan. She'd been maneuvering toward it for years now. She kept telling Maomao to quit wasting her time with medicine already, but that was never going to happen. What, was she simply going to swap her interest from pharmaceuticals to singing and dancing? Not a chance.

As Maomao took in the room, she saw that everything was hugely ornate: each bottle of wine and every sitting mat was of the highest quality. *Surely they wouldn't notice if I helped myself to a furnishing as a souvenir,* she thought, but then shook her head. No, no, that wouldn't do.

Calling courtesans to one's private residence was substantially more expensive than holding a banquet at the brothel. All the more so when the courtesans one summoned were women any one of whom could charge a year's wages in silver for a single evening. To ask all of the Three Princesses of the Verdigris House—Meimei, Pairin, and Joka—to be present at once was as good as to announce that money was no object.

Maomao was just one of those who had been brought along in

support of the night's three stars. She'd learned to be mannerly, but she couldn't hold a tune, nor could she play the erhu. And dancing? That was out of the question. The best she could hope to do was to keep a close watch on the guests' drinks and make sure they never ran dry.

Maomao forced the muscles of her face into a smile as she began to pour wine into someone's empty cup. Her only saving grace was that everyone was so enraptured by her sisters' singing and dancing that they didn't so much as glance at her. One person had even started a game of Go with a member of the support staff.

While everyone else laughed, drank, and enjoyed the show, though, she spotted one person looking down at the ground. *What, bored?* Maomao wondered. He was a young man dressed in fine silk; he rested a small cup of wine on one knee, sipping from it occasionally. A gray gloom clung to him. *They're going to think I'm not doing my job,* thought Maomao, who had a way of turning serious about anything she happened to be doing. She grabbed a good, full bottle of wine and sat down beside the melancholy young man. His sleek, dark bangs hid much of his face. For the life of her, she couldn't see his expression.

"Leave me alone," he said.

Maomao was puzzled: his voice was oddly familiar. Her hand moved almost before she could think; any thought of propriety or politeness had vanished from her mind. Careful not to touch the young man's cheek, she lifted his hair.

A gorgeous countenance greeted her. Her reserved expression promptly changed to one of total astonishment. "Master Jinshi?" There was no gleaming smile on his face now, no sweet honey in his voice, but still she would have known that eunuch anywhere.

Jinshi blinked several times in succession, studied her for a second, then said uneasily, "Who . . . Who're you?"

"A question I'm often asked."

"Anyone ever tell you you look very different with makeup?"

"Frequently."

The conversation gave her a sense of déjà vu. She let go of his hair, and it fell back over his face. Jinshi reached out and tried to take her wrist. "Why are you running?" He looked sullen now.

"Please don't touch the entertainment," she said. It wasn't her decision—it was the rules. They would have to charge extra.

"Why the hell do you even look like that?"

Maomao refused to meet his eyes as she said uncomfortably, "It's . . . part-time work."

"At a brothel? Wait . . . Don't tell me you . . ."

Maomao gave Jinshi a glare. So he liked to question people's chastity, did he? "I don't take customers myself," she informed him. "Yet."

"Yet . . ."

Maomao didn't elaborate. What could she say? It certainly wasn't outside the realm of possibility that the madam would finally manage to force a customer on her before she was able to pay off her debt. Although thankfully, under the influence of her father and sisters, it hadn't happened so far.

"How about if I bought you?" Jinshi drawled.

"Huh?" Maomao was about to tell him not to joke when an idea flashed through her mind. "You know, that might not be half bad."

Jinshi caught his breath, startled. It was the face of a pigeon spooked by a peashooter. Apparently, the lack of sparkle opened the door to a great wealth of expressions. Lovely though the ethereal smile was, it

The Eunuch and the Courtesan

almost didn't look human. It was nearly enough to convince Maomao that he must have two *hun* spirits within a single *po* spirit: two transient yang souls for the single, corporeal yin spirit.

"It wouldn't be so bad, to work at the rear palace again," she said.

Jinshi's shoulders slumped. Maomao looked at him, wondering what could be the matter.

"I thought you quit the rear palace. Because you hated it."

"When did I ever say such a thing?" In fact, Maomao was convinced she'd all but begged to stay on in order to pay off her debt, and it had been Jinshi who'd had her fired. The place had its troubles and difficulties, no question, but Consort Gyokuyou's ladies-in-waiting had been good women. And food taster was an unusual role, not one to which most people could—or would—aspire. "If there's anything I didn't like about it," Maomao said, "I suppose it would be that I wasn't able to conduct my poison experiments."

"You shouldn't be doing those anyway." Jinshi rested his chin on his knee in place of his cup. His look of outright exasperation spontaneously slipped into a wry smile. "Heh. I know, I know. It's who you are."

"I'm afraid I don't follow you."

"Anyone ever tell you you're a woman of few words? Too few?"

"Yes," Maomao replied after a beat. "Often."

Jinshi's smile gradually grew more innocent. This time it was Maomao's turn to look annoyed. Jinshi reached out again. "I said, why are you running?"

"It's the rules, sir." The information didn't seem to dissuade Jinshi, whose hand didn't move. He was staring fixedly at Maomao. She was getting a bad feeling about it.

"Surely one touch is all right."

"No, sir."

"There won't be any less of you afterward."

"It takes my energy."

"Just one hand. Just a fingertip. Surely that's all right."

Maomao had no answer. He was persistent. She knew him; knew he didn't give up. Maomao, helpless, closed her eyes and let out a deep breath. "Just a fingertip."

The instant the words were out of her mouth, she felt something press against her lips. Her eyelids fluttered open, and she saw a daub of her red lip color on Jinshi's lithe fingertip. He pulled his hand back almost before she realized what had happened. Then, to her amazement, he touched the finger to his own lips.

That sneaky little . . .

When he pulled his fingers away from his mouth, a spot of scarlet was left on his finely shaped mouth. His face relaxed a little, and the smile became even more innocent. A flush entered his cheeks, as if a touch of the lip color had gotten on his face.

Maomao's shoulders were shaking, but Jinshi's smile looked so profoundly youthful, almost childish, that she found she couldn't rebuke him. Instead, she focused on the ground.

Damn, it's catching . . . Maomao's mouth formed a tight line, and her own cheeks were turning pink. She knew she hadn't used any rouge. Then she realized she could hear laughter, chuckling men and giggling women, and she discovered everyone was looking at them. Her sisters were grinning openly. Maomao was terrified to imagine what would come next. Suddenly she wanted to be anywhere else.

Gaoshun appeared veritably out of the blue, his arms crossed as if to say: *Finally. That's one job done.* It was all enough to make Maomao's head spin, and later she hardly recalled the rest of the evening. She never forgot, though, how her sisters hounded her about it afterward.

Some days later, a gorgeous noble visitor appeared in the capital's pleasure district. He came with money enough to make even the old madam goggle—and for some reason, an unusual herb grown from an insect. And he wanted one young woman in particular.

Fin.